BANNERLESS

BANNERLESS

Carrie Vaughn

A John Joseph Adams Book
Mariner Books
Houghton Mifflin Harcourt
BOSTON NEW YORK
2017

For information about permission to reproduce selections
from this book, write to trade.permissions@hmhco.com or to
Permissions, Houghton Mifflin Harcourt Publishing Company,
3 Park Avenue, 19th Floor, New York, New York 10016.

www.hmhco.com

Library of Congress Cataloging-in-Publication Data is available.
ISBN 978-0-544-94730-6

Book design by Jackie Shepherd

Printed in the United States of America
DOC 10 9 8 7 6 5 4 3 2 1

*For Paolo, who might not know that
he got the ball rolling on this one*

BANNERLESS

A Suspicious Death

Enid came downstairs into a kitchen bright with morning sun blazing through the one window and full of the greasy smell of cooked sausage. Olive already had breakfast —sausage, toast, cream—set out on the table. In her dress and apron, her dark hair pulled back with a scrap of cloth, she was already at work—but shouldn't have been, in Enid's opinion.

"How are you feeling?" Enid asked, hoping to keep worry out of her voice.

"I wish people would stop asking me that," Olive said, not looking up from the batch of dough that she was kneading, folding and punching it into the counter as if she could make it disappear.

Three other batches of dough sat rising in nearby bowls. Serenity household didn't need that much bread. Olive would probably trade it around the rest of Haven town.

Enid couldn't help herself. "How long you been up?"

Olive's smile was strained. "Up before Berol this morning."

2 · CARRIE VAUGHN

Berol worked the early shift at the goat farm outside town. He was usually the first one up.

"You sure you shouldn't be resting? You don't have to work so hard."

"I want to be useful. I have to be *useful*."

You are, Enid thought. Maybe part of Olive resting was just leaving her alone to mourn the miscarriage and recover in her own way. Which maybe meant making too much bread.

"Tea?" Olive asked as Enid sat and took up a knife to smear cream on a slice of toast.

"Sure."

Olive smiled broadly; such a little thing could please her. She bustled between the stove and counter to get the pot ready —of course, she already had water heated. When the tea was poured, Enid wrapped her hands around the earthenware mug to soak in the warmth, breathing in the steam, and tried not to nag too much.

They made small talk about the weather and the town, the late-summer market coming up and which of the outlying households might travel in, which of their far-off friends might visit. Usual gossip about who was sleeping with whom and whether the grain harvest was going to be over or under quota, and if it was over, would the committee let a couple of fields go fallow next year, though some would grumble that with a surplus the town could support a couple more mouths, hand out a couple more banners. Folk always wanted more banners.

After breakfast Enid helped clean up but only got as far as wiping down the table. Olive had already taken the plate and cup from her hands to put in the washbasin.

"What're you up to today, then?" Olive asked.

"I'm off to see if the clinic needs any help. Work's been slow lately."

"It's good that work's slow, yeah?"

When Enid had work, it meant something had gone wrong. "It is."

She put a vest over her tunic, took her straw hat from its hook by the door, and went outside. Didn't get much farther than that and stopped, seeing Tomas coming down the walk toward her.

Tomas was a middle-aged man, his silvering hair tied back in a short tail, his face pale and weathered, laugh lines abundant. Average height, a commanding gaze. He wore his investigator's uniform: plain belt and boots, simple tunic and trousers in a dark brown the color of earth, much deeper than any usual homespun or plain dyed brown.

A charge lit her brain: they had a job.

"Up for a tough one?" he asked in greeting.

"What is it?"

"Suspicious death out at Pasadan." His frown pulled at the lines in his face.

Enid stood amazed. She had investigated thefts and fraud, households that tried to barter the same bags of grain or barrels of cider twice, or that reneged on trades. She'd broken up fights and tracked down assaults. She had investigated bannerless pregnancies—women who'd gotten pregnant either because their implants had failed or, more rarely, because they'd thought to have a baby in secret. Keeping such a thing secret was nearly impossible—to her knowledge no one ever had. Though she supposed if they had managed to keep such a secret, no one would ever know. If you asked most folk, they'd say a bannerless pregnancy was the worst of the work she did.

The hardest, because she would be the one to decide if the case was an accident that could be made right, or a malicious flouting of everything the Coast Road communities stood for.

Murder had become rare. Much rarer than in the old world, according to the survivor stories. It still happened, of course; it always happened when enough people lived in close-enough quarters. But Enid never thought she'd see one herself. And maybe she still wouldn't; suspicious death was only *suspicious*, but Tomas seemed grim.

"Maybe you'd better come in and explain," she said.

///

TOMAS MADE HIMSELF at home in the kitchen, settling into a chair at the table.

Olive, still at the counter kneading bread, looked up. "Hey! Company! Can I get you some tea—" The bright greeting was habit; she stopped midsentence, her eyes widening. It was the uniform. Always a shock seeing it, no matter if an old friend like Tomas wore it.

"I'd love some tea, thanks," Tomas said. "How are you, Olive?" His tone was friendly, casual—an everyday question, not the pointed one Enid and the rest of the household had been asking her for the last week, and so Olive was able to give him an unforced welcome.

"Just fine," she said, wiping her hands on a dishcloth then scooping fresh leaves from their jar into the pot. "If this is about work, I can leave you two alone . . ."

"It's all right," Tomas said. "You're busy—stay."

Olive finished prepping the teapot, then went back to her dough, slapping the fourth batch into a smooth loaf, round and puffed and smelling of yeast.

"So what's this about?" Enid asked. *Suspicious death* was frustratingly nonspecific.

"A committee member at Pasadan requested the investigation. Man in his thirties, no other information."

"That's maybe thirty miles south, yeah?" Enid asked. "Not a big place."

"Couple hundred folk. Stable enough, mostly subsistence farming and some trade. Healthy community, everyone at regional thought."

"But are they really thinking murder?"

At the counter, Olive stopped kneading and glanced over, blinking disbelief.

Sam wandered in then, barefoot, shirtless, all wiry body, brown skin, and ropy muscles. Her Sam was thin but powerful. Folk thought he was weak, until he hefted fifty-pound bags of grain on his shoulder with one hand. He stood fast in storms.

"Murder? What?" he muttered sleepily, then saw Tomas and the uniform. "Oh, it's work. I'll go." He started to turn around.

"Stay, Sam," Tomas said. "Have some tea."

Sam looked at Enid for confirmation, and she hoped her smile was comforting. This would be all right; this was her job, after all. And Sam was family, part of what made her able to do the job. Someone to come home to.

"Morning, dear," she said, and kissed his cheek.

He sank into a chair at the kitchen table and accepted a fresh mug from Enid. "Murder, you said?" He tilted his head, a picture of bafflement. Who could blame him?

Tomas continued. "No one's said the word 'murder,' but they want us to check." He turned to Enid. "You up for that? You're due to carry this one as lead."

"Well, yes. Someone's got to, I suppose. But—are there witnesses? What happened?"

"Don't know yet. They've saved the body. We'll see what we see."

"If they've got a body on ice, we ought to hurry," she said.

"I was hoping to foot it in a couple hours, after we've had a chance to go through the records."

Well, that was her day planned then, wasn't it?

"Is everything going to be all right?" Olive asked.

They all looked to Tomas, the elder and mentor, for the answer to that, and he took a moment to reply. How did you answer that? Certainly, most things would be all right for most people. But they never would be again for the dead man, or the people who loved the person he'd been.

"Nothing for you to worry about," Tomas said. "That's our job."

Our job. Investigators, moving through communities like brown-draped shadows of ill tidings.

"Oh, I'll always worry," said good, sweet Olive, and the smile she gave them was almost back to normal. Then she sighed. "At least it's not a banner violation."

She'd become deeply sympathetic to households caught in banner violations. Wanting a baby badly enough could make someone break the rules, she'd say, and then insist she would never ever do such a thing herself, of course. But she could sympathize. After all, you could follow all the rules, earn a banner, and then nature plays a cruel trick on you.

On the wall above the kitchen door hung a piece of woven cloth, a foot square on each side, a red-and-green-checked pattern for blood and life: their banner, which the four of them had earned. They'd all come from households that put their banners on the wall as a mark of pride. This was their first, and they could hope there would be more. Then Olive had miscarried. They had a banner and no baby to show for it. Enid kept telling Olive that they had time and more chances. No one could take the banner away.

///

ENID AND TOMAS arranged to meet at Haven's archives, where they'd go over any records they had on Pasadan, looking for . . . anything. Something not right. Something that stood out and might explain any anomalies they found once they got there.

After Tomas left, she went to change into the uniform, the earth-brown tunic and trousers. Along with it, she put on the attitude she'd need to convince people she was in charge and her word was law.

Serenity household's cottage had a handful of rooms. The kitchen and workspace, several bedrooms. Olive and Berol had the downstairs one, Enid and Sam the upstairs. There, she sat on the bed, her brown tunic laid out next to her, her pack open at her feet, taking a moment to gather her thoughts. Sam found her there with her guard down, holding head in hands, just for a moment.

He settled beside her, his weight creaking the ropes under the mattress, making her sway.

"Don't you have to get to work?" she said, straightening, combing fingers through her short hair to cover her unease.

"We're just putting the walls up on the new barn at End Zone. It can wait. You going to be all right?"

"Yes, yes," she said. "It's probably a misunderstanding. Can't really be a murder, can it?"

"One way or another, you'll figure it out."

"Nice of you to have faith in me."

She stretched out her hand; he took it and squeezed. His darker coloring contrasted with the pale sand color of hers. Both hands were calloused and weathered, rough, catching against each other. Pulling herself over to him, she gave him a long kiss, which he happily reciprocated. She hoped she would be back to kiss him again soon, and that he was right and she would figure this out quickly.

Back in the kitchen, Olive was clearing up her workspace. Finally finished with the bread.

"I shouldn't be more than a few days," Enid said, backpack over one shoulder. "Tell Berol I said hey, yeah?"

"Enid. I was thinking." Olive paused, staring at her clean hands. Avoiding looking up. "I was thinking maybe you should try. Maybe it was meant to be yours."

It. The banner. The baby.

How could Olive say that so easily to a woman about to leave for a death investigation? Olive was the one meant to be a mother; Enid couldn't seem to stop traveling. Enid teared up at the unfairness of what had happened, but she held herself calm—the uniform might have helped—and replied firmly, avoiding any tone that could be mistaken for anything but resolve. "I stand by what we decided. Don't go dismissing yourself so easily, my girl. The banner is yours."

She went to Olive, kissed her cheek before heading for the door. Olive appeared both exhausted and grateful.

Olive clasped her hand for a moment. "Careful, Enid. This sounds like a rough one."

"Don't worry," Enid said. "We'll be back before you know it."

"Better," she said sternly.

SERENITY WAS ON the outskirts of the town of Haven, situated on the Coast Road. The place occupied a wide, grassy valley, bounded by distant rolling hills and lots of sky. Pasture, cultivated fields, orchards, and vineyards, and the households that tended them, spread out along winding paths and the shadows of old roads. The settlement that clustered around Haven was home to a couple thousand folk. Sometimes, especially on the big market days, the place even felt crowded. But mostly it sprawled.

The walk from Serenity to the clinic in the middle of town didn't take long, maybe twenty minutes, straight down the Coast Road. Enid passed a handful of other households, some garden patches, and workshops. The forge was lit, metalsmiths working, and voices carried from the potters'. Chickens muttered from coops, and goats chuckled from behind sheds.

Other Haven townsfolk were out and about; they started to wave when Enid came up the road, but saw the uniform and then held back. The uniforms changed people, and it didn't matter how familiar their faces were, most folk never treated them quite the same while they wore the brown. Enid could smile and wave back all she wanted; nothing seemed to change that.

The archives were in the cellar under the clinic building in the middle of town. One of the few surviving structures from before the Fall, it seemed incongruous next to the other buildings, which were all stucco and plank boards. The clinic was made of smooth concrete and metal, austere and oddly geometric, like a piece that had fallen out of a puzzle. An array of solar collectors covered the roof except where skylights peered through, and drainpipes fed into a cistern. The windows were tall and narrow, unadorned. A porch had been added, and orange and lemon trees edged the walkway.

Most of the space around the clinic was taken up with the town square, which hosted once-a-month markets and communal herb gardens. A couple of nearby households worked to maintain the gardens and process the herbs, drying them for cooking, preparing them for medicinal and household use. This late in the summer, the air in this part of town smelled heady, almost overpowering, with mint and sage and lavender and a dozen other scents rising up and becoming rich and languorous. The air was hot and sticky; Enid's hat kept the sun off.

The packed dirt of the main road through town had once been asphalt. It had decayed decades ago, so folk tore it out. This was way before Enid's time, but when she was young, Auntie Kath told stories about it, about the bones of the world from before and what they had to do to survive. The shadow of that world remained, the streets in the same places and the foundations of buildings still visible. But a new skin had been put over it. This was all Enid had known, but Auntie Kath used to sit on the shaded porch of the clinic and look out, murmuring, *It's so different now.*

Tomas waited for her at the cellar's slanted wooden doors. She nodded at him, and he opened one of the doors and gestured her down.

Down a set of concrete stairs, the clinic's cellar opened up. A switch turned on a string of lights, powered by the solar panels on the clinic roof. The ceiling was low—so much so Tomas had to slouch—but the space was wide and filled with shelves, trunks, wooden crates, and plastic bins. Much of it was like a museum—odds and ends from before the Fall that folk thought might be useful someday . . . or might never be useful again but someone had thought worth saving, keeping dry and safe. The place had a musty, disused air that tickled the nose.

Books—hundreds of them—comprised the bulk of the

collection. The founders of Haven had looted a couple of libraries, so the stories went. Practical books on farming, food preservation, irrigation, medicine—everything they thought they might need. But also an odd collection of novels, commentary, magazines, and newspapers—things that would have been disposable back then. Now, they seemed like a time capsule. Artifacts of a lost world. And then the diaries, the journals, the accounts and letters written by people who lived through the Fall. History, now. During their training, investigators were required to read the extant diaries and journals, to understand people, to understand where their world came from and why their rules existed. To try to keep all that from ever happening again.

A small desk in the corner served the investigators as an office, where they could review evidence and keep accounts of previous cases. Their collective knowledge. Committee records were kept here as well, pages bound into simple books with leather covers recording harvests, births, deaths, storms, local happenings, events of note. Local histories, local portraits.

There wasn't much. Various committees and investigators had only been keeping records for about twenty years or so; the notes didn't go all the way back to the Fall. Folk then had more important things to worry about; paper had been scarce, and they weren't convinced there'd be anyone around in the future to look at records. At some point, though, someone decided that writing things down might be useful. Planning resources and crops and babies and everything was easier if you could see the patterns. So, now they had records.

Enid and Tomas found the relevant volumes; each took half to read, and the tedious work began. They'd only been at it twenty minutes or so when Tomas asked, "Do you remember Auntie Kath?"

"Of course I do."

"She talked about how they didn't know what they needed to save. They couldn't save it all, so they had to choose. How later she wished there were things people in the early days of Haven had saved."

"Like cameras. Or latex gloves." Enid not only remembered—she could almost hear the old woman's low, rough voice going on about it.

"Plastic wrap," Tomas added, and they both chuckled. Plastic wrap had been an obsession with Auntie Kath, who insisted the item had a million uses, and she brought it up every time one of those uses occurred to her. No one had ever really understood what she was talking about.

"Someday we'll dig into an undisturbed cellar or an old archive and find some plastic wrap," Enid said.

He shrugged. "We've gone this long without it. No one's missed it since Kath died. But I wonder if this is how they felt. Trying to learn it all because we don't know what we need to know. But it isn't possible. We'll miss something but have to hope we won't."

They studied the records, hoping to get a picture of the town of Pasadan, to guess what they might find when they got there. But they couldn't predict, not really. Columns were labeled, lists of numbers written carefully in different hands, in fading ink. Names of Pasadan's committee members, short descriptions of them that in the end didn't say anything at all. This might have been any of a dozen small settlements on the Coast Road. But this was the one requesting investigation of a death.

They wouldn't really know a thing about the town until they got there.

Fifteen Years Earlier

The Worst Storm

The storm started with gusts that threatened to throw Enid across the yard at Plenty household. She had the job of putting away tools and tying down tomato plants and squash vines, hoping they wouldn't get too torn up. The sudden blasting wind turned what should have been an ordinary chore into an emergency. Some of the plants in the garden were already flattened. Enid's fingers shook, trying to get a last piece of twine knotted. She'd seen storms before; this felt like something else, electric and ominous, black clouds on the horizon expanding to fill the sky.

Peri, her mother and one of the town's medics, shouted at her from the door of Plenty's cellar. "Enid! Leave it! Come in now!"

Rain started, huge drops driving into the ground and into Enid. They actually hurt, icy slaps on her skin. Sheets of it would soon follow, soaking everything. She ran to the cellar along with the last few straggling household folk. The wind howled.

One of these last was Tomas, who still held the hammer he'd been using to help to secure doors and windows. He was a lithe man with brown hair in a tail, his tunic stained with sweat and dirt.

"This is some fun, yeah?" he said, grinning. He had to put down the hammer and use both hands to haul the cellar door shut.

"What?" Wide-eyed, she gaped at him. It hadn't occurred to her that on some level this might be *fun*.

"Get in, you, come on." Peri patted his shoulder, urging him down the thin wooden stairs, and put her arm around Enid. Her hair was coming loose from her headband; sweat matted strands of it to her face. "You okay?"

"Yeah," Enid said, but she wasn't sure. The adults had this pensive air, brows furrowed, biting their lips and looking up at the ceiling as if they might see through wood and dirt to what was happening in the sky overhead. Hanging on to their children just like Peri was doing.

Plenty was a prosperous household, with a half-dozen kids under eighteen. The baby was crying, and no one seemed to mind. Having to huddle in a cellar during a storm seemed like a good reason to cry. On the other hand, Tomas sat on the steps by the door, hand resting on the handle, like he wanted to reach through the wood and touch the storm. Thriving on the sense of urgency.

"You look like you want to go out and watch," one of the household women said to him.

"I kind of do," he answered. There was nervous laughter. A crack of thunder startled them into silence. Rain rattled on the doors like a million hands clapping.

Windows had been boarded up, doors bolted, rain barrels drained and secured, windmills lashed down. Livestock penned into barns and chickens into coops. Everything that could be harvested had been. Nothing more to do but wait it out.

Even in the cellar, the wind pounded, slamming against adobe walls, whistling through cracks in the door. Enid had never heard anything like it. She didn't want to admit how the fierceness of it scared her. This wind could pick them up and carry them away. The rain was loud as thunder, the thunder like earthquakes.

It seemed to go on for hours. Enid found her own place sitting with her back to one of the dirt walls. Wrapped in a blanket, she hugged her knees to her chest and failed to sleep.

Most of Plenty's thirty members had crammed into the cellar; a few had stayed at Haven's clinic to help anyone who needed it. They had lanterns, plenty of water, blankets, food, and a bucket in a corner roped off for a latrine. But the time dragged. Most tried to sleep, but the next crack of thunder would wake everyone, and they'd go back to studying the ceiling, gripping one another's hands.

"How bad is it, you think?" someone asked.

"Worst I've seen," another answered.

"No, remember that one that flooded the river? Washed out Angel household? They never did rebuild, did they?"

A discussion ensued, all the old people talking about what storms they remembered, what the previous worst storm really was, and whether it was twenty or twenty-five years ago. People only fell quiet when the rain picked up and got so loud nobody could hear anymore.

The oldest among them was Auntie Kath, and she was old enough to remember before the Fall; she'd been a teenager in Haven's earliest years. So, of course, folk turned to her for the definitive answer.

"Oh, no, not even close to the worst," she said, shaking her head. A chair had been brought to the cellar for her, and she sat there, blankets piled on her. One of the little kids curled up asleep at her feet. Her frame was shrunken, bent, her hair thinned to wisps. Her vision was long gone. She didn't work anymore, but the folk of Plenty cared for her, a precious grandmother to them all. The last who remembered. "The one that shut down L.A. was the worst. This isn't anything as bad as that. But really, the storms don't seem as bad when you don't have as much to be broken by them." She chuckled in her rattling voice.

This was definitely the worst storm Enid had ever been through, but she was only twelve. Listening to the others, she was pretty sure there'd be worse someday. She tried to think of what that might look like and decided Tomas had a point: she was curious to see what a worse storm could possibly look like. How bad was *really* bad, if this was only *sort of* bad?

More hours passed. The air in the cellar grew close and humid. The little kids were crying along with the baby now. Enid was trying hard to be grown-up about the situation, but she thought about crying too. Or convincing Tomas to maybe open the door, just a crack, and let them have a look outside. People kept trying to talk to her, and she was tired of answering the same questions: yes, she was fine; no, she didn't need anything to eat; and even if she was scared, she wasn't going to admit it.

Several times, Peri went around to check on everyone and came to Enid last. "How're you holding up?"

"*Fine,*" she said, her face wrinkling. What if the storm never let up? There'd been talk of flooding, of lightning strikes and fires. What would they do if anything like that happened here?

Peri smiled wryly and ran a hand over Enid's hair. "It shouldn't be too much longer."

"How do you know?"

"Because there's never been a storm in all of human history that lasted forever."

"Can't I go out? Just for a minute, just to look around." Just to get away from the crying, the people fussing, the heat . . .

"Look at Tomas. He's being patient." In fact, Tomas was still on the stairs, hunched over. He seemed to be asleep even, despite the noise, the stuffiness, the still-pounding rain. "Just a little longer. Try to sleep, all right?"

Enid huddled back in on herself and glared.

More hours passed. The world quieted, wind letting up, rain slackening. The building above them stopped rattling. Restless murmuring started, folk asking one another when they might open the door and go out to see what damage had been done.

A hard pounding—a human pounding—knocked at the cellar door, and Tomas was right there to crack it open. The lingering rain was enough to soak the edge of the steps and Tomas's tunic, but he didn't seem to mind. He called a greeting to the visitors.

Two soaking-wet men in brown investigator tunics leaned in. The beard on one of them dripped water. This one spoke loudly, as if he had been shouting over the storm for hours and hadn't noticed the quiet. "Tornado touched down. Ant Farm and Potter north of town got hit. Some of their folk are missing; they need help."

"Right." He pushed open the door, turning to Enid. "Latch it closed behind me, yeah?"

"I want to go," Enid said, not thinking before starting up

the stairs, as if she were a cat hoping to slip out the door before he could shut it again. "I can help." She was done with sitting, done with listening to the breathing and the chatter and the crying. She didn't know if she could help, really. But she wanted to get out and *do* something.

"Enid," her mother commanded. It was uncanny, how her mother could make the name sound like "stop."

She looked pleadingly at Tomas, who considered a moment.

"You're a spark, kid," he said, then to Peri, "I'll look after her."

Peri shook her head. "I don't think—" But Enid had already scrambled up after him. "Fine, then. But don't get in the way," she ordered, grabbing a cloak to shove at her. Enid took it, nodding. "Is it okay for the rest of us to come out?" Peri called to the investigators.

One of them looked into the sky and said, "Give it another hour."

"Right. Enid, be careful."

"I will."

///

TOMAS HAD BEEN training to be an investigator for the last couple of years. Enid still wasn't used to seeing him in the brown uniform. He looked almost sinister wearing it; he didn't smile as much. He wore it now because the other investigators seemed to think they needed the authority. In a disaster, they needed people to follow orders, and the uniform increased the chances of that.

This wouldn't be the last time Enid followed Tomas on an investigation, but she didn't know that then.

The rain had turned everything to mud: the garden, the pasture, and the paths between houses—all of it had become a soupy mess, melted brown earth slipping under their feet, a stink of rain and rot rising up. Some of the fencing around the household grounds had blown over. Branches on the big cottonwood in back had broken off, and now hung on by naked strips of torn wood. Cleaning this up was going to take weeks. The plants and vines she'd worked so hard to shore up were all ripped and drowned. Rain still fell, but it seemed tired now. It would have been a pleasant drizzle, if it hadn't just followed a typhoon. Enid took a big breath of wet air, which smelled strongly of dirt and ozone, but was still fresher than the close stink of heat and bodies in the cellar.

They had a solar car still charged up; Enid perched in the back among the tools they'd brought: ropes, hooks, crowbars, shovels, a first aid kit. Things for digging, breaking, rescuing, and she wondered what they expected to find. She also kept very quiet, surprised that they were letting her come on the trip and determined not to get in the way. To actually be useful. Small price to pay for getting to see what all this was about.

One of the affected households had gotten a runner out to Haven to get help. The investigators had been sheltered at the clinic; one of them was a medic as well. They set out as soon as the rain let up. Still, several hours had passed. Things could have gotten much worse in that time.

After bouncing and jolting over rutted, washed-out roads, slipping in mud, nearly stalling out in places where the road had washed out entirely, the solar car ran out of battery halfway to the plain where the households of Ant Farm and Potter were located. The adults seemed to expect that, merely collecting the gear and setting out on foot. Enid carried coils of rope over her shoulder and hugged the first aid bag to her chest. A lane branched off, emerged from a copse of trees, and from there they looked out onto a wide field.

Plenty and the rest of Haven had been waterlogged and roughed up. But Potter, the first of the households they came to, was shattered. A windmill lay on its side; trees had fallen, tangled roots reaching to the sky and dripping mud. The first plank-board cottage they came upon had completely fallen over. Clothes and pots and glass and furniture lay scattered among broken wood, as if some giant had come and smashed the thing with a hand.

"They didn't have a cellar," the bearded investigator said despairingly.

"What did this?" she asked, awestruck.

"Tornado," Tomas answered simply. While Enid might have known the definition of a tornado, understood the concept of one—a great funnel of wind bridging earth and sky, generated by colliding storm fronts—she had no idea what that meant in reality. What had all this looked like while it was happening? What had the howl of wind sounded like?

The household had two other buildings: a workhouse and a small barn for goats and chickens. The workhouse, little more than a shed, was smashed and blown across half a pasture. The barn was still mostly standing, and they found four survivors there, three adults and a kid of about ten, soaked and huddled together under the wall that had only fallen halfway in.

"Bret and Smoke, did you find them? Did you find them?" one of the survivors demanded as Tomas and the others coaxed them out of their hiding place. They stood blinking into the pale sky, like new chicks.

Since they didn't have a cellar, they had fled to a nearby ravine for shelter—as low and as close to underground as they could get when the worst of the storm cell had passed overhead. But Smoke had stayed behind to save a few things from the house, fetch water and supplies they would need while they hid, as well as knives and tools that would be difficult to replace. After the howling winds had passed by, the others returned to find the cottage smashed. Bret had urged them to stay sheltered in the remains of the barn while he went to check on their neighbors and then go to Haven for help. He was still at the clinic, his household-mates were relieved to hear. But they hadn't found Smoke.

While the medic sat with the survivors, tending small wounds and shock, the investigators started a search. Enid helped pick through the cottage's wreckage. Systematically, starting at one end and working through it together, they turned over boards, broke through walls with the crowbars. The thing hardly seemed like a house anymore, even when she came across an intact clay vase, still with a soggy flower nestled inside. A rag doll. A woven blanket, matted with mud. A sodden mop of feathers that turned out to be a dead chicken.

"Here!" Tomas called finally, and Enid and the other investigator ran over.

Tomas had broken through a wall to find a body. He knelt to touch it, but with a lack of urgency. Part of Enid told her to hold back, that she didn't need to see this. She didn't want to —she should never have come. But she'd wanted to come, she was here—she should see it all.

Caught up in broken boards, the body was of a youngish man, tan skin gone ashen. Half his shirt was torn off, along with the skin underneath it, a great gash across his chest, but rain had washed the blood away. He had shoulder-length black hair and the start of a beard. His eyes were closed, one hand clenched around a hammer.

"Well," the other investigator muttered. "That's that, then."

"Was it blood loss that got him?" Tomas asked.

The older man shook his head. "There's a wound on the skull, here. Probably a combination of things, when the house came down on him. He shouldn't have gone back." He shook his head. "You want to tell them, or should I?"

Tomas answered, "Which would you prefer?"

"I think I'd rather untangle this guy here, if that's all right."

Tomas nodded. "We ought to get to Ant Farm as soon as we can. If it's anything like this, there's a lot more work ahead."

"Yeah. Enid, could you help me lift this?"

She stood frozen a moment. She had wanted to help. She had wanted to work, but she hadn't imagined this. Tomas lingered a moment, as if waiting to see what she would do. That more than anything prompted her. "Yes. Yes, I can."

Tomas turned to the barn to deliver the bad news, and Enid helped prop up the broken boards while the investigator extricated the body and carried it to the soaked grass, to lay it there neatly for his people.

In the meantime, a loud cry of grief came from inside the barn.

The rest of the household emerged soon after and came to see their dead and to gather whatever they could from the wreck. They'd move on to Haven, rejoin Bret, and decide what to do from there. Rebuild or find another household to join.

Picking through the cottage's rubble, one of the survivors picked something up: a foot-long square of cloth, woven in a red-and-green pattern, still recognizable even soaked in mud. A banner—very likely the banner authorizing the child who clung to the woman's cloak now, unwilling to let go and maybe still get washed away. She held the banner to her face and cried, her whole face puckered. The kid hugged her tighter, and they held on to each other for a moment. The woman never let go of the banner, as if it were an anchor that would keep her from drifting into a void.

When the investigators and Enid arrived at Ant Farm, the household folk were trying to herd together a handful of goats and a pair of horses who'd fled the half-fallen barn. They'd also found shelter in a ravine, but the tornado hadn't struck here directly as it had at Potter. They did have a couple of hurt folk—one with a concussion, another with a broken arm.

They hitched one of the horses to a wagon for the trip back, to carry the injured to the clinic at Haven. Enid found blankets, passed around water, carried tools. She looked around with a sense of growing disbelief and wondered how any of them were going to get through this.

Toward nightfall, the group started back to Haven. The storm clouds were breaking up—they even caught a hint of deep blue twilight sky, blazing against the gray they'd lived with for the last couple of days. Still, night was close, and they decided it would be better to travel at night than wait to get back to Haven. Enid and Tomas walked ahead of the wagon, carrying lanterns to light the way. The medic walked behind, to keep watch on the injured. They stopped on the way to pick up the survivors from Potter.

They traveled slowly, checking the road for hazards, avoiding flooded spots. The horse's hooves sucked in the mud. The night was damp, turning colder by the moment, and Enid's wet cloak didn't do much to warm her. She shivered.

"You all right?" Tomas asked her.

She didn't know. But if she kept walking, she'd get back home, and then she'd be all right. "I probably shouldn't have come. Wasn't much help."

"You did fine." His smile was kind, but she was still unhappy. She'd never forget the way that body looked, twisted and fragile.

This was not the last body she and Tomas would examine together, but she didn't know that then, either.

The Body

Enid and Tomas walked partway to Pasadan that afternoon and spent the night at a way station outside the village of Tigerlily. Along the way they passed a couple of solar cars, as well as horses and wagons. In a month or so, when the harvest trade fairs started up, the Coast Road would fill with cars, horses, wagons, and travelers, carrying with them a party air.

They waved and offered greetings to folk, who returned the hails cautiously, eyeing their uniforms, unsuccessfully hiding their trepidation — no doubt wondering where the pair was headed and what poor household had drawn the attention of investigators. Enid was used to the anxious look-overs by now, and even found them amusing. Most folk would never come under the scrutiny of her or any other investigator. But everyone worried they might, and what did that say about people in general?

Tigerlily had a solar car for communal use, usually reserved for the old, the young, and the injured. Enid and Tomas requisitioned it, to save time but also for the sense of authority.

The people of Pasadan would hear the hum coming down the lane and look up. Their arrival would be an event. *We are here now,* would be the message, delivered by the investigator and her enforcer, and those in the village would pause, daunted by the authority without consciously realizing it. An investigator's power wasn't something Enid wielded so much as donned like a coat. They wouldn't really see her and Tomas at all.

Tomas drove the rest of the morning until the early mist had burned off and the sun was high and warm. Bouncing, swaying on its low tires, the car came over the crest of a hill to a valley that looked imaginary, constructed to be beautiful. Green meadows covered shallow hills, and the road curved around to a wide vista cut through by a river, lined with copses of cottonwoods and perfect squares of cultivated fields, grains nodding and rippling in a breeze, all of it lush and welcoming. Far on the western horizon, a hazy gray line marked a distant ocean. The Coast Road continued west and south around a set of hills to a series of fishing villages along the ocean, another two weeks' walk at least.

A friendly sign marked the turnoff, a whitewashed plank nailed to a couple of sturdy posts. PASADAN, written in artistic black with little flourishes at the beginning and end, with a couple of painted strands of ivy for a border. It was charming.

The town came into view; they got a look at it from above, before the road descended. Pasadan was set on a grid—it might have been built on the bones of a small town from before the Fall, the old concrete and steel knocked in and cleared away for salvage, the asphalt rotted, a new town built on the old. Square paddocks of fenced-in green pastured sheep, goats, a few horses. There were chickens and geese. Houses and communal buildings clustered along dirt paths, and a group of windmills stood on the side of a hill. Noise drifted from workshops; smoke rose up from a forge and another shop that looked like a glassblower's. Color fluttered from clotheslines, stretched along the edges of the pastures. It was all clean, well organized, pleasant. Enid couldn't find fault with the place, not from this far out. Finding any cracks would take time. Speaking to people, looking at the body, poking around for anomalies. Discovering what had caused enough suspicion to call for an investigation in the first place.

"They must have someone who's good at building fences," Tomas said. The place did seem to have a lot of them, from pens for goats to pretty whitewashed planks surrounding garden squares, more decorative than functional. Tomas was probably right—someone here was building fences for fun.

The car trundled down a gently sloping road. Tomas steered it around a pair of switchbacks before leveling off and heading toward the first of the buildings, a sprawling whitewashed structure built half into the hillside. He asked, "Strategy?"

"We present ourselves to the village committee and ask to see the body," she said.

"And if they refuse? If they've gotten rid of it since the request for an investigation went in?"

"One of them requested the investigation," Enid said. "If they got rid of evidence since then, that'll be on them." If there was dissension within the town's committee, set the factions against each other until the truth, or something close to it, came out. There'd be a lot of interpretation. "If it's an accidental death, the evidence should be clear enough. The committee here should welcome an investigation."

"No one likes an investigation, Enid."

That was true enough. Especially a place like Pasadan, which seemed to have never had one. How much of a shock were they in for?

They had seen people moving around from the first: some-one in skirts at a laundry line, a teenager herding geese toward a pond, a blacksmith stepping into the street to stretch his back or to look into the clear sky to gauge the weather. No one had a reason to glance up the winding lane that led out of the val-ley until they heard the car's motor. The kid with the geese first, then the blacksmith. The kid ran to the large whitewashed building, probably the community hall and committee rooms, a way station for travelers. This was where Enid and Tomas would be living while they conducted their investigation. She hoped this didn't last much longer than a day or two.

By the time Tomas guided the car up to the communal building, a crowd was there waiting for them. The three in front were likely the committee members, gray sashes hurriedly put over their shoulders, standing rigid as walls. The rest stood a little ways behind them, leaning in to hear—but not too close. Spectators. A chorus, to report on gossip. A general mood of anxiety made everyone frown, but no one held anything that might be used as a weapon, no pitchforks or knives in view. Tomas had weapons—a staff and a packet of tranquilizers. Mostly for show. She'd only seen the tranqs used when some-body lost their temper. Sometimes, people lashed out. And if they did, Tomas would be ready. But right now, everyone just seemed cautious.

The committee trio waited: a white-haired old man, tall, ar-thritis twisting his hands; a second man, bald, short, and round, with narrow eyes and skin like amber; a woman, younger than the others, with her hair in a dark braid, her gaze lowered. Bit-ing her lip as if thinking hard about something. This would be Ariana, then. She'd requested the investigation. Enid wanted to get her alone to talk as soon as possible.

The white-haired man, however, glared daggers. Very

likely, he was the committee chair, Philos. The other must have been Lee.

Enid and Tomas left the car and came forward. Tomas stayed a little behind, leaving no doubt who was in charge. Ah, yes, that would be her. She wasn't a big woman, but she wasn't small either. Average height, with some weight and muscle on her. Tomas and his wood staff would be the one the folk of Pasadan glanced at nervously. The threatening one.

She donned a placid smile, as if nothing at all could ever be wrong. "Hello. I'm Enid. This is Tomas. The regional committee called for an investigation after a request was submitted. We'll make it as quick as possible. Would you three like to step inside so we can talk?" She didn't look at the crowd that had gathered, the folk she didn't want listening in.

The old man and committee chair, Philos, didn't move. He looked her up and down, clearly sizing her up.

"You seem young," he said. He glanced at Tomas. Wondering maybe if he was really in charge, if he was supervising some sort of training assignment. She wanted to snarl at him —would regional send a trainee on a possible murder investigation? Truly? Maybe he thought so. Such stories were told about investigators, after all. That they had too much authority, wielded too blithely. Trouble was, no one had found a better way to do the job.

"I've worn my uniform for three years, sir," Enid said. "Tomas is my enforcer. I hope we can take care of this unpleasantness quickly."

"It was an accident," Philos said.

The woman, Ariana, rolled her eyes. Commentary on a long-running argument? Enid was able to catch her gaze then and raise a questioning brow.

Jaw set, she stepped forward with sudden resolve. "Investigators, welcome to Pasadan. I'm Ariana. This is Philos and Lee. We'll help in any way we can."

"Thank you. Let's go inside, shall we?" Enid gestured at the door that she hoped led to some sort of conference room.

"Come, Philos," Ariana murmured through gritted teeth.

The man's posture flinched just enough to let him turn and lead the others to the door and inside. Enid and Tomas followed. Enid lingered long enough to look over the gathered crowd and offer a friendly smile.

No one smiled back, and no one seemed put at ease. Investigators didn't make a lot of friends and weren't often welcome. Not while they were wearing their uniforms.

She'd guessed right, and the front room of the community building was a group meeting space: committee meetings, public hearings, petitions. During some periods it might have been used for harvest, food or wool processing, or town-wide activities during bad weather. The place had a cement floor, windows and skylights letting in plenty of natural light, and a faint agricultural air of hay and soil. A long wood table and chairs sat on one side of the room, along with a blank chalkboard. An all-purpose room, clean and worn with use. Enid approved.

The three committee members clustered by the table; Enid guessed they'd usually sit on one side of it during hearings but that they didn't know what to do now. They were so rarely the object of a hearing, and not the ones in charge.

"You must be tired after traveling," Ariana said, bustling as she defaulted to the role of a good host, eager and hopeful. "Would you like to rest first? We have a good way station here, a shower for washing up if you like."

As lovely as a shower sounded, they didn't have time. "Later," Enid said. "Why don't we sit and discuss business first."

In a moment they were arranged at the table, the committee members on one side and Enid on the other, as if this were a normal meeting after all. Tomas ranged around the room, hands behind his back, studying the walls and window frames as if he were a carpenter running an inspection. Philos kept glancing over at him. Wondering what Tomas was up to, no doubt. While the enforcer was on his feet, the others would never relax, and that was all to the good as far as Enid was concerned.

Enid waited a moment. Resisted asking if everyone was comfortable; they likely wouldn't answer her.

"We received the initial report. A man was killed. Sero," she said.

"It was an accident," Philos repeated.

"Why do you say that?" Enid asked him.

"He fell and hit his head." Very decisive.

"Did anyone see it happen? Is there a witness?"

No answer. The three glanced at one another, then quickly looked away. Afraid to reveal too much, even by looking. So no one saw, or no one would reveal anyone who did see.

"What was he doing when he hit his head?" Enid asked.

"Working. He was in his workshop," Philos answered.

"You're sure no one saw him?"

"I . . . we . . . we don't know. We're not sure."

"Do you know who saw him alive last?" Enid asked. She spread the question around. The second man, Lee, hadn't spoken yet, merely nodded or shaken his head in agreement with the others. Ariana looked like she wanted to speak, but not if it meant interrupting Philos. She watched him closely, as if waiting for cues.

"Ariana?" Enid prompted.

Again, she set her expression. Steeling herself. "No.

Sero . . . Sero was a bit of a loner. We don't know who might have seen him."

They'd had almost four days to get their story in order. Enid would have to keep asking the same questions until something slipped out. Question them again, separately. She'd have to find out where he lived, who interacted with him regularly, if the dead man had been acting strangely.

"I understand you submitted the investigation request, Ariana?"

She started to speak, but Philos interrupted. "She did so against the recommendation of the rest of the committee." Lee seemed to be biting his lips, not looking up, not willing to stand with Philos's declaration. Ariana glared at them both, and Enid wondered if Lee had assured the committeewoman that he agreed with requesting an investigation, just as he agreed with Philos about not requesting one. Philos continued, "It was an accident and not worth the time or effort of an investigation."

"Always worth the effort, if the truth is under debate," Enid said. "Pasadan won't be penalized for the wasted time, if that's what you're worried about."

His mouth pressed shut, his gaze shadowed. He was worried about something else. Out of the corner of her eye, she saw Tomas standing by, listening close.

Enid said, "Ariana, how quickly after Sero died did you send the request?"

"I . . . I'm not really sure, because we're not really sure when he died. He might have been there some time. But once he was found . . . not long, a couple of hours. We were just all so shocked; it just seemed so odd."

"The committee could have handled it. *Should* have handled it," Philos said. He and Ariana glared at each other, across Lee, who looked like he'd rather be somewhere else.

This sounded like Ariana went behind the others' backs.

"There wasn't much discussion about it between you, then?"

"Oh, there was some," Ariana said.

"It was loud," Lee added. His voice was deep, which Enid hadn't expected.

Philos turned to Ariana, his jaw stiff and lips puckered. He either wanted to spit or swear. And how many secret conversations had been going on between these people over the last several days? Sending for investigators was an end run around the debate, then. Dissent within Pasadan's committee. This was already more complicated than Enid had hoped.

"I'd like to have a look at the workshop where he died. And I understand the body is still available?"

"Is that really necessary?" Philos asked.

"Philos, please, no trouble!" Lee hissed, reaching out then flinching back, as if he'd tried to touch fire. They were treating the man like he was cracked glass that might shatter.

Philos turned on him in a silent reprimand, glaring. Enid had a memory of children fighting.

At the moment, Enid didn't like Philos. He seemed to be the kind of person who liked being in charge, who liked being the first to know things and didn't like being left out, and who didn't much like parties.

"I don't know if it's necessary or not," Enid said brightly. "But I'd rather look and find out it's not needed than skip it when it is. We'll go look at the body first, then look at where he died, and figure out what we need to do next, if anything. All right?"

"How long do you think this will take? Until we get this all cleared up? I just—it's my job to protect this village. I don't want any unnecessary disruption." Philos suddenly seemed aware of the bad impression he was making.

"The disruption has already occurred, sir," she replied. She caught Tomas twitching a smile at that.

Ariana led them out to the street. Philos and Lee followed, the former tense with anger, the latter deferential. Tomas kept a respectful distance, looking them all over. The trio kept glancing at him over their shoulders.

Most of the spectators had left, but a few lingered, inventing chores that brought them close to the committee house, hoeing patches that didn't have weeds, feeding chickens that were probably used to scratching somewhere else. They looked up, watching the group's progress. As if they could tell anything by seeing a group of people walk.

Ariana's household, Newhome, was close by and had a couple of cottages, a barn, a windmill, and a cistern. They kept geese and chickens for eggs and meat, wove cloth, and Pasadan's medic lived here. They also had a root cellar, which was where they'd stored the body. The doors were outside, angled up against the barn, opening to stairs that led down into a chill darkness.

"He's in here," Ariana said, gesturing in.

"Thanks. Your medic had a look at him?"

"Yes, briefly. Wasn't much he could do; Sero was clearly dead. But Tull arranged to have him carried here."

"Can you wait out here, please?" Enid said. The request sounded so reasonable, no one could say no. The committee members didn't look happy about it, but they agreed.

Enid and Tomas both held hand lanterns, fully charged, and turned them on as they went down the steps into the cellar.

The place was small, maybe twelve feet square, typical of most underground storage spaces. Dirt floor and walls, four-by-four posts supporting the ceiling. The dry chill raised goose flesh on Enid's arms. Foodstuffs had been cleared off the shelves on one wall, or the cellar had already been empty. A canvas sheet draped on the floor across from them clearly covered a body, just under six feet tall, lanky. The pole-and-canvas stretcher that had been used to carry the man was still underneath him. Enid passed her lantern back and forth over it but couldn't find any details out of place. It was all very neat and clean, but the room smelled like a corpse, musty, underlay with a stomach-turning sweetness. The place was cool, not cold, so the body was rotting.

She put on leather gloves and pulled back the sheet. The edges had been tucked under the body, and it took her a moment to slip them free without jostling the corpse too badly.

"Would have been better if they left it in place," she said.

"Not in this heat," Tomas answered. "That they saved him at all suggests they're not hiding anything."

"Well, not hiding anything *obvious*," she said. "I get the impression Philos and Ariana aren't the best of friends." Tomas gave a huff of agreement.

She revealed the body.

He was in his thirties, with pale skin, sharp features, and a dark beard of a few days' growth. His eyelids were swollen shut; his cheeks and the rest of him were bloated, belly starting to distend with rot. They would need to cremate this one soon. The investigators got here just in time.

He wore plain homespuns, an undyed pullover shirt and drawstring trousers. Good, solid leather boots, aged, scuffed at the heels and toes. He might have worn these boots his whole adult life. His body seemed untouched, unscathed, unremarkable. His hands were calloused. He still had the dirt of his last job under his fingernails and worn into the cracks of his palms. He was a laborer.

Then there was his head. She tilted it gently; the body was far past rigor mortis and pliable. The hair on the back of his head was matted with blood and smelled sour. There'd been a lot of blood, caked as thick as a piece of felted cloth, tracking rivulets from his ears. Deep bruising darkened the back of his neck—blood had pooled inside him. Even in the cool of the cellar, flies buzzed. Gently, she prodded his skull—the back of it was cracked, like a piece of broken pottery. She winced. Whatever had happened, he'd likely died instantly. At least there was that mercy.

Now, if she could only make a guess at what had inflicted such an injury. A fall would have broken his skull in one pattern; a strike with a weapon would cause a different one. She wondered if she ought to try to perform a rudimentary autopsy. She'd never done one before. Since she wasn't a medic, she wasn't sure she'd even know exactly what she was looking at if she peeled back the skin. Didn't take an autopsy to tell his skull was broken. And the body was getting ripe.

She used her hands then, feeling along his head, tracing back from his ears and down his neck, searching for patterns. She recited her findings to Tomas.

"It's a broad wound. There's a dent maybe two inches wide along the entire back of the skull."

"A club, then?" Tomas asked.

"Or the edge of a table. Anything with that shape." She prodded a little more firmly—broken bone flexed under her touch. Flesh soaked with clotted blood felt wet, thick. That might even have been his brain. Her stomach turned, and she avoided lingering any further on that thought. Being sick over this wouldn't help her standing here.

The wound was deep; her probing fingers seemed to keep sinking into the man's brain. It went at a slant—deeper along one edge than the other. So yes, he might have fallen against something with an edge.

"Shine the light there, would you?" she asked, scooting back as she took off her gloves. Taking out a pad and pencil from her tunic pocket, she sketched his skull and marked the shape of the wound in it, showing the radiating pattern of broken bone around it. So she would remember. Grim work.

"It looks like an accident, doesn't it?" Tomas said.

"Except that Ariana saved the body and called for an investigation."

"Maybe she just wanted to be sure."

Enid didn't like it. It would be easy to call this an accident and walk away. "We'll see."

She put her pad and pencil back in her pocket and slipped her gloves on again. After arranging Sero's body neatly, smoothing away any sign that she'd examined him, she replaced the canvas cloth over him. Rested a hand on his shoulder for a moment, so that at least one person gave him a kind farewell. They should burn him by nightfall. After their next stop.

Back aboveground, back in the light, Enid asked for a washbasin and soap and scrubbed her hands and washed her gloves, flattening them and leaving them to hang on her belt. The committee waited, strained and silent.

Enid needed some time. "Ariana, might I have a cup of water? It's a little dry down there."

"Yes, of course, this way."

Enid drew the woman off from the others, moving around

the cottage to an outdoor pump by the cistern. She guessed Ariana might speak more openly without Philos glaring.

Ariana filled a clay cup, and Enid asked, "Why do you think it wasn't an accident?"

The dark-haired woman bit her lip, lowered her gaze. Deciding what to say—or working up to speaking what she'd kept to herself. "No one much liked Sero. I'm sorry to say it, but it's true. He wasn't part of any household, just lived off by himself and made do somehow. I don't know absolutely that he didn't just fall. But . . . it's strange. It's all so strange. And no one wants to talk about it. That's mostly why—that no one will talk. And Philos has been so . . . so *determined*. Not that he's ever *nice*, but the way he's so set against this . . ." She heaved a frustrated breath, made an offhand shrug.

"Like he's hiding something?" Enid suggested.

"Yes. Exactly," she said bleakly. "You—do you think it was an accident?"

"Could have been," Enid said honestly. "I want to look at where it happened before I decide."

Enid finished off the cup of water and gathered the troop to move on to the next location. A few folk from the town watched, pretending not to.

"Well?" Philos demanded. "Did you find anything useful? You saw, didn't you—he fell and hit his head. Could have happened to anyone."

Yes, and such accidents were relatively common. A person fell from a ladder; a child fell from a tree. A man died in a storm. Accidental deaths were tragic, striking as they did like lightning, leaving survivors unprepared for the aftermath. That could be what happened here. Ariana was shocked and confused by the death, felt she must do *something,* that by being on the village's committee she had some kind of responsibility.

So she called an investigation where none was needed, because Sero didn't have a household looking after him and someone had to. Or she could be absolutely correct, and more was going on here.

"I have a few more questions, Philos. I'm sure you understand."

Philos raised his hands like he wanted to argue, but Enid glanced at Tomas, who didn't do anything at all, and the committeeman stayed quiet.

Moving down the gridded streets, they passed nicely kept cottages and workshops. The sound of a baby crying came from one house, a couple of kids laughing behind another. A productive town, then, earning banners and children, all of them cared for.

Ariana led them past all that to where a dirt path branched away from the street, leaving the grid to curve around to an isolated homestead. A small house sat up against a copse of trees and tangled undergrowth, along with a cistern and a chicken coop, weatherworn and empty. Another fifty feet along stood a shed made of rough plank board and roofed with shakes. Wasn't much—wouldn't stand up to a bad storm. But it would keep the sun and rain off and store tools and jobs in progress. No chimney, no windows. The double doors at the front were closed. The workshop, then, where Sero had died.

This was a man who had wanted to live alone, who hadn't wanted neighbors. Or the neighbors hadn't wanted him. Didn't have a household, likely didn't want one. It happened sometimes. Living with a household wasn't required, but living without was . . . odd. Harder, going through the world alone. Enid got a chill, thinking about not having Sam and the others to come home to.

She tried to see the man through where he had lived. All

very practical. Functional, if not particularly nice to look at. "How did Sero earn his keep, then?"

"He was a handyman, mostly," Ariana said. "Wasn't dead weight. Did small jobs all over the town. He did good work. It's just that he was alone."

"Something wrong with him," Philos said. "He wasn't friendly. But what can you do? Maybe he earned his keep, but he'd never earn a banner, that's for sure."

"Not everyone wants to," Enid murmured.

Ariana said, "He had a power auger, from back before the Fall, and a solar battery to run it. It was his, passed down from parent to child till he got it. He took really good care of it, kept it running. Everyone asked him to work—he could do fences and foundation posts in half the time. He even went out to some of the other towns on jobs."

That explained the neat rows of fences and fence posts everywhere in Pasadan. Sero had probably even helped with the sign along the road.

"I think he liked that machine better than people," Philos said.

Enid couldn't really blame Sero. A machine like that from the old days, still running, still useful? Such artifacts were becoming rarer and rarer. Things wore out. They broke, and getting the parts to fix them was tough. Such a thing was precious, and she was impressed that he'd made such good use of it.

"Who's got the auger now?" Enid asked.

"It'll go to community stores," Ariana said. "Since he didn't have a household, it belongs to everybody, now. But we left it here, until you got here."

It wasn't unheard of, people fighting over precious objects. Someone might have wanted to take the machine from Sero.

"He kept it in the workshop?"

"Oh, no," Ariana said. "Something like that he kept in the house. The workshop was just a workshop."

"Well, let's have a look at where he died."

The group of them walked down the second path. Enid and Tomas pulled a little ahead, and she asked him in a low voice, "Thoughts?"

"They might just need an outsider to come in and make the decision for them," he said. "I feel like we're breaking up an argument between children."

"Yeah."

The shed was old, rickety, with wide cracks between shrunken gray boards. A place to keep rain off and little more. From the outside, nothing looked amiss. This time, she didn't need to tell the committee to wait outside. They held back. Lee had his hands clasped tightly together.

Enid unlatched and pulled open both sides of the double door, and Tomas followed her inside.

Exactly what she expected to see here. A table with a couple of vises attached to it sat along one wall, which was hung with hooks holding up tools, everything from hammers to wrenches to saws and snips. Surely he must have been friends with the town's blacksmith, to have such a set of tools. A hutch under the table was filled with pieces of lumber; a second held scrap metal. With the front of the shed open, she could see the house and path from here, and also into the trees behind the homestead.

The floor was dirt. An irregular dark spot by the wall proved to be blood. The color stood out, brown and baked. There seemed to have been a lot, and it soaked into the dirt before drying into crust. Flies congregated, buzzing away when Enid approached, stepping carefully.

"Well, this is it," she said, sighing.

"And the wall," Tomas said, pointing.

There it was, the killing blow: a two-by-four framing the wall. The perfect match for the shape of the dent in Sero's skull. A smear of blood marred the color, and strands of Sero's dark hair were imbedded in the splinters. He'd hit the post, hard. Must have fallen straight into it. An investigation never got easier than this.

If he'd been just a couple of inches on either side, he would have hit the planking instead of the post, and the force of the blow would have been distributed—or the planking, old boards only lightly nailed into place and not driven in the ground, would have split. He'd have had a bad headache, maybe even a concussion, but he'd have lived, likely. Of all the terrible luck.

Enid looked around the rest of the workshop, carefully taking in every inch, putting together the rest of the story of what had happened to the man. What had he been working on? Had he slipped? Taken a bad step?

The floor was clean of debris—Sero kept a good shop here, sawdust and scrap swept away. The dirt was scuffed and marred, signs of feet dancing, tripping. Multiple feet. More than one person here. She knelt to study the impressions more closely, then stepped back to get a better idea of the whole picture. There, someone had come in through the door, discovered the body. There, those straight lines, and where the dirt looked like it had been pressed down—they'd set down the stretcher to put the body on it. There must have been quite a few people in and out here, dealing with the aftermath. A clear picture of what Sero had been doing, where he'd been standing, had been erased.

"We'll have to talk to whoever found the body, find out

what they saw," Enid said, sighing. "Four days gone, memories aren't going to be too sharp."

"We'll figure it out," Tomas said.

She went over every inch of the place, studying tools that might have bits of hair and blood on them, anything on the walls that might tell her what happened, and made notes of what she saw. Observations, not conclusions. The bench had a couple of pieces of metal, some files, and shavings spread out on it. This must have been what Sero was working on before he died, filing down some parts, doing some kind of hand tooling. A bolt, a plate with a sleeve—hinges, he was repairing hinges. Maybe for a gate on one of those fences he'd built. Otherwise the place was neat. He kept it organized, tools all in their right places. She mentally measured the space between the bench, the marks his feet might have made while standing there, and the spot on the wall that had likely caved in his skull. Compared that to the height of the body. He would have had to take a couple of steps back first.

The basic physics of the scenario didn't seem quite right. Why would he have needed to step back? What had he been doing, really?

When they finished inside, she walked out and around, searching the exterior walls and ground, just to be thorough. The path from the shed to the house was well traveled. Likely, whoever had found the body had come that way, as well as those who'd carried out the body—and anyone else who'd come to look.

Which was why she didn't expect to find footprints around the back of the shed, disappearing into the grasses of the meadow that ran along the tree line. The scuffed tracks of someone running—not up the path like everyone else, but around the back and away. Enid didn't think there'd been rain the last few days. No way to tell how old they were.

"Tomas?" she called, nodded to the ground when he came up beside her. She measured the foot marks against her hands and made a note her in book.

"A witness?" he said.

"Yeah, maybe." She wondered how in the world she was going to find the person who had made the tracks. Or how she could get the person—their prime witness—to just come forward.

She straightened, looking across the back of the shed, the meadow, the trees, trying to imagine the scene. Sero fell against the post. Someone had come across the body—or maybe even seen him fall—then ran.

Then she saw the blood on the wall, a brownish streak smeared on the wood, dried like ink, as if their runner had stumbled and put out a hand for balance. A runner with bloody hands.

Five Years After the Worst Storm

Enid was sweeping out the front room of the clinic while her mother, the on-duty medic, came in from outside, eyes bright with gossip.

"What is it?" Enid asked, pausing, resting the broom against her shoulder.

"Franie's moving to Bronson with that guy he hooked up with. They got the okay to start a papermaking workshop."

The most banal kind of gossip, but still Enid's mouth opened and she made a startled noise. "Franie the *reprobate*?"

How did Franie of all people convince someone to shack up with him, much less get the go-ahead to start a household? A functional, purposeful household? Franie, who'd seemed to spend most of his childhood knocking over baskets of apples during harvests and picking fights with Enid whenever she stood up to him, who'd grown six inches in a year and put on muscle and become passionate about *paper* of all things.

How had Franie the reprobate managed to fall in love?

"You're the only one who calls him that anymore," Peri chastised her.

"*Someone* has to remember what he was like." She started sweeping again in earnest, though the floor was already mostly clean—she'd swept the day before, too.

Her mother studied her. "You don't have to do that. It can wait, if there's something else you'd rather be doing."

"I'm just trying to be useful," she said, working the broom with more force than was really necessary.

"You are," Peri said, a little sadly it seemed like. "But you're not particularly happy, are you?"

"That's irrelevant," Enid muttered, digging the broom into the next corner with renewed determination.

"Do you think you'll want a banner someday?"

"How am I supposed to know that?" she shot back, then ducked her head, ashamed at the outburst. Everyone was supposed to want a banner. To work to get a banner. Uphold your quotas, make your household and community a better place. Prove you could care for any children you brought into the world.

Enid was beginning to suspect she didn't actually want a banner, ever. She would be happy to let someone else, someone who really wanted it, have one instead. And that meant one less thing to worry about.

But she was still lonely. The implant in her arm, which she'd had since she was twelve, also seemed irrelevant. It wasn't like she'd made use of it.

Enid had tried to fall in love. They all had, their cohort of teenagers in and around Haven, supplemented by the teenagers who came in from surrounding villages and households for markets. They kissed. They experimented. They tried to figure out what all the fuss was about. And some of them *got it.* Dived into sex and came back to gatherings with flushed faces and bright eyes and tales about how great it was, how great *they* were; and they walked hand in hand and lost interest in their friends—and then fell out of love and hooked up with someone else, trading partners and stories, and Enid didn't understand it. She could go through the motions, but invariably they'd all be sitting around a midwinter bonfire one moment, and the next she'd be alone because everyone else had gone off with one another and she hadn't noticed. Maybe she was broken, she'd think. And now even Franie had figured out what to do with himself and Enid couldn't pick on him anymore. She was getting left behind.

Lost in thought, she'd swept the same piece of floor for a full minute, and Peri sighed loudly.

"I love you, my child, but you need a *job*." Peri flapped her arms as if waving away a cloud of gnats before disappearing back into the exam room.

Enid wanted to go. Just away. And when she said that, her mother and Tomas and everyone else said she should talk to the committee about courier jobs, that she should think about apprenticing with a road maintenance crew. But she resisted, like she resisted everything.

It was a week or so later when it finally happened, when everything changed—when *he* dropped on her like a tornado, the best worst storm.

///

ENID WENT TO Haven's one-day-a-week market to run errands for the household: delivering eggs to be traded for what Plenty didn't make for itself, picking up cloth from the weavers at Barnard Croft. The day was hot, sticky. Awnings and shelters had been set up along the road around the town square, and people clung to the shade they provided, fanned themselves with woven reed fans, and batted flies away from baskets of fruit and baked goods. The carts and trestle tables were spread out enough that people had space to move around, close enough that they could chat and make the day feel a little bit like a party.

At first she'd taken her time, looking over the stalls and carts for anything new, anything interesting, any new faces to say hello to. The big harvest market wouldn't come up for a month yet, so this was the usual crowd with the usual set of bottled mead and cider, canned fruits and jams, pottery, baskets, boots, knives, clothes, and hats, and the odd bit of livestock like goats and ducks. Enid unloaded the eggs and collected the fabric, thick wool for winter blankets and jackets, which was heavy and a pain to carry around in summer heat. She'd stuffed it all in a backpack, slung over her shoulders. But the pack got heavier, her whole back turned sweaty, and she just wanted to get home.

At the edge of the market, from the open space in front of the clinic, she heard music. At first a light guitar, then singing. The voice was . . . astonishing. She'd never heard anything like it. A clear tenor, resonant, so the sound carried and became fuller and better rather than flat and more diffuse. Haven had local musicians, folk with guitars and drums and fiddles, and they'd come out for parties and markets, good enough to dance to and sing along with. But none of them sounded like this.

She drifted toward the music to see who made it, leaned up against a tree at the back of the gathered crowd, dropped her pack of cloth to the ground, and listened.

The young man at the center of attention, singing and playing as easy as anything, seemed otherworldly. Clean shaven, nut-brown skin, long brown hair pulled back in a tail. He wore a plain tunic and trousers, scuffed boots, and a bright red vest with patterns embroidered on it—no one would miss him in a crowd. He sat on a wooden stool that had been brought down from the clinic porch, guitar nestled in his lap, one foot stretched out. Like someone out of a story.

This wasn't a boisterous party sing-along. The musician sang, and people listened quietly. In awe, even. This was art; this was beautiful. One song, a light melody that everyone knew, ended and he started another, and this one—haunting, in a minor key with a drifting chorus that told a strange story of sailors lost at sea and ghost ships returning during storms —she'd never heard before. Maybe he'd even written it himself.

She couldn't stop listening. She couldn't leave. Finishing another song, he caught her gaze across the heads of his audience, gave her a smile—bright, wry, welcoming—that made her feel like they'd known each other forever, and that he was here just for her. Her heart flopped over. She managed to smile back, even wave a little, though she felt goofy and crazy doing so. He'd think her silly. He'd laugh at her. She tried to smooth back her ratty hair, which she suddenly wished she hadn't chopped so short last year in an effort to feel new and different.

But no, at his next break, when he set down his guitar by the bench and the audience drifted off, he held her gaze and came toward her. This was her chance. If she wanted to flee, she could. If she didn't want to talk to him, preferring to nurse her burning little crush from afar, she could do that. He gave her plenty of time. But she waited, unable to control the beaming smile on her face.

He came right up to her. "Hola," he said. Up close, she saw his eyes were a gray blue, magical.

"That was really great," she said. "Thanks for playing."

"Thank you for listening," he said, and they stood for a moment, grinning at each other. "Hey—this is my first time in Haven. You think you can give me a tour of the place? If you'd like to take a walk with me, that is?"

She didn't think she could smile any wider. And those *eyes*. "Yeah, sure, I just have to drop this off at home. I'm Enid, by the way."

"I'm Dak. Nice to meet you."

Later she decided she'd fallen in love with him on the first note she heard him sing. Seeing him only confirmed it, and holding hands with him was inevitable. *Perfect*, even. They spent that whole day together. He played some more, and she listened to every song. That night, at the close of the market, townsfolk gathered to build a fire pit and roast some kebabs over it. She and Dak sat side by side through it all, and when he leaned in close, nuzzled the hairline behind her ear, and whispered if she'd like to take another walk with him, she grabbed his hand and led him off to the orchard over the hill. They found a sunken dip between roots that was both dry and out of sight, pulled each other down, rolled in the grass, one ending up on top, then the other. She'd felt such a desperate craving for him, she didn't know where to start: take his tunic off or hers, knot her fingers in his long luscious hair or grab tight to his back. They were body to body, legs locked together, and she still wasn't close enough to him.

Auntie Kath talked about the early days during the Fall, when sex was the most reliable form of recreation and pleasure they had. And how that warred with the terror so many of them felt about having children. They could barely take care of themselves in this new world with no electricity or running water or reliable medicine or reliable *anything*. The early epidemics wiped out a measurable percentage of the population, and after that the ancient diseases came back—cholera and dysentery and everything—and confidence in the world vanished. But they really liked sex.

Enid hadn't understood until now. Until right this moment, when it all became clear. If you lost everything else but could still have sex, things wouldn't seem so bad, would they?

Hormones, she'd been taught. The flush of hormones was soaking her system and making her crazy. But right here, in the middle of it, the heat was real, and Dak filled the sky.

"You're so *pretty*," she breathed, pressing her hands to his cheeks, sliding them down to his chest. She couldn't feel him enough.

He laughed, kissed her again and again, everywhere, all over her body. He found nerves in places she hadn't known she had them. Her own body turned new and weird and messy and breathtaking.

For a long time after, they lay still and exhausted, her clinging to him and him lying flat, looking up at the sky filtered through branches filled with new apples. The sky grew chilled, and the goose flesh rising on her arms made her snuggle closer to his warmth. Dak hummed a song, the melody vague so that she couldn't follow it.

///

ENID WOULD ALWAYS remember exactly when she got her first implant: it was after her first bad storm. Still the worst storm, according to her own memory. The next morning, after returning to Haven and staying up most of the night fetching water and blankets and seeing the refugees settled, she'd felt an aching, bruise-like pain deep in her gut and for a moment wondered if she'd been injured somehow, if the stress of the storm had hurt her. Then she went to use the latrine and saw blood spotting her underpants when she pulled down her britches. She wondered if stress could cause internal bleeding, flashed yet again on the memory of that body and its ashen, gaping wound, and panicked, wondering if she was dying. Of course, she wasn't hurt and wasn't dying, and if she'd been thinking straight and not sleep-deprived and traumatized, she'd have known exactly what was happening: she had started menstruating.

Peri shared her cloths for the blood and came with her to the clinic the next day for her implant. Enid felt small, fragile, and defiant. The clinic was still crowded, a few of the worst-injured cases still occupying beds where medics could keep a close watch on them, and other survivors sheltered in safety until they could make plans. Enid felt odd, being here for such an ordinary reason when there were folk here who'd almost died. Everyone must have been staring at her; they must have known why she was here. Everything was different now. She hated that it ought to be so. To so randomly be declared an adult. Not really, of course — she still had to go to classes and help with the same set of kids' chores. But this was a sign that time was pressing on her, and an unknown future was opening up.

"You're very quiet," Peri said. Enid didn't answer, because she didn't know what she was supposed to say.

"It's just routine," her mother said. "Nothing to be scared of."

"Not scared. Sad." Her eyes started pricking, tears burgeoning, and her anger that she was about to start crying made her want to cry even more.

Peri squeezed her shoulder. "You'll wake up tomorrow and everything'll be just the same, you'll see."

Even with the storm, even with all the injuries, the medic on duty, Alvin, seemed to know exactly why they were here, with Peri's hand resting on Enid's shoulder.

"Implant time?" he asked.

"I'll do the honors if there's space in the back exam room," Peri answered.

"We'll make space."

They ushered out a woman and child with a bandage on his head—not the ones from Potter, Enid thought. They didn't look twice at her. But then, they had bigger worries. Enid decided that nobody was staring at her; it just felt like it.

Enid sat on a chair while Peri went to the pharmacy in back and returned with a jar. Using tweezers, she pulled out the sterilized implant, just a little capsule an inch or so long, thin as a toothpick.

This was one of the bits of technology they'd worked hard to save after the Fall. Because if you could manage birthrate, you could manage anything, and they had the statistics to prove it. Before the pre-Fall supplies ran out, medics figured out how to derive the hormone from what they had on hand, how to develop the little cellulose, slow-delivery packets. Didn't look like much, really. Not a big deal at all.

"Ready, kiddo?"

Her mother hadn't called her "kiddo" since she was eight. Ironic that she did so now, when Enid was supposed to be growing up. Peri had done this dozens of times, but Enid still sort of wished one of the other medics was on hand. Then maybe she'd feel a little less like a child.

First came a swipe with a numbing agent that made the skin of her upper arm tingle. Then a swipe with alcohol. Then a tool that looked like an awl, at which point Enid decided not to look anymore. After a pinch and a weird sliding sensation under the skin, it was over. Peri held gauze over the spot, so Enid couldn't see exactly what it looked like. Time enough for that later, she supposed.

While Peri was cleaning up, putting tools in the pot by the stove to be boiled later, Enid asked, "Why do only girls get implants?"

Peri turned. "Oh sweetie, that's a good question. It's a holdover from the old days. Women carry babies so it's up to them to manage it. Except when it isn't." She shrugged away a lot of explanation there. Complications, Enid thought.

Then her mother came over and put her hands on Enid's shoulders. "I have to give you the speech, now. Ready?"

Enid nodded. She'd heard this before; they all heard it growing up. But this recitation had the air of ritual to it.

"You understand that this is an honor, yes? Children are precious, and this means you are willing to earn the right to bear a child of your own someday, and not leave it to chance."

"To prove that I can care for one."

"Yes. It's a privilege, not a right. Understand?"

"I understand."

"I know you do," Peri said, and kissed her forehead.

Back out on the clinic's porch, she looked out at people working to clean up roads and salvage what they could from the gardens and fruit trees surrounding the building and felt herself even more at a loss than usual. She had an implant. What did she do now?

"Is that Enid?"

Auntie Kath was back at her usual spot, sitting in a rocking chair on the clinic porch, taking in the world as it passed by. Kath couldn't see, but Enid was pretty sure she knew everyone in town by their footsteps on the wooden boards, maybe even by the way they breathed. She seemed to have emerged from the cellar exactly the same, none the worse for wear.

"Yes, ma'am." Enid came over to sit next to the chair. Auntie Kath always had time for her.

"You sound sad."

"I started bleeding last night."

"That's a big deal," Auntie Kath said.

"I guess so."

"So you're here for your first implant, is that it? There's nothing to be scared of."

Why did people keep saying that? She knew that. She started to rub that arm and its fresh tiny wound again, then clasped her hands tight to keep from fidgeting. "I know. I just thought . . . it would happen later. Or something."

She chuckled. "Isn't that always the way?"

Early afternoon, sun finally came through the clouds, lighting the town gold. The puddles of water and dripping trees gleamed. For a moment, the scene looked alien.

Enid sighed. "Does it ever get easier?"

"Does what get easier?"

"Everything," Enid said. That was the kind of answer that made the adults chuckle at her.

But Auntie Kath didn't laugh. She looked over that same golden scene, damp and newly born from the storm, as if she could really see it. Maybe the light felt different to her.

Her voice stretched as if speaking brought pain, she finally said, "Oh, yes, it's so much easier. You'll never know how hard it was."

Auntie Kath was the last one who remembered.

Enid had a million questions, but she didn't press. Auntie Kath could usually be persuaded to tell stories from before the Fall, about what things had been like then, about what had changed, all the work they'd done to get from there to here and how many times they were sure they wouldn't make it. But right now she sounded breakable. More breakable than the blind old woman usually did. She said goodbye to Auntie Kath, who squeezed her hand and waved her off and told her to keep her chin up.

///

DAK STAYED AT Haven longer than he'd intended. When market day ended, he'd meant to head north to the next town, the next set of markets. He traveled the Coast Road, timing his arrival with various midsummer markets and festivals, trading music for a bed and food. He seemed to do well at it, too. He rarely stayed longer than a few days in one place. But he stayed in Haven for over a week, for her. She thought she'd burst. She spent every moment she could with him, hardly any at home, until Peri said, "Are you ready to move out, then?"

"What? No," she said. But maybe she could see about asking Dak to move in . . .

"Then maybe get some of your chores done before you run off today, hmm?"

Enid had been letting things slide. She hadn't thought anyone noticed. But no, everyone had noticed. Tomas was the next person to stop her.

He was a lead investigator now; the brown uniform was a little less scary than it had been when he first started training, but it was still the brown uniform, transforming him into something larger and distant, and even after years she was still getting used to it. He was wearing it now, which meant he was on the way out to a case. He didn't seem too grim about it, but then again he wouldn't.

"You okay, Enid?" he asked, as she was hanging laundry to dry, fast as she could. Dak was down in the square giving music lessons to kids. They were going to have dinner together later. But if she could get free a little early . . .

"Yeah, I'm fine," she said, not looking up. "Where you off to?"

"North this time, to Hel. Shouldn't take long."

"Can you talk about the case?"

"I'd rather not yet." He lingered, watching her. Studying her.

"What is it?" she said, pausing to look at him.

"You've made a friend," Tomas said.

Enid blushed so hard, her face hurt. Went back to hanging shirts and towels, quickly, with intense focus.

"As long as you're having fun. Just be careful. He's not likely to stick around."

"I know that," she said, indignant. Tomas was in a lecturing mood. But still, a brief panic rattled her. When would Dak leave? How long did she have? Would it be unreasonable to spend every moment with him until then? Chores could wait.

"You know he probably has lovers in every town up and down the Coast Road."

Now Tomas was just pestering her.

"So? That's his business," she said, trying to sound mature and worldly, but her tone was petulant. Defensive. She realized she didn't know anything about Dak except that he could sing better than anyone and she loved every bit of him, down to every last pore. Because she was finished with the laundry, and because she wasn't willing to wait to see how else Tomas could tease her, she stormed off, empty laundry basket propped against her hip.

Dak planned to leave the next morning, it turned out. He was properly apologetic, properly attentive. They had a picnic dinner in the orchard, the heady scent of ripening apples and hot summer air lingering. Someone had given him a bottle of mead for his singing, and they sipped at it. He lounged against a tree and held her tight against him, stroking her hair, making her feel as loved as she could wish. And at least he told her he was leaving. He could have just left without a word while she raced all over Haven looking for him, and people would regard her with pity.

"Are you sure you can't stay? Plenty has room, I know we do. You . . . you could stay." And she imagined the dozens, the hundreds of other lovers up and down the Coast Road, all telling him the same thing.

"I'm not really the settling-down type, Enid. You know that. Folk up the road will be looking for me."

She'd only known him for a week, and yes she knew that about him. "Doesn't hurt to ask. Where you from, anyway? You have a household to go back to, to winter over, maybe?"

He shrugged, pursed his lips. Glanced away like he did when he was trying to remember the next song or story. "Oh, it's just a little place. A little bit south and a little bit east. Or maybe a lot south and a lot east. Been a while since I've been back there." His gaze returned to her and his smile went back to charming.

"Any family?"

He shrugged again. "As much as anyone, I suppose."

And that was that, he wasn't going to tell her, or he didn't want to. Maybe something terrible had happened. It seemed sad, not having a household of one's own.

She said, "I just want to make sure you have someplace to go to. If you need it. You can't wander forever."

"You'd be surprised." He kissed her gently. "I'll be back this way. I promise."

That was enough for her. But then it would have to be, wouldn't it? So they made passionate, satisfying love under the trees. It was still new, and she wanted more. She could see how practicing would make it even better. Dak sent her back to Plenty in the foggy late hours of night. In the morning he was gone. She didn't go looking for him.

///

BUT HE DID come back.

Autumn market this time, just a month or so later. Once again, Enid heard his voice in the town square before she saw him, and her heart nearly stopped. She approached cautiously, getting it into her head that he wouldn't remember her, that he would ignore her if he did. That he wouldn't care, and he wouldn't want to carry on with her. All she wanted was to kiss him; she was aching for it.

He was sitting on the same stool in the clearing outside the market, playing the same black-lacquered guitar. A new song this time, one she hadn't heard last time—and how many songs did he know? She leaned up by the same tree, crossed her arms, and waited.

When he looked across his audience, he saw her. And he smiled. Might even have hitched a note in the song he was playing. Finished the song, slung his guitar over his shoulder, and rushed up to her. Touched her cheek and kissed her till her hands clenched into the fabric of his shirt.

"Enid, how are you?" he said, but only when he pulled back for air. She just grinned.

They picked up together as if he'd never left. Let anyone give her a hard time about Dak now; she'd face them down. This time, he planned to stay several days longer than usual.

Enid might have expected another lecture from Tomas—or maybe an apology—but he'd been away on a case. His return in the middle of a market day ended up being something of an event.

Out in the square, Dak was between sets. Enid had brought him a sandwich and sat with him while he ate, watching the people at the market stalls. He'd lean to her ear and make up stories about this or that person, and she'd laugh; if she knew the person, she'd lean to his ear and tell him if he was right or wrong. They sat hip to hip, shoulder to shoulder, and she was happy.

There was a commotion, and the crowd parted as a solar car came up in front of the clinic. Tomas was driving. He parked, climbed out, and helped out the others who were with him: a young woman, a man a couple of years older than her, and a middle-aged woman. The young one was maybe a year or so older than Enid, wearing a skirt and tunic, her hair braided up around her head, and she was crying. Tomas's hand rested gently on her shoulder as he guided her up the porch to the clinic door, followed by the other two. Folk of her household, maybe?

Dak caught her staring and caught the implications of an investigator shepherding a group of people who were all clearly unhappy.

"What's going on there?" Dak asked.

"That's Tomas—he's in my household. I can ask him when he comes back out."

"An investigator in your household? What's that like?" He wrinkled his nose, as if the thought bothered him.

"He's just Tomas. He gets serious when he's wearing brown, that's all."

"You'd never even think about saying the wrong thing at home, I bet, with one of them around."

She glanced at him. "It's not like that. Not really." She didn't think about it most of the time—most of the time, he wasn't in uniform. "It's not about saying the wrong thing. It's about not hurting people. Really, I'd be worried about disappointing Tomas even if he wasn't an investigator."

That evening, she broke away from Dak long enough to go home for a bit. Dak was performing in the square, and she planned to join him later. This was her chance to corner Tomas in private.

"That looked rough," she said. "At the clinic today, with that woman."

"Bannerless pregnancy," he said.

Her stomach dropped. Could be a million reasons why such a thing happened, but it reflected badly on everyone: the woman, the father, their households, a whole town sometimes. It had never happened in Haven in her lifetime, but there were stories. "Oh no. How bad is it?"

"Not too bad," he said. "Looks like an implant failure. No one's fault at all. The clinic's checking it out. Once they confirm, we'll all have to decide what to do next."

If the implant had failed, the woman's household would likely be awarded a banner retroactively—if they could feed an extra mouth, if they didn't have too many mouths already. If they couldn't support a new mouth, the woman might be asked to transfer to a household that could, that would maybe welcome a baby. If the woman wanted the banner and the baby, ways could be found to make it work. If she didn't want the baby, there'd be a termination. No banner at all.

Enid tried to think of what she would want in that situation, and she couldn't imagine it. Mostly, it made her fervently hope that her implant never failed so she'd never be in that situation. Dak had suddenly made her implant relevant.

"I see your boy came back." Tomas turned the interrogation back on her.

And still, she blushed. She thought she'd be over that by now. "Yes. He said he would."

Tomas hid a smile, indicating what, Enid couldn't guess.

She waited for him to chastise her or offer her some token of unwanted advice. "Well?" she demanded finally. "Aren't you going to tell me to be careful, to watch out, to not trust him?"

"No," he said. "You already seem to know whatever I could tell you."

She stormed out, and she thought she'd be over that by now as well.

Back at the square, where a late-market party had sprung up, she and Dak sat by themselves, eating pot pies and talking. She passed on what Tomas had said about the young woman at the clinic, about the bannerless pregnancy.

"It sounds like it'll all turn out okay," Enid said. "Not like those terrible cases." She didn't have to explain—the ones where people cut out their implants, hid their pregnancies, hoping no one would ever know. Whole households colluded sometimes, keeping pregnancies and babies hidden. But people always found out; people always seemed to know. No one ever wanted to be in that situation, a whole town or a whole region rejecting you, cutting you out because you couldn't be bothered to play by the rules. Shamed and shunned. And the poor children who never asked to be bannerless—but people always knew. Because if you had too many babies, if they couldn't be fed, if there was another epidemic or famine, they couldn't take care of everyone, and the Fall would happen all over again.

Dak ran his hand up her arm, fingering that raised bit under the skin behind her bicep. "Would you ever do it? Sabotage your implant to have a baby? Skip the whole banner?"

"Oh no," she said, horrified. What a terrible thing to do to your household—they might all be held accountable, if she tried to go behind their backs like that. If she wanted a baby, she'd work for one. "I'm not sure I even want a banner at all. Plenty of other people to worry about that sort of thing. I like things the way they are."

"Me, too." He put his arm around her shoulders and nestled her close, kissing the top of her head. As warm a gesture of agreement as she could ask for. He didn't need a household—of course, he wouldn't think of banners. He might earn enough for himself, but how could anyone feed another mouth traveling the way he did?

///

THE MARKET ENDED, Dak stopped playing for audiences, and Enid felt the timing as a gnawing in her gut. She leaked tears for no apparent reason. Dak would leave. He said he traveled south during the winter months, to the fishing villages on the coast. He had places he could stay if storms came up. He'd traveled like this for a couple of years now; he wasn't worried.

She hated it but wouldn't say anything because her voice would come out whining and terrible—and then he'd never come back, would he? She would tell him she'd miss him. Kiss him and try to remember him, in case he didn't come back.

Enid went to find him in town—he'd been sleeping on the clinic porch, since the weather stayed warm—and saw Tomas talking to him. She held back, trying to stay out of sight while watching, to suss out what was happening. Tomas wasn't wearing the brown uniform, but his stance was pure investigator, pure intimidation. Dak had his arms crossed, smiling a flippant smile and looking anywhere but directly at Tomas.

Enid wanted to kill Tomas. This was none of his business. He had no right to interfere. Furious, she decided that rather than kill him, she'd avoid him. Avoid him forever.

Except before she could march off, he spotted her, because that was the kind of thing he was good at. He finished talking to Dak, who made a half bow at him before going to fetch his guitar where he'd leaned it against a bench, and Tomas left the square—walking straight toward her.

"Really?" she spat, to get in the first word, so she wouldn't have to find out what righteous declaration he'd make to her. "Was that really necessary?"

"What do you think I said to him?" Tomas said.

She had to shrug, because there were so many things he might have said. "Probably something along the lines of 'Hurt her and you'll regret it.'"

"Exactly right," Tomas said, grinning. "You should be an investigator."

"Just leave me alone, will you!"

And so he did, continuing on toward home, smiling a little. Not even Dak taking her hand and kissing her forehead could make her smile after that.

"Ignore him," she said, fuming. "Whatever he said, just . . . he's just making a pest out of himself."

"He's only worried about you."

Yes, she knew that. She ought to be grateful that she had people looking out for her. But they didn't know Dak. They didn't know *her*.

"I've been thinking," he said, after she'd settled down a bit. "You like your household, yeah? You're close to it?"

"Lived there my whole life," she said.

"But you're not looking for a banner or anything. You don't have a real job yet, right?" A vocation that would root her in place and draw her forward through her life. No, she didn't. She still got by helping anyone who needed it, and that seemed all right.

"I can't seem to decide," she said.

"That's all right, you know. Not deciding."

"I know that."

He took both her hands and turned to face her. "I wondered if maybe you'd like to travel with me for a bit? It's a good chance to see some of the world. That's always a good thing, I've thought. If you don't like it, you can come back, easy as that. But . . . you seem like you might want to travel." He smiled that bright, sunny smile that could light up the night.

She matched his grin. This . . . this was what she'd wanted all along, but it hadn't even occurred to her to ask. And she didn't have to because he just *knew*.

"That sounds amazing," she said, and suddenly she could see into her own future. She would get *away*. Make her way as best she could, like Dak did.

She would travel the Coast Road.

Blood on the Wall

Enid showed the smear of blood on the wall to Tomas.

"I suppose, on the one hand, this just got interesting," Enid said.

"I think I could have done without interesting this time." Tomas leaned in close, studying the shape of the mark, the shadow of whoever had left it.

Enid had read about investigations from before the Fall, which appeared to be highly organized and detail-oriented. There was a science to it—forensics—that had complex tools and procedures. There'd been machines to show the insides of a body, which would have shown exactly what had happened to Sero's skull. They'd been able to record images in order to study the victim and the scene over and over again, as much as they needed to after flies and rot set in. Test blood for poison, or even identify individuals from a drop of blood or strand of hair. Back then, they'd have had the ability to peel the images of fingerprints from that smear of blood on the outside of the shed. She could compare those prints to everyone in town and find out exactly who had run away after Sero died. Who'd been there long enough to get fresh blood on their hands. Who might have seen Sero fall.

So much hadn't been important during and after the Fall, so it hadn't been saved. If one of the old investigators had been at Haven from the start, maybe the knowledge, the tools, the abilities would have been passed on, and not just the vague knowledge that those things had once existed. On the other hand, Haven had desperately needed the doctors and biologists who had founded the place. They had saved vaccines and been able to reconstruct antiseptics and basic antibiotics. Without them, nothing at all might have survived.

The whole idea of forensics seemed a bit magical to Enid, and she wasn't sure the world really missed it. Wasn't sure they needed it—until they did. Maybe she could try to bring some of that knowledge back. Someday.

In the meantime, this suspicious death had turned into a real investigation.

A rangy calico sidled up around the outside of the shed, meowing. Tomas reached down to offer to pet it, and the cat considered his outstretched hand a moment before stalking off, tail up, clinging to the wall. The beast might have belonged to Sero or might have been a general mouser, haunting barns around town.

"I wonder if it saw anything," Enid joked, then spent a moment really truly wishing cats could talk. Just to tell her what had happened here.

"Could still be an accident," Tomas said. Reminding her not to make snap judgments. "That mark could have been left by whoever found the body. Someone who didn't want to be seen, didn't want to talk about it, and went into hiding. The person they think found the body may not be the one who really found the body."

"One way or another, that's our prime witness. Whoever it is," she said. She didn't relish interviewing every single person in town to suss out a witness who didn't want to talk, but if she had to, she would. "Well, let's deliver the news."

Face set, determined to get through the next few days as efficiently and fairly as possible, she went back to the committee, where they waited on the path toward the house. Probably looking on and wondering what had fascinated them so. Well, now Enid and Tomas would have to tell them. The next few moments would determine how the rest of the investigation went.

Lee had been pacing but stopped when the investigators approached; his hands reflexively opened and closed into fists. Ariana's arms were crossed so tightly, she hunched in on herself, as if wanting to hide. Philos stood between them. He might have been talking, but the others didn't seem inclined to listen. A committee at odds.

Enid went to Ariana first. "Ariana. Good instincts."

Instead of looking pleased, Ariana's mouth opened. "What? But . . . but . . ." Her disbelief stammered out. So, Ariana had hoped she was wrong. Or she hadn't really believed the death was suspicious and had called an investigation anyway. She didn't look like a woman who'd been validated, but one who'd had a roof nearly fall on her.

Continuing, Enid said, "I have reasonable suspicion of unusual circumstances surrounding Sero's death, enough to warrant further investigation. I'll proceed accordingly and hope to have everyone's cooperation."

She anticipated an outburst from Philos, but she'd expected it to focus on her. Instead, the man turned on Ariana. "Now look what you've done! This wouldn't be happening if you'd just let it go—why couldn't you just let it go! None of this *matters!*" His hands clenched; Ariana bared her teeth, ready to shout back.

Tomas stepped between them, silent, his gaze leveled at Philos.

Everyone shut up.

"I'll need to talk to whoever found Sero's body, whoever last saw Sero alive, and to anyone who might have seen who came to and from the workshop that day." Four days ago now. Too much time had passed already.

Lee, the quiet one, spoke, his voice shaking. "We don't even know who all that could be . . . it could be anyone!"

"Then, I'll talk to everyone," she said. She wouldn't even be able to pin down an approximate time of death. Just when the body was found, and then count back from there. "First—who found the body? Who reported that he was dead?"

Silence. They either didn't know or didn't want to say.

This was going to be a long couple of days.

///

WHILE THE OTHERS scowled at her, Ariana finally revealed that a man named Arbor had discovered the body. At least, he'd been the one to go get help. Enid went to speak with him and his household first, while Tomas started interviews to find out who'd seen him alive last.

Arbor was part of Baker's Hill, a small household at the edge of town, closest to Sero's homestead. The heads were a couple of older women; Arbor was the son of one of them. A few younger folk had joined them over the years. They had an orchard and a small herd of goats they used to make cheese.

They gathered at the kitchen table in their comfortable adobe house. Enid turned down an offer of lemonade and asked them questions. What had they seen? When was the last time they saw Sero alive? Who else had they seen at his homestead? Had they spotted anyone running away that morning?

No one else in the household knew anything. They shook their heads, ducked their gazes. They kept to themselves; Sero kept to himself; they rarely spoke; they didn't keep track of him. He was a loner. Strange, they kept saying.

Convinced that most of the household really didn't know anything, she let them all go except Arbor. They fled through the kitchen's back door, and he stared after his mother and the rest as if they'd abandoned him to monsters. His hands rested on the tabletop, one clutching the other, and he wouldn't meet Enid's gaze.

She'd managed a quick look at his feet; his shoes seemed larger and wider than the steps she'd found outside the shed. He probably wasn't the one who'd run away. Probably.

Arbor explained that he'd recruited Sero to help him dig new latrine pits the afternoon of the day he died. When he didn't show up on time, Arbor went to find him, first checking the house, then knocking on the front doors of the shed, then opening them and finding the body.

"So the shed doors were closed?" Enid asked. "Did Sero normally close the doors when he worked?"

She let Arbor think a moment, his head bent as he searched memory. "No," he finally said, brow furrowed. "Not in this heat; he'd leave them open to let in air. I know I've seen him working there with the doors open."

Then someone had closed the doors before running away from the body. "Did you touch the body?" she asked.

"Oh no! No. I—I didn't have to." His gazed flickered nervously to the table, then back to her. "There was so much blood, and flies. He was dead; I didn't have to go near him. I didn't even go inside, really."

"So you didn't get blood on your hands? On your shoes, maybe?"

"I don't think so. No, I didn't."

"You ran to get help. Where did you go?"

"To Newhome household, to find Tull."

That meant up the hill to the main part of town. Not back behind the shed. And he didn't have blood on his hands, confirming that he hadn't been the one to make that smear of blood. Someone else had been there first and closed the doors before fleeing, slapping up against the wall.

"What else did you see?" Enid asked.

He described just what Enid would have expected: sprawled body, a pool of blood. Nothing else out of the ordinary. He had fetched Tull, the medic, who went to check the body, then called on the committee. Ariana first, who'd ordered the body taken to her cellar. The scene must have looked like it required an investigation, and she must have been eager to pass that responsibility along. Well, this was why they had investigators, wasn't it? At least they were starting to build a timeline of what had happened. Arbor had found the body early afternoon, four days ago.

"Sero was usually reliable, then?" Enid asked, calmly and without accusation, going over the same information, searching for telltale gaps. "He agreed to do a job and he'd be there?"

"Well, yes. Mostly. I was ready to be angry at him if he'd forgotten what we agreed on."

"But he hadn't forgotten."

"No." Arbor's hands rested in his lap. "Was there something else I should have done?"

"No, that's fine. You didn't see anything else in the shed? Any sign of commotion, anything knocked over? Any kind of weapon?"

The man wouldn't meet her gaze. "Can't say I looked around enough to see anything. Just the body. The blood."

"Did you notice anything odd that morning?" Enid pressed gently, hoping to jog a memory. He seemed keen to scrub his mind clean of any such recollection. "Anyone else going to talk to Sero, anything out of the ordinary?"

Arbor, short and stout, bearded and balding despite being a relatively young man in his late twenties, said, "No one ever went there. I'm not sure what you think anyone's going to tell you."

She expected such evasions and offered only calm. "I'm only trying to be thorough. Any scrap of information, even if it doesn't seem important, might help me understand what happened. It seems odd that Sero would just fall, doesn't it? With the floor that clear?"

"Maybe he died then fell. Heart attack. Something like that."

"Maybe," she agreed, and wondered if an autopsy would tell them if there'd been some other cause. Maybe the medic would be up for performing an autopsy. "Are you sure no one else ever went there?"

Arbor bit his lip, looked away. "If anyone went there, it was likely to talk to him about a job. Find out what he was working on, who he was doing jobs for. Maybe someone else will know."

"That's a good idea. I'll ask around. Let me know if you think of anything else, yeah?"

She started to get up from the kitchen table when Arbor reached after her.

"He was bannerless, you know," he said. "That's why he was alone. That's why he didn't get along with anyone. Why no one liked him."

The one did not follow the other, in Enid's experience. If Sero was the product of an unauthorized pregnancy, that was on his parents, not him. He'd have been adopted out, taken care of. No one ought to hold it against him; ideally no one even ought to know about it.

But people did know. Somehow, they always did.

She frowned. "You seem to be telling me he deserved to die the way he did."

Arbor sat back as if she had slapped him. In the next breath he looked down, shoulders hunched. Proof of shame. Because he knew better; they all did.

She imagined that Arbor was not the only one who would say that Sero was bannerless. That this had somehow happened because of it. Because being bannerless meant a person lacked protection. Lacked a home and safety. As if the child ought to be made to suffer for the parents' infraction, all through his life.

Enid would say to them: *The whole community couldn't see fit to offer him protection, then? Is that what you're saying? Did he not earn his keep for building all your pretty fences?*

They'd all get that hunched-in, shamefaced look that Arbor had now.

She stood from the table, grateful not to have to thank him for a glass of lemonade. "If you think of anything, if you hear anything, come find me or my partner, Tomas. All right?"

He hadn't met her gaze but once or twice during their whole talk; now he looked straight at her. "Yes, ma'am," he said. "Yes."

Enid next spoke with the town's lone medic, Tull. Used to dealing with procedure and questions, he was the only one not instantly put on guard by the uniform. He kept a small clinic near the committee house. In so many respects, this was such a nice town—so many places didn't try to recruit or maintain a medic. Pasadan had so much, and yet here they were, in the middle of an investigation.

Tull and Enid stood outside the clinic's front door, taking advantage of the cooler air outside. His testimony didn't hold any surprises.

"It was a mess," Tull said, shaking his head in memory of the scene. "He was dead when I got there. But even if I'd got to him quick, I couldn't have helped. Not with a head injury like that."

"He didn't have any other injuries or health problems that might explain what happened?"

Tull shook his head. "No, no. Not that I know of."

"Was anyone with you when you examined the body?"

"The whole committee. The two guys I had with the stretcher—one of 'em's my assistant I'm training up."

"Anything strange about how the committee members acted around the body?"

"Just the way they argued. I mean, of course they argue, that's what a committee does, right?" He chuckled. "But sometimes people get funny around death. More stressed than usual.

Ariana was in tears. Wanted an investigation right off. Philos argued against, said they could take care of it."

"I get the feeling Philos and Ariana don't get along," Enid prompted.

He shrugged, seemingly unconcerned. "Philos isn't used to being questioned. Ariana asks a lot of questions, you know? But I don't think anyone has complaints about them or their work, if that's what you mean."

Enid nodded. "I'm just trying to understand what happened. Part of the job of coming into a town like this."

Tull asked, "Do you really think something's wrong? Obviously it was an accident, right?"

"What do you think?" Enid asked. "Accident or not?"

"You mean, did someone push him?"

See? Enid told herself. It wasn't just she who thought it. "There's blood on the outer wall and a set of footprints running around the back of the shed. Any idea who they belonged to?"

"No," he said, astonished. His gaze turned inward, thoughtful. He breathed again, "No."

"If you think of anything, let me know, yeah?"

"Of course, of course."

This was a man looking at his community in a whole new light. Mysterious bloody handprints had a way of doing that.

After her talk with Tull, Enid met back up with Tomas. He hadn't had much luck with his interviews, either. Just more of the same: Sero had been a loner; no one talked to him; no one had any idea who might have seen him last. Or who might have run around the back of that shed. And did they know that he was bannerless? Most everyone had taken care to point out that he was bannerless. All very rote.

ney felt they could authorize the cremation of Se-
afternoon. Whether they might learn more from
matter—it wouldn't last long enough. Tomas
oversaw the arrangements—one of the households already
had the pyre set up in a clearing about a hundred yards away
from the center of town; they were just waiting for the word.
Sero didn't have a household, but this one stepped forward to
take care of the job because of the goodwill they'd earn with
the committee for doing so. Or maybe they really were doing it
to be nice. One could be optimistic. Probably it was a little of
both. If the committee had to name a household to do the job,
it would reflect badly on the whole town.

A middle-aged man in a blue tunic and well-loved straw
hat supervised the pyre, a simple mound of dry wood and kin-
dling. He stood waiting with a torch and lantern. A bucket of
water sat nearby.

"Any words?" he asked Enid and Tomas, who stood by,
watching. Sero's body, wrapped in an old length of sheeting for
a shroud, seemed small. Just another part of the fuel.

Enid shook her head. "Just . . . thank you. For this."

The man nodded, lit the torch from the small lantern
flame, and set the pile burning in a half-dozen spots. A great
crackling fire roared up in moments, pressing out heat. Enid
and Tomas stayed to watch for a time, until the top layer or so
turned to gray ash and the whole thing started to sink.

The man would stay and tend the fire, see the whole pyre
burned through. But he was the only one. Ought to be friends
and family and children here in the clearing, well-wishers surrounding the fire. Ought to be here drinking, singing songs,
telling stories about the departed, crying out their grief. But
Sero didn't have anyone. Not even the committee members
came; Enid had expected Ariana at the very least. Instead, the

only witnesses to the pyre were a couple of investigators—strangers—and a man sitting on a stump, who watched the flames and poked at the logs because he seemed to like fire on principle. It felt wrong and made Enid sad. But the chance to fix it would have been years in the past. Decades. Assuming there was even anything to fix. If Sero had been contented alone, why should anyone complain now?

At the edge of the town, a couple of figures stood. Two people, a man and woman. Younger, in their early twenties maybe. She couldn't make out much more of them with the sun at this angle. But Enid spotted them in time to see the woman storm off and the man bow his head and follow. Not quite observers, but something.

Those two. She would talk to those two next.

The wind changed; the smoke drifted, and the smell of burning wood couldn't entirely mask the stink of the burning body. Enid touched the attendant's shoulder and thanked him again, then said to Tomas, "Time to get to work."

"Yeah. Saw those two watching?"

"I did."

Pasadan wasn't that big. Shouldn't be hard to find anyone. Of course, the two figures had vanished. Fled. But she was patient. They'd turn up.

"Something to hide, then?" Tomas asked. "Or is it just the uniform?"

"I always assume it's the uniform first. You've worn it so long, you take it for granted, the way a whole village freezes up when one of us comes along."

"But the effect is so very useful," he said, grinning. Indeed, she'd seen cases where a guilty party would throw themselves at an investigator, unburdening their souls of every slight they could think of, just at the sight of the uniform and the implication that their mistakes would inevitably be discovered so they should immediately confess and beg for mercy. Muddied the water, sometimes. So Enid assumed anxiety when folk avoided her.

On the other hand, someone had fled from that work shed. Someone in this town must know something.

They reached the first dirt lane in the town. Tomas gestured right; the man was out of sight, but the young woman was marching steadily to a house a ways down.

"Why don't you go ahead?" Tomas said. "The both of us will just spook her. I can find the other one."

"Right," she agreed, and continued on, while Tomas went the other way.

When the young woman arrived at the house, she circled around back. Enid followed to see her take up a basket and begin pulling linens off a clothesline. She might have been trying to look like she'd been there for some time. A pale kerchief tied back her black hair, and she wore a yellow skirt and tunic and laced-up sandals; her face was round, still babyish though her body was full grown and curvy.

"Hola," Enid called as she came around the corner, giving the woman plenty of warning. Her quarry turned sharply but didn't look surprised. Basket against her hip, shirt dangling from a hand, the woman froze. Enid said, "Please, don't stop. I just have a couple of questions; we can talk while you work."

The woman looked like she didn't entirely believe Enid. When she reached for the next piece of laundry, she moved at about half speed and didn't glance away from the investigator.

"What's your name?"

"Miran. Of Sirius household." A towel dropped into the basket, and she reached for the next as if afraid of startling it.

"I'm Enid. I saw you watching Sero's pyre."

Miran ducked her gaze, nodded. "I was curious. I'd heard it was finally being taken care of."

"Did you know Sero very well?"

She shrugged as well as she could with a basket on one hip. "No. But no one did. He kept to himself. He was . . . odd."

"So I've gathered. Do you remember the last time you saw him?"

"No. Can't say I do. I mean . . . I'm sure he was around. He was repairing the fencing at Sirius, but that was a couple of weeks ago. After that . . . maybe in the square? Just walking along? You take it for granted, right? See people but don't see them."

People became part of the background noise of the world, like birdsong or clouds. Enid tried to name everyone she saw on her way out of Haven two days ago, and wasn't sure she could. So yes, she understood.

"Do you remember how you heard that he'd died?" Enid asked. "Where you were, what you were doing, who told you?"

The woman swallowed—she didn't want to say. Worried, perhaps, that she would implicate someone. Her dark eyes were large, blinking. "I think everyone must have heard the news all at once—that's how fast word traveled. It was so strange, so sudden. Philos, maybe? Or Ariana? Maybe both of them together. I know they came around to all the households here in the village to say that he was dead and that he'd be burned soon. As if any of us would go watch—"

"They encouraged people to come watch the pyre?" Enid asked. Other people; the committee members clearly hadn't felt that request applied to them.

"I think . . . they hoped someone would. They knew it would look strange if there was no one there. But they must have known that no one would watch; it isn't like Sero was friends with anyone."

"So you heard the news from Philos or Ariana, when they came around to make the announcement."

"But we all already knew. We just . . . knew."

That instant wave of rumor. And the memories had already blurred, because people had gossiped and shared their own impressions and decided that yes, this must have been how it had happened; Sero must have just fallen, an accident. Of course.

Enid and Tomas might have to talk to everyone in town. The prospect daunted her. Well, she reminded herself, *someone* had to do the worst jobs.

"Who was with you back there, watching the pyre?"

Miran swallowed, as if trying to keep back the word. Enid left the question hanging until the girl said, "Kirk. It was Kirk. He's . . . he's just a friend; we just happened to be there."

"What's his household?"

She studiously folded the next sheet. "Bounty."

"Thank you, Miran. I may have more questions later, all right?"

She nodded, not lifting her gaze. Enid left her alone to her laundry and her anxiety.

Enid had gotten the sequence of events of how and when the body was discovered and what happened after. She hadn't learned anything about what happened before, except that at some point some people must have visited Sero about jobs around town. She started looking for brand-new fence posts, unfinished construction, or freshly painted anything. All those extra household jobs that folk sometimes needed help with, so they'd ask their neighbors. While it seemed that nobody spent any social effort on Sero, they were happy to ask him to work.

And was he happy to do it? Did he ever argue about it? Did anyone hold a grudge against him?

No need to go spinning stories. She just had to find the person who'd rushed around the back of the work shed. Who'd gotten blood on their hands. Ask them what had happened. Then it would all be clear. She could hope.

She spoke to a half-dozen folk around Pasadan about obvious recent repairs at their households. All of them looked back at her, wide-eyed and startled, taking in her uniform and her serious expression. She tried to appear neutral—merely a sponge for information, nothing to worry about. Didn't seem to help. They shouldn't have been surprised; surely they'd heard about her and Tomas's arrival just as quickly and thoroughly as they'd all heard of Sero's death. But still, they all seemed just that tiny bit guilty at her presence.

Everyone she talked to who'd had a fence built in the last ten years had gotten Sero to build it for them, because of his auger. Most said they had spoken with him more than a week ago. The jobs had all been finished days before his death. Did anyone know who else might have been talking with him about new jobs? Who they might have seen going to his house? Anyone at all? No one knew or could recall.

The households here were all neat, well cared for. Nothing too big or unreasonable. No one exceeding what they needed, no one going hungry. By outward appearances, Pasadan was ideal. Except for Sero, the outcast.

Enid went to examine Sero's house next. Maybe he kept records.

It was as simple as a house could get. A front room with a small wood stove, water pump and basin for a kitchen, a table and chair for sitting. A single chair—none for guests. A back room that held a canvas cot with a faded quilt spread over it, a closet with a few changes of clothes, a couple of towels, and a spare blanket. A door led to a water closet and shower. A solar cistern on the roof meant hot water. Or at least comfortably warm water. It was simple, but it was enough. A person could be happy here, she imagined.

A set of shelves in the front room held tools and buckets of spare parts. He might have brought some work here instead of keeping it all in the shed. The solar-powered auger Ariana had mentioned had pride of place, hanging on a rack in the corner, the battery and power cords tucked up underneath it. Sero had kept it in amazing shape. The steel bit was as long as her arm, polished to a shine and sharp. The housing for the motor wasn't as pretty; a faded green, it had layers of scratches and dings on it. In places the plastic had grown brittle and chipped. Strips of canvas held parts of it together.

On one side, a series of four names had been painted in black ink. The older names were faded: Ray Macintyre. Carter Macintyre. Aldus of Bansai. And then last: Sero. Just Sero, as if he didn't identify with anyone or anyplace. Not Sero of Bansai, Pasadan, or any household. The auger had been passed down, and it was clearly a legacy Sero had cherished. She wondered: Did he have an heir in mind? Had he ever intended to try for a banner, to pass the ancient machine on to someone else? Maybe he hadn't. Maybe this had been enough for him.

Making a cursory search through the bedroom, Enid looked in the shallow closet, pushed aside the few tunics and clothing hanging on pegs, and found a banner on a hook in the back. A red-and-green section of woven cloth, a foot and some on each side. Embroidered along one side in bright yellow thread: SERO.

Some households did that, sewed in the name of the baby

represented by the banner. Olive and the others at Serenity planned on doing so with theirs.

Sero *had* been born with a banner. A parent or someone of the household he'd been born into had stitched his name on the cloth that the household had earned to have him. Whatever had happened to that household, whatever reason Sero had had for going off on his own, he'd taken the banner with him. A mark. A declaration.

He must have known of the rumors about him. That was half the point of such rumors, holding them against their object. Sero could have nailed that banner to the outside of his house, told everyone the truth. But he hadn't. He'd just wanted to be left alone.

Sadly, Enid brushed a bit of dust from the cloth and let it be.

///

ENID MET TOMAS walking back to the committee house. The scent of wood smoke hung about him.

"Pyre's done, then?" she asked.

"Just about. How'd your talk go?"

"Her name's Miran; the guy with her was Kirk, and she was careful to tell me they're just friends. Sero did work for the household a couple of weeks ago, but she can't remember the last time she saw him. You find anything?"

His expression went from pensive to sly. "I have two witnesses say that in the days before he died, they saw a young woman named Miran go to Sero's house twice." He looked like a cat who'd just dropped a mouse at her feet.

"Huh. She didn't mention that."

"Right?" he said.

84 • CARRIE VAUGHN

"So what's going on here?"

"Somebody's hiding something."

"Well, yes, clearly. Could they have had a thing going? Miran and Sero?"

"And hiding it because everyone would have disapproved," Tomas said.

"You've picked up on that too, hmm?" She was thinking of the auger, the list of names, and whether Sero might have wanted to add to that list.

"It's a thread at least," he said.

She turned to him. "You're so calm! Doesn't it make you angry? The way everyone wants to brush this away like Sero didn't matter? He's got no one standing up for him."

"Better to stay calm," he said, like he always did. "See more, when you're calm. You know that."

"Yes. But I want to knock some heads together."

"You usually do," he said, grinning.

There was a disadvantage, doing this job with someone who'd known her so long. She scowled in reply. "So we need to get a timeline down and see where we follow it out to—"

Enid stopped. A group of people was in front of the committee house. Ariana, a couple of others from the town. The way they hunched in together suggested serious conversation. Likely, discussing the arrival of a certain pair of investigators and what they might find.

One of the people there had long brown hair that brought out the angles of his face, sharp chin and defined cheekbones. Nut-brown skin. She'd have recognized this older version of him soon enough. Especially if he'd been holding a guitar.

And then his voice. "—they're here now, nothing to do but deal with it and hope they finish quickly—"

She knew that voice; it hadn't changed. It was like hearing the familiar, nerve-breaking crack of pottery shattering on hard ground. She hadn't seen him in ten years, and she hadn't ever expected to see him again. Yet somehow, she wasn't surprised to see him now. As much traveling as she did—as he must still do—it was inevitable. And all she felt was frozen.

He looked out at the newcomers, caught her gaze. She thought she saw surprise there, eyes going round in a moment of shock. He knew investigators had arrived, but no one had told him their names. That one of the investigators would be *her*. His performer's instincts quickly took over and settled his expression into a pleasant smile.

"Dak," she said with her next breath. Disbelieving.

"Enid," he said. "Been a long time."

Sea Glass

The Coast Road was somewhat misnamed—it ran inland for a third of its length. Miles west of Haven lay a series of hills and the ruins of the old cities that had been flooded, destroyed, and abandoned at the time of the Fall. Folk didn't much go out that way. But south of the ruins, the Coast Road bent westward around the hill country and finally reached the ocean. Fishing and seaside villages clustered there. Enid had never seen the ocean and was looking forward to it. Dak promised to show her.

Along the way, several byways branched off from the Coast Road—the Long Road to the eastern plains, the Sierra Road north to the mountains—and one could travel along these for weeks and still come across households and villages that were part of the Coast Road communities. This late in the season, Dak kept to the main road, where he was more sure of the welcome he would get. High summer, when harvests came in and before the autumn storms hit, was the time to go exploring.

Enid and Dak never had to walk more than a day to the next village, and between those larger settlements, dozens of households had rooted in along the Coast Road. Most could be counted on to put up a couple of strangers for a night or two, especially if they helped with chores and sang some songs, making at least an effort to earn their keep. They knew one of theirs might need the favor returned someday.

Some of the villages they went to were more structured than Enid was used to. More formal, more . . . rigid. In a village called Saved, for instance, Dak found a spot that looked like a central gathering place and began tuning his guitar. Before he'd sung a note, a committee member arrived to explain to him what rate of exchange he could expect: an hour of playing for a place to sleep, six songs for a meal. Dak would look on these bargains with amusement, especially when the committee member seemed relieved that he wasn't going to haggle. He sang because he liked it, and because he could usually count on some recompense for it. Meals, drinks, even a hat or some mending for his boots. But Saved wasn't like Haven, where what people gave him seemed more like gifts or gestures of gratitude than payment.

Some places, though, were very strict about recompense and fairness. Very serious about resource management, and they considered music to be a resource like any other. Wouldn't want anyone to get more than they'd earned, because that was what doomed the old world. Enid could understand, she supposed, but it didn't feel the same as sharing.

Enid had credits from Plenty—a letter that stated she had the backing of her household, that she had resources if she needed them—and her own muscles and effort to support her. She reassured herself that she wouldn't need Dak to sing for her bed as well. Usually, she did chores: weeding, chopping wood, some light cooking, and mending. A little of everything. She didn't mind; she wasn't dead weight. Dak even taught her a few songs, harmonies they could sing to add an extra kick to his music. She could hold a tune, but her voice wasn't artful, didn't draw people in by its tones the way Dak's did. She didn't sing much—and she'd rather listen to him anyway.

And they made love. Sometimes at the excuse of a picnic lunch or for no reason at all they'd leave the road, run off to a beautiful copse of willows along a pretty creek, and end up tumbled together, peeling off their clothes to soak up the sun and each other. Rainy season was coming—best get all the sun they could while they had the chance. Did they really need an excuse to roll around in the wild for an afternoon? They had food—not a lot but enough—they had water, and they had each other. They had exactly what they needed and no more. It was a good way to live, she thought.

Dak wanted to be south by the time of the first rains. More shelter there, he said. They could walk in the rain, but it was best if they had a place to dry out each night.

A week out, they saw the ruins.

The Coast Road went into some hills, rising gently enough that the walk wasn't difficult, and they almost didn't notice until they paused at a crest and looked out to what felt like hundreds of miles in all directions, if not to the ends of the world, then maybe to the ends of *their* world. Pockets of settlements huddled in valleys up and down the road; smoke from their hearth fires rose up, and flocks of bleating sheep dotted windblown pastures. Clusters of windmills reached up hillsides, spinning lazily.

But west, not so far in the distance as she would have expected, was the big ruin, what had been a city of millions a hundred years before. Enid couldn't imagine a million people in a space like a city, much less in the whole world, though folk who talked about such things said there must have been billions of people still living—we just couldn't get to them to count, and the world was too big. These days, there was a lot more space between people. A lot fewer roads and radios connecting them.

The city was a gray mountain that had collapsed on itself, its ruins projecting from the surrounding landscape like the shards of a broken bone. Those struts had been buildings once, towering hundreds of feet tall, and the space between them had been wide streets. Hard to make out more details than that—from where they stood, it was mostly a stretch of color, a gap in the land where something had been taken away. The air over the city was hazy, almost smoky, as if the ruins produced their own atmosphere.

Through the years of the Fall, the dense settlement had been inundated and washed away. Pieces broke and couldn't be repaired until all of it was broken. It was a marvel, how quickly a structure became a ruin. "If we didn't save it, it didn't get saved," Auntie Kath used to say. Meaning, they could only save so much. Those first years, they did triage on the whole of civilization. Auntie Kath said that they'd been shocked: much of the old world was gone or useless within a decade or two. They looked around one day, and the Fall was over, and they were living After.

You could only save what you worked to save—what everyone came together to save. If you didn't work to save anything—you saved nothing. That was the city in ruins.

Looking at it, Enid felt both revulsion and longing, urging her to flee from it and race toward it at the same time.

"Auntie Kath says they used to talk about ways to save the cities. There just weren't enough people, and then the buildings started coming down, and it wasn't safe to go there anymore. But I'm thinking it might be safe now—everything that's likely to fall down has probably already fallen, yeah?"

"But is there anything worth saving in there?" Dak said.

"I don't know." That was why she wanted to go check. And to bear witness. Had Kath ever gone back, after helping to build Haven?

"Who's Auntie Kath? You talk about her a lot."

"She was the Last." And yes, the word felt like a title rather than a description. The Last of them. There might have been others up and down the Coast Road—even now, there might still be folk who remembered what it was like before. But maybe not. Someone with vague childhood memories of things like television and airplanes wouldn't be able to explain, not like Kath. "She was alive before the Fall. Really old when I knew her. But she told stories."

"Must have been great stories."

"Yeah, they were. I learned a lot."

"Anything useful?"

She looked at him. "Everything's useful to someone, I imagine. I want to know everything."

"But really. I bet she talked about things like airplanes and orchestras. You think anyone will ever see an airplane fly again?" A laugh touched his voice; he sounded like he was mocking her.

"Then maybe it's even more important to know about it."

"That can be your job, then. The Knower of Things."

Yes, he definitely seemed to be laughing at her, though he had the decency to hide his grin. She frowned and scuffed a foot at the dirt.

"The old world fell because it was broken, Enid," he said. "We left it behind because it was broken."

Yes, that was so. But Auntie Kath had so loved to talk about that broken world.

She asked, "You ever been there? To the ruins?"

He didn't answer right away, and she didn't know what that meant. Was the answer yes, but he didn't want to talk about it? Or no, but he didn't want to admit not leaping into such an obvious adventure? Was he preparing a story, some bardic tale for her?

"I got close, once," he said finally, pointing toward the gray gash on the horizon. "Decided I was going to march straight in and see what I could see. But—there are people living there. Rough scavengers. I didn't like the way they looked, so I turned back."

"Did you think they'd hurt you?"

"Me, or the guitar. Either way, I didn't go."

The idea that he'd been scared seemed like a confession. She took his hand, sure that both of them were telling themselves stories about what the ruins were really like and about what kind of people could possibly be living there. Enid couldn't imagine. Whoever they were, they never came to the Coast Road, and that said something about them.

She wanted to go there. Maybe not right now—she could almost feel Dak pulling away from that hulking ghost on the horizon. Not leaning toward it, as she was doing. Someday. On the way back. Which was when she realized that she wouldn't do this forever—she'd go back to Haven someday. She didn't know when, but that wasn't important.

Oddly, the world seemed to open more, not less, knowing she had a place to go home to. It was an anchor in a safe harbor, no matter what happened. She was Enid of Haven.

"Let's go, hmm? We should reach Firepit by dark," he said, tugging on her hand until she followed.

//

ALL THIS WALKING was productive, even if it wasn't useful.

Enid developed a long swinging stride and toned muscles that may not have been strong but could keep going as long as she needed them to. She learned how to start fires in the rain, how to look for good sources of water, and how much time they had before a storm opened up on them judging by dark clouds on the horizon. She flinched at the particularly dark clouds, even years after that last big storm. In every town they stopped at, she looked for cellar doors. A place to shelter, to stay safe.

How much credit was all this worth, and how did she measure the experience? Could she ever use these skills, or was she being frivolous? Maybe she could be a courier, delivering messages up and down the Coast Road, dropping off packages, guiding travelers. Knowledge was a resource, and she could do a million things, learning what she was learning while traveling with Dak.

Funny thing was, Dak didn't seem concerned about earning his keep or contributing to the community or any of it. "We'll just see what happens," he'd say, and, "I'm sure it'll work out." They'd show up at the next village or household, Enid would say she was from Haven, and people would smile and cluck over her. They all knew about Haven, the closest thing the Coast Road had to a center. Then Dak would slip his guitar out of its case and strum a few chords, and people would come to him like hens to seed. He was always right—he'd play, and people would feed him, exactly the sort of exchange their whole world was built on. That the music was intangible, impractical, didn't seem to matter. Dak's arrival was special, and folk could usually afford to trade a couple of apples and a meat pie for the novelty of it. Dak was almost always a better musician than the local variety who hadn't been practicing every day of their lives.

Now and then they came to a household or settlement that couldn't spare a couple of apples or anything at all. Enid learned to recognize them: the buildings were run-down, the gardens sparse. There might only be a single windmill. The people would look tired, and they didn't smile at the sight of Dak's guitar. A household or town might have a million reasons for not thriving—a couple of bad harvests, drought or disease, or bad management. After a couple of lean years, a place might turn around. Or it might break up, its members putting in for transfers to other settlements, scraping together credits to put toward starting over somewhere else. Asking for help. Didn't happen often, but it did happen. Regional committees were there to make sure such folk were taken care of. No one ought to starve.

Even if all they could do was thank him, Dak stopped and played at these settlements anyway. "It's what I do: I play and sing," he said, suggesting this wasn't how he made his living, that he could earn his keep some other way. But it was good he and Enid always carried some extra food in their packs.

One time, they encountered a turnoff and started down that path to see what households were there, but after only a mile or so, they saw a post with a sign nailed to it, driven into the middle of the road.

QUARANTINE.

The sign looked new, the wood freshly cut.

Enid stood staring at it for a long time, part of her desperately wanting to run ahead to see what was wrong, see if they needed food, if there was anything at all she could do to help. Did they have a medic? Should she go get one for them? Bring medicine? Was it flu or hemorrhagic fever or something else? She wanted so much to help. Dak gently touched her shoulder and urged her back. "Enid, come on. Sign's there for a reason; we need to go."

If the place needed help, they would have left a note asking for it. Enid searched and didn't find one. So they were protecting travelers with the quarantine sign, and that was good. But she wanted to help.

"We'll leave word at the next way station," she said. "Pass the news on to the regional committee if they don't already know. Right?"

"That's right," Dak said. "That's a good idea. We should get going now."

They walked on.

Sometimes, she and Dak would approach a place with that tired look, the air around it too silent—no clucking chickens, no loom beating a rhythm or blacksmith's hammer clanging, no voices—and some instinct would tell them not to stop. They'd keep going on to the next place, or spend the night under the stars and talk about what the point of it all was, working to feed yourself and your friends if you were all just going to die in the end.

"Humanity's made it this far," Dak said on one of these nights. "Might as well keep going, yeah?" Enid thought of Auntie Kath, who might have had doubts about how far humanity had really come.

FIVE WEEKS IN, Enid saw the ocean for the first time. The real ocean, not a straight gray haze along the horizon as seen from the hills. Close enough to hear water shushing along the sand, splashing back in on itself. Dak knew a spot where an old town from before the Fall had just about finished rotting into sand and crabgrass, a dozen big storms over the last century pulling down buildings and dragging streets into the sea. All that lingered were some squares of concrete foundations, some rusted shells of cars, fallen poles, and symmetrical mounds of vegetation hiding whatever was underneath. The town had been there because of a beach, a slope of clean yellow sand stretching toward the water. The beach was still there, and they spent a night on it, having sex and laughing because the gritty sand got everywhere.

At sunset Enid rolled up her pants and waded into the surf, letting the chill waves crawl over her feet, like some living thing was tasting her skin. Little translucent crabs skittered out of the way of the water; ropes of brown kelp slumped onto shore. She dug her toes in the wet sand and found bits and pieces of broken shells, and also a couple of chunks of sea glass the size of her thumb, irregularly shaped. Pale green and creamy white, rubbed smooth and frosted by endless trips through the surf.

Not at all practical, but too beautiful and mysterious to leave behind. She tucked them in her satchel.

Half a day's travel from the beach, they reached the first of the fishing villages. Enid thought the place was magnificent; community buildings and various households clustered on a hill above a curving harbor. A couple of wooden docks were built out on the water, and a dozen boats moored there, most with shining white hulls and tall masts, sails on them wrapped up and bundled out of sight. Some of the boats had apparently survived from before the Fall. Their hulls were fiberglass, carefully cleaned and patched and maintained over the decades. They seemed like pale birds bobbing up and down on the rippling water.

Fintown was one of the welcoming places. The main road led down the hill, right through the middle of the town, and around the curve of the harbor. People were out on the docks coiling rope or mopping the decks of the boats. On a patio outside a long work building, a group of people cleaned a mound of silvery fish. The air reeked of fish. They knew Dak here—one of them looked up, saw the musician, and called out. Then everyone was smiling, greeting him by name. Enid had to smile, too. She felt like a hero in a story, walking in to this kind of welcome. This was likely part of why Dak traveled like he did.

"Dak!" a particularly enthusiastic voice shouted from the dock.

He looked for a moment and laughed when a tall man with frizzy dark hair ran up from the docks. "Xander!"

The musician rushed forward, and the two came together in a big thumping hug, in the way of good friends who'd been too long separated. Then Dak took the other man's face in his hands and kissed him, long and lingering, on the mouth. The other man—Xander, apparently—clutched Dak's sides and pulled him in.

Enid lagged behind, her smile frozen. She knew those gestures. Muscle memory in her own body could feel them, or the echo of them. Dak kissed her just like that. She had to remind herself to keep breathing.

She had expected this. She knew, abstractly, to expect this. Tomas had been right from the start, that Dak would have lovers up and down the Coast Road. She had known that he would be right. But maybe, deep down, she hadn't actually believed it.

She hadn't expected to feel so . . . *angry*. Her heart scrunching up into a tiny crooked ball. She had thought herself better than jealousy. But she'd had Dak all to herself for weeks now. She'd gotten used to it.

Suddenly, she wanted to leave. She didn't know if she'd ever be able to eat fish again.

"Been over a year, yeah?" Xander said. The man had a lopsided grin and bright dark eyes. He spotted her over Dak's shoulder when she made her feet stroll forward to insert herself in the reunion.

Dak then seemed to remember her and gestured. "Xander. This is Enid of Haven."

"Hola," she said, smiling by remembering the sea glass in her bag and reminding herself that it really was beautiful here. Xander offered his hand, and she shook it as if she were glad to meet him.

"Dak finally talked someone into taking to the road with him, did he?" Xander said, a laugh under his voice.

And just what was that supposed to mean? She lifted an eyebrow at Dak.

"I wasn't doing anything else, much," she said, before Dak could say anything that she wouldn't be able to argue against.

"It's good he has someone looking after him, then," Xander said, playfully cuffing Dak's shoulder. "Keep him out of trouble."

"There's no trouble," Dak said. "None at all. Hey, think it'd be okay if we stuck around for a few days? Keep out of the next rain?"

"Of course," Xander said. "Always. Come on, let's get you in to rest."

He led them up the road to the fourth enclave back from the shore, a household made up of a couple of cottages and a parcel of land with the usual complement of cisterns and chickens. Xander gave them an enthusiastic tour of the household, called Petula Dock. The back cottage was sleeping quarters; the front was a kitchen and workroom, clean and lit from above by a skylight in the roof. In addition to the cottages and land, the household's folk maintained two boats, a larger fishing boat and a smaller sailboat. They fished some, but mostly worked to maintain the dock area and harbor. Xander promised to show them the docks later and take them sailing.

The next couple of hours were a busy blur. Late in the afternoon, Petula Dock's members drifted in from work and chores, looking for food, interested to meet the visitors. Xander told Enid their names, and she forgot them instantly — she was tired, fuzzy, and maybe hungry. The household had two kids under eighteen and a brand-new banner, but no baby for it yet and no one obviously carrying. Enid didn't pry, but she did wonder. Most of them already knew Dak, and they all asked when he would play them something. They were polite to Enid, and she tried to stay unobtrusive, not to disturb what felt like a family reunion. Xander and Dak stayed side by side. Enid felt off balance, caught between the familiarity of the close-knit domestic scene and also not knowing anyone. Even Dak seemed like a stranger to her here.

Fisher — Enid *did* remember her name, it seemed so obvious — was the head of the household, a middle-aged woman with luxurious black hair braided down her back and a billowing tunic tied in place with a multicolored woven sash. She ducked into a cupboard and emerged with a dark, enticing-looking bottle. "Guests call for brandy!" she announced, holding it high, and everyone cheered.

"Pear brandy," Xander leaned in to explain to Enid. She must have looked blank or confused—she'd heard of brandy but had never had any. "Sunshine household up the way's got a still, a good one from before the Fall."

"Ah," she answered politely, starting to understand. The still was a little bit of old technology that managed to survive, and the whole village was proud of it. This was special; this was important.

And this was why everyone liked Dak. He spontaneously triggered parties wherever he went.

Fisher poured little fingers of the brandy into cups and passed them around. Enid tried it—it burned going down and left a light, summery aftertaste of fruit and flowers that she imagined would taste best in the middle of winter, next to a hearth fire. She took seconds and started to relax. Food seemed to magically appear—a fish-based stew that had been simmering all day. The household's youngest kid, eight years old, had to show Enid the socks she was knitting; she was just learning to knit and very proud of herself. Enid was attentive and felt like she earned her dinner just for that.

The rain Dak had predicted started up after dark, sounding as a light pattering on the skylight overhead. They all looked up.

"Raul, is the coop closed up?" Fisher said.

"Yeah," the stocky, good-natured man answered. "Did it when I came in."

The rattling grew heavier, and Fisher sighed. "This one's going to last all night by the sound of it."

The rain's patter was comforting, lulling. But it also made Enid feel trapped—they'd likely be here at Petula Dock until the weather broke, and who knew how long that would be.

Dak had already left the gathering by then. First time since leaving Haven they'd been apart. Xander was gone, too. Nothing surprising about any of it. And yet. She sipped the brandy, listened to the talk around her, and tried to be content. Gratefully accepted a pallet of blankets in the common room for her bed. Curled up to sleep as Fisher banked the fire in the wood stove to embers.

One of the benefits of walking all day: she never had any trouble sleeping. Even now, simmering in some vague emotion between anger and abandonment, her tired body pulled her under.

///

GRAY MORNING LIGHT came in through the skylight, waking Enid early. She felt fuzzy and unhappy—took a moment to remember why, and missed Dak's warm self, who should have been snugged up beside her but wasn't. She got up and dressed to escape the reminder.

Rustling in the kitchen drew her in, and she found Fisher starting water boiling for tea.

"Morning," the woman said brightly. "Get a cup from the shelf there and I'll pour you some."

A shelf above the sink had a dozen or so mismatched earthenware mugs. Enid chose one. She kept looking at the door for Dak, who kept not arriving.

"Plans for the day?" Fisher asked.

Enid shook her head, then belatedly thought she should maybe try to keep the conversation alive. Try not to feel quite so superfluous. "You? Anything special planned?" She winced, because the question sounded silly out loud. Sounded like a crutch.

If Fisher thought so, she didn't react. "The boats won't go

out today because of the rain, so I'll mostly be doing chores and repairs around here."

"Can I help?" Enid asked, rather more desperately than she intended. "Anything you can teach me—I learn fast."

Fisher considered her, seeming to take a moment to decide whether to classify her as "guest" or "temporary household member." Or maybe "Dak's current accessory," which brought Enid back to being angry so she shoved the thought away. Enid didn't really know which category she fit in, either. This would decide.

"Ever prep fish jerky?"

They'd need a way to preserve the fish they caught. Right. "No. Show me?"

"Drink up your tea and we'll get started."

Getting started involved preparing four big buckets of little silvery fish from yesterday's catch that one of the other households had spent the night cleaning, filleting, and brining. Fisher brought out a set of racks, and Enid helped arrange thin strips of fish on the racks, careful not to let them touch.

At the back of the household, partway up the hill, sat a smokehouse, a small square shed that wasn't big enough for much of anything else. Wood, scrap metal, and a chimney reaching up, pouring gray smoke. Fisher had already started a smoldering charcoal fire in the base. They had to deliver the racks they'd prepared to the smokehouse in a misting rain— they worked together, trotting up the hill with Fisher holding the racks while Enid held a light tarp over them, getting soaked herself. All the racks loaded into the shed. The fish would stay for a long time at a low temperature, drying out more than cooking, until the moisture burned away through strategic slats at the door. Enid took it all in.

"We'll rotate the racks partway through, and the whole mess will be ready to seal up this afternoon."

Back inside they dried off, changing shirts, hanging the wet ones by the stove to dry. After, Enid helped clean up the mess in the kitchen, and then gratefully accepted another cup of tea. She hadn't realized how chilled she'd gotten until she held it in both hands; before, the work had kept her warm.

Fisher talked, and Enid asked questions to keep her talking, about the household, the town, their work.

Petula was an older household, on its third generation. A dozen banners were pinned up on the wall of the common room, including the new one, recently awarded. Some of them were old and faded, the next newest some eight years old. The kid it represented, the knitter Hild, ran around with a hyperactive amount of energy, harvesting herbs from the garden and digging weeds and talking about beehives, and then suddenly running out to Fintown proper on some mission or other. Petula had invited in new members over the years, as necessary. Fisher reminded her of some of the names and faces she'd forgotten the night before. Vinya made rope from hemp; Raul was a carpenter; Bin worked the scales at the docks, recording daily catches and quotas. The place had the same rhythms and energies that measured life at Plenty, but with different trappings, such as talk of how the sea looked and what storms brooded on the horizon, fish and seabirds and life on a rocky coast instead of hilly meadows.

The older woman finally made her feel welcome in her own right.

Fisher's son Stev, represented by a banner on the wall some twenty years old, joined them that afternoon. He hadn't been there for brandy the night before, Enid was pretty sure. He was short, stocky, with a shock of black hair and a small face in a seemingly large head—eyes set close together, wide lips. A near-constant smile. He moved carefully, as if he had to take an extra moment to be sure he had a good grip on a spoon, a chair, his own feet sometimes. He stirred the stew, delivered a pot full of kitchen waste to the compost pile in back, swept the floor after. If he'd been a child, Enid wouldn't have taken a second look at him—he spoke like a child. But he wasn't.

"Can I show Enid my rocks?" Stev earnestly asked Fisher.

"Ask her if she wants to see them."

Stev looked at her, his eyes alight, and carefully asked, "Would you like to see my rocks?"

"He has a rock collection," Fisher explained softly, nodding encouragingly.

"I'd love to see it," Enid said, and Stev beamed.

He raced off and returned with a wooden crate filled with fist-sized rocks of every description, yellow sandstone and smooth beach rocks, granite sparkling with crystals and a dozen other earth-colored, unidentifiable samples. Stev had collected them all and told her exactly where each had come from—the beach north of town, the garden, the hill above the docks, and so on. A whole catalog of rocks ended up spread across the floor in the common room. Enid dutifully pointed to her favorites, and Stev arranged and rearranged them in categories of his own making. When it was time for dinner, Fisher asked him to clean up, and he did.

Enid tried not to stare after him—was chagrined that part of her recoiled from him. She quashed that feeling. But she stared all the same.

"It's a genetic anomaly," Fisher said, after he'd left to put his rocks away. "After he was born, the midwife brought a book about it from Haven for me. They called it 'Down's' before the Fall."

"I've heard of it," Enid said. She might have read the book Fisher spoke of or one like it in the Haven archives. She'd never met anyone like Stev before.

"We think the banner is everything," Fisher said. "Once you've got that cloth to hang on your wall, you've done it, observed the quotas, earned a kid. But it's just the start. There's so much can go wrong." She smiled broadly at the door her son had left through. "Not really what you expect when the committee hands you a banner. But you know what? He's part of our house. He earns his keep." She bustled for a moment, pulling bowls out of a cupboard, handing them to Enid, who took them to the table. Found a pitcher and filled it from the pump at the sink, then looked around, distracted, for something else to do. "Thank goodness for the household, so he'll always have someone to look after him."

Stev couldn't look after himself. Like Auntie Kath couldn't, at the end. Enid had a moment of panic, a heartbeat where the bottom dropped out of her gut thinking of what would happen if she got hurt out here on the road, camping in the middle of nowhere with Dak, and she fell and broke her leg or hit her head. What would happen? Who would take care of her? Would someone find a car or wagon to carry her back home? Would anyone be so kind? She'd been so blithe. How easy to set off with a satchel, a canteen, and a couple of packs of dried fruit, when you'd never had to worry about who would take care of you. She had just done it.

"Are you mad for a baby, Enid?" Fisher asked, winking. Still thinking about banners. "Some girls are at your age. Vinya's trying now—it's her turn."

"I hadn't really thought about it," she answered. "Not now, I mean. I'd never earn a banner wandering around the Coast Road with Dak, would I?"

"Hmm," she said, noncommittally.

This was the moment Dak came in, blinking between the two of them with a look of panic. Enid rolled her eyes.

"He emerges," Fisher said.

"Didn't miss anything, did I?"

"Just tea," Enid said, pouring a fresh mug from the pot Fisher had brewed and pushing it over to him. "You should have some."

His look of panic vanished, and he seemed happy enough to slide into the seat next to her and kiss her cheek. Just like that, and she thought, *Really?* She wanted to yell at him. No, talk. She wanted to *talk* to him, like an adult. He should have warned her. She could handle anything with a little warning. She refused, utterly, to ask where Xander was and what they'd been up to all morning, and all last night. But she couldn't think of anything apart from that to say, and the kitchen became unbearably silent. Even the sound of Fisher washing dishes at the basin seemed muted. As if she was trying to be quiet, to overhear what they might say.

Dak finally broke the quiet with, "You seem to be getting along well then, yeah?"

Fisher pressed her lips in a pitying look that Enid glanced away from before she'd have to respond. Brightly, she said, "Enid, I have a couple of errands I need doing this afternoon, if you don't mind getting out in the rain. We trade eggs for bread with a couple of households down the way."

"I'd love to help," Enid said.

"You can also spread word that I'm playing at the community house this evening," Dak said. "Folk might like getting out for some music, after being cooped up with the weather like this."

Or he could offer to go with her, tell folk himself. Or she

could tell him she wanted to talk to him. Right now, she decided, she just wanted to get away.

"All right," she said, with forced cheer.

///

SHE AND DAK finally talked at dinner. Sort of. They took their bowls of stew to a bench outside, sitting under the eaves to watch the rain, a gentle but persistent drizzle that beat on the world.

"You've been quiet," he said, after a long moment.

She looked at him, and then away.

"I've never seen you angry," he said. "It looks strange on you. I'm not sure what to do about it."

"I'm not angry. I'm insanely jealous," she said, deadpan, studying the carrots and potatoes in her bowl.

He laughed, and she blushed. Embarrassment, this time. She wasn't a child, but she felt like one at the moment, and it hurt.

"Xander's an old friend," he said. "What did you want me to do, ignore him?"

"Tell me?"

"Ah." Then, after they'd eaten a couple more bites, "I suppose you'll want to leave, move on to the next place, then?"

"You can do whatever you want to." She shrugged. "And so can I. It's nice here. I don't mind staying." But she was still angry.

He put a hand on her leg, brushed it up so it rested at her hip. Tilted, so his nose was in her hair, smelling, nuzzling. So all she would have to do was turn her face and he would kiss her. "I'm sorry. I didn't mean to hurt you. I didn't think. Next time, I will."

She tucked that *next time* away in the back of her mind to consider later. For now, she turned her face and caught his lips.

He spent that night with her.

///

THE RAIN BROKE the next day, and Xander took them sailing on Petula Dock's smaller boat, a little single-mast craft, maybe twenty feet long. Antique, he said, one of the old ones with a fiberglass hull. The community took good care of it, working hard to keep it cleaned, patched, and repaired. Not big enough for real fishing, it was mostly used to patrol the harbor, mapping hazards and changes in the coastline after storms, and helping when the bigger fishing boats got in trouble. When people had time and the wind was fair, it was perfect for spending a nice morning on the water.

Enid was annoyed to discover that she liked Xander. He told jokes, many at his own expense, about how clumsy he was and how he had terrible taste in men while raising an eyebrow at Dak, who merely chuckled. He could set her at ease with a smile and was kind to her—he seemed to recognize that Dak had dragged her into this without warning her. He sympathized. As if Dak had done this before.

She liked the sailing. It was new. It felt like an adventure.

"Some people get sick from the rocking," Dak told her. "It's nothing to be embarrassed about."

She hung on the side of the boat, watching the silky dark water slip past, trying to follow the patterns the waves and the wake of their passage made. She dared to reach out, dip in her fingers, and they made ripples to join with the others. The water was cold, slippery.

She didn't get sick.

The canvas sail went up the mast, cracking and rippling in the wind. Xander worked lines and watched the fabric, turning the boom to take advantage of the wind. When it filled, the sail was a beautiful field of clean, taut white. The boat jumped with a burst of speed and raced away from shore.

Dak sprawled in the boat, arms stretched out and face turned up to the sun. He might have been napping. Xander sat in the back, keeping hold of the tiller to steer. Enid watched the water, looking for . . . anything. She'd never seen so much water, and it smelled wet and briny and rippled in colors before her eyes. Fish lived here. Whales, even. She wanted to see it all.

She asked Xander questions, which was how she learned the parts of the boat, how they fished, and what she should be looking for.

"We don't see many whales," he said when she asked. "But you want to look for spouts. They come to the surface and blow out air through their blowholes. It's like a mist shooting straight up a few feet. You'll see that before you see anything else."

She watched until her eyes watered but didn't see anything.

They'd brought along canteens of water and sandwiches for lunch. Xander lowered the sail and they drifted, rocking from the movement of the waves, and he told stories about being a kid on fishing boats, the strange things they pulled up sometimes, rusted artifacts of the old world like bicycle wheels and street signs crusted over with algae and barnacles. Usually they tossed such things back, but onshore was a kind of pre-Fall graveyard where they sometimes brought and stashed such items of steel and rust.

Enid might like to see it, but she asked more about the fishing, imagining spending days on the water, and maybe *that* was what she might like to do with her life. Find a household on the shore that would take her. A complete change from the way she grew up. Maybe that was what she wanted.

"It's hard work, Enid," Dak said, a laugh in his voice. "All hauling and cleaning and weighing and watching your quotas—around here they ding you hard for going over. Overfish and there's nothing left. And it all stinks."

"I don't mind it," she said. But not loud enough for him to hear.

The wind picked up in the afternoon. They'd sailed a ways down the coast by then, out of sight of the village, into sight of the next one. A couple of fishing boats came close enough for Xander to wave at the people in them. They all seemed to know one another. Soon, though, the wind slapped at the sails, which jerked taut and pulled at the boom. Xander wanted to get back before the weather turned.

By the time they docked, Enid was confident enough to help put the sail away and throw the line out to Xander when he jumped to the dock to tie up the boat. All in all, it made for a satisfying day. She'd been wearing a hat but her arms had still gotten a bit sunburned—sun reflecting off the water made it more intense. It felt like an accomplishment. Like she had something to show for the day.

Dak slapped Xander's shoulder, gave Enid's hand a squeeze, and announced he was going back to the house to take a nap. That left them alone.

She stared after Dak, not realizing she was doing so.

"Are you okay?" Xander asked. They were collecting their canteens and bags from the boat, getting ready to walk up the path to the houses. She wanted to see this graveyard of artifacts first.

"In what sense?" she shot back, without thinking.

His smile was gentle, and she couldn't be angry. None

of this was his fault. He was stepping as softly as he possibly could, and she was grateful.

"In the 'Dak' sense."

She sighed. "He doesn't owe me anything. I don't need anything."

"But wanting."

"Yeah," she agreed.

"What do you want?" he asked. "I mean, I know right now you want Dak. I get that, for sure. But without him, what do you want? What brought you all this way down the road with him?"

"Not really sure," she said. "But this . . . I'm really glad to have seen all this." She stared at the ocean, its expansive breadth, the endless rippling sameness of it. Storm clouds gathered on the horizon and piled high, brought in by a sudden wind that tasted of brine. "I might just keep walking, with or without him."

"You can always stay here if you need to. With or without Dak."

She didn't know she needed that encouragement until he said it. She grinned back warmly.

Back at Petula, Dak was sitting on a bench outside, arms crossed, head resting against the wall. As if he'd gotten this far and couldn't wait for that nap any longer. She hesitated a moment, watching him, setting sun turning his skin golden, his brown hair draped around his shoulders. His face looked young; his lips rested in a vague smile. He couldn't have been more alluring if he'd posed this way on purpose, as if he were a piece of art.

She had an idea. Second-guessed herself on that idea, then went back to it, and then considered a third time. And then decided to just give in to the urge. If it went badly, so be it.

Dashing the last few steps, she threw herself on the bench, sliding right up to press against him, and wrapped her arms around his middle, holding him tight. Held her breath as she waited to see what he would do. Let it out with a sigh when he laughed and put his arms around her.

That was what she wanted. What she'd hoped he would do.

"Having a good day, I take it," he said.

"Hmm." She hugged him harder, resting her head on his shoulder. She could almost hear his heart. Tipping her head up, she didn't wait for him to kiss her, but touched his chin and held him still so she could kiss him. If she wanted something, she decided, she ought to ask for it.

He seemed perfectly happy kissing her, and she melted against him. And all was again right with the world.

When she heard footsteps on the path, she assumed it was Xander finally returning from the docks. But no, there were two sets, and unfamiliar voices in conversation. She and Dak broke their kiss and looked out.

Two figures in brown uniforms approached. Both she and Dak tensed, their bodies braced by instinct. Enid took a breath and relaxed as she saw the people wearing the uniforms—a short, dark-skinned woman with a kind smile, and the man who must have been her enforcer. He carried a staff, wore his blond hair braided, and kept a short strand of his beard braided as well. She didn't know them, but they likely knew Tomas.

Dak turned anxious. Worried. She glanced at him, his uncharacteristic frown.

The investigators approached.

"Hola," Enid called out to them, to break the tension that was threatening to knot them up.

"Hola!" the woman called back. "I'm Nala; this is Holt. Is this Petula Dock household?"

"Yeah," she said.

"And how long have you two lived here?"

"We're not actually part of the household; we're just visiting. I'm Enid from Haven—do you know my friend Tomas? He's an investigator."

The man, Holt, answered with a smile. "Yeah—worked with him on a couple of cases up north. Good guy."

Enid beamed. Maybe not as good as seeing someone from back home, but still a connection.

Nala looked at Dak. "And you are?"

"Dak," he said. "I'm just traveling a bit. That's all." As if he was trying to provide an alibi.

But they weren't here for Enid and Dak. Nala gestured. "The head of the house inside? That's Fisher, isn't it?"

"Can I ask what this is about?" Enid asked. Pure curiosity.

"I want to hold off on that until I speak to the folk I need to. You'll hear about it soon enough, I imagine."

The two investigators went in through the archway to the household's inner yard.

"Well, you were very helpful," Dak said, scorn in his voice, as if she had done something wrong.

"Yes?" she answered.

"You know they can't be here for anything good. Don't you wonder why on Earth they'd be investigating Petula?" He looked out, worried. "Xander needs to know about this."

"They might just be here to get information. It doesn't mean that Petula's done anything—"

But Dak was already running down the path to the docks, looking for Xander.

Complications

W hat are you doing here?" Enid asked Dak, who laughed at her astonishment. It was a stupid question; it just fell out. Tomas wryly crossed his arms, like he was holding in words. Dak seemed to avoid looking at him, without *appearing* to be avoiding him, of course. Maybe they could each just pretend the other didn't exist.

"I live here," he said. "And I can see exactly what you're doing here." He gestured at her, indicating the uniform.

This probably wouldn't be the best time to ask him if he knew Sero, when was the last time he'd seen the man, and where he'd spent the morning four days ago.

They lingered in the shade of the committee building, surrounded by the heat and buzz of the afternoon. She could feel sweat on her brow and wanted nothing more than to take a shower and sit for a few moments.

"You know each other?" Ariana asked. She looked back and forth between the two of them, mid-gesture. More astonishment.

"A long time ago," Enid said simply.

"A very memorable time," Dak added.

She ducked away, embarrassed, frustrated that she was blushing. Tomas didn't offer rescue. But then he'd never much liked Dak.

Ariana's smile was tight, polite. "That sounds like a good story."

"Oh, I doubt it," Enid said. Again the words seemed to just fall out. Of course, Dak laughed again. She hadn't been trying to be funny.

"So do you know what happened yet?" Ariana asked.

"Still working on that. We may need to talk to everyone in town, just to get our timeline down, to know when Sero was last seen. You won't mind if I asked you a few questions?" Enid regarded Dak appraisingly; she couldn't imagine him rushing to share information. Maybe he'd surprise her.

"Not even starting with, 'Hey, how are you, what have you been up to lately?'"

She matched his smirk. No reason to poke at each other, but here they were. He was more likely poking at the uniform, she reminded herself.

Ariana laid a hand on Dak's arm, a friendly, familiar gesture. "You should play tonight, Dak. Get people's minds off all this."

The couple of townsfolk who hadn't drifted off — to avoid questioning, likely — jumped in eagerly. "Oh, please do, it's been weeks!"

"Why not?" he told them. "We'll put a fire in the pit up here, and maybe you all can scare up some food to share? We can welcome our investigators properly."

The others ran off to spread the word, leaving Ariana and Dak standing side by side before Enid and Tomas. Clearly a united front. Intimate, even. Were they together? Dak said he lived here now—as part of Ariana's household, she'd bet. Well, good for him.

"We still have a few questions to answer," Enid said evenly, professionally. "The investigation may take a couple of days. If you can show us to your way station, we'd appreciate it."

"Of course, it's just behind the committee house," Ariana said. She and Dak exchanged an indecipherable look. Rather than trying to find meaning in it, Enid decided it wasn't any of her business.

Within half an hour, an impromptu party gathered around the side of the building, where a fire pit and a cluster of benches and chairs were located. Dusk was settling in, bugs coming out. Someone brought out a cask of cider. It was exactly like she remembered all of Dak's grand entrances, the way the man could start a party anywhere he went.

She lingered at the door of the meeting room, watching, wondering who knew what and why they weren't speaking to her. She'd gotten into the mindset where everyone looked suspicious.

"Come sit," Dak said, coming up to her and gesturing to the fire. He'd gone to get his guitar, its strap slung over his shoulder in that all-too-familiar way. "Tell me what you've been up to."

"Can't." Couldn't maintain objective distance for an investigation during a party. And she couldn't imagine folk being in a mood for celebration with a couple of investigators on hand. "They'll be happier if we're not there."

Tomas also lingered outside, near a corner of the building. Standing watch, seemed like. "Someone might want to talk about the investigation," he explained. It happened sometimes, a local with something to say, but without the pressure

of formal questioning, coming to them under cover of darkness or some other pretense. But Enid suspected this was an
excuse for him to get out of their way. She almost wished he
wouldn't.

But she and Dak did need to catch up with each other,
didn't they? Might as well get it over with. "Why don't you
come in for a couple of minutes? You won't need to go play
while everyone's cooking."

Inside, she pulled chairs from the table and acquired a couple of mugs of cider while Dak explained that he still traveled
a week or so out of every month to play for markets and festivals, usually only when invited in advance these days.

"I'm mostly settled now. Newhome—Ariana's household
—took me in, the poor chumps. I teach the kids in the town
reading and writing, a little music." His guitar leaned against
the table beside him. Every so often Dak glanced at the doorway as if worried. Enid didn't know if it was the uniform or
the sense that Tomas might be outside, eavesdropping, or se-
cretly wanting to throw him in a pond.

"You and Ariana?"

"We're friends," he said. The phrase could have meant anything when Dak said it. "She was kind to take in a stray."

"Strange to think of you settled down." He shrugged, as if
he couldn't explain it either. She gestured to the guitar. Worn
blond wood instead of the black lacquered one he'd had before. "You found a new one."

"Yeah. Wasn't as hard as I was afraid it would be. This is
actually my second new one. Best one yet. If someone's out
there building guitars, the world can't be all bad, yeah?"

"Right," she said softly.

His presence had no bearing on the investigation, but she

would have preferred to do without the distraction. She'd gone for months without thinking of him. Years. Why should he cause her any worry now? Her lips twisted wryly, regarding him, trying to figure out how much he'd changed, if at all.

"You get back to Fintown often?" she asked.

Dak shrugged. "Haven't been that way in a few years."

"Ah." Enid had traveled to Fintown just two years ago—delivering copies of records, not because of an investigation. Xander was co-head of Petula Dock these days. Still sailing. Strange, to think she'd been there more recently than Dak. She and Xander had only spoken of him in passing.

A knock came at the door. Enid expected Tomas, but Ariana leaned in. "Is everything all right?" The question was tense; her hand gripped the door frame. Laughter sounded from outside. Night was settling in, and the fire would be going strong by now. Dak's absence would be noted.

"He'll be out in a few minutes," Enid said. Ariana took the hint and ducked out, biting her lip.

"What about you, Enid?" he asked, when his own tale reached a suitable end. "You've been busy, I take it." He gestured at her, or rather at the uniform she wore.

"I have," she agreed. She thought for a moment about what she could say, how to explain Serenity, Sam, her career—all of it—and no words seemed adequate. So she settled on broad summary. "Life is good."

"Bien, bien," he said. Another long silence passed. He studied her, and she him. She was used to dealing with long silences. He very much wasn't. "You're still in Haven, then?"

"I am. I started a small household with three others. We do all right. I travel quite a bit."

"I imagine you do."

Enough with the small talk. She resisted the urge to straighten, to lean in as if this was a serious interrogation. "I'd like to ask you . . . did you know Sero?"

"Not really, no. He was a loner. That's why he lived out on that patch by himself. No one ever visited him. No one much even talked to him."

"He never came out to the fire pit for gatherings?" she said, gesturing toward the party outside. "Not even to hear you play?"

"No. Can't charm everyone, I guess." His smile turned lopsided, and she chuckled at the joke. "Ariana said you think it's a murder. That can't be right, can it? I heard it was an accident. He just fell."

"Possible murder. We're still asking questions, looking for possible witnesses."

"She was pretty upset," he said.

"A lot of people are. I can't blame them. Can you remember the last time you saw Sero? Maybe just walking around town, working on some of those fences?"

"I'm afraid I can't. You know how it is, you walk around and see people . . . they're like part of the scenery." He didn't even have to think about it.

She took a chance. "Can you remember what you were doing in the morning four days ago?"

He never stopped with that smile, even now. "You're interrogating me."

Her lips curled. "Just asking a few questions." She wondered what Dak saw when he looked at her now? Not that she ever really knew.

"As it happens, I was away. Playing for the market at Porto. Only got back the next day and heard about the accident then.

If I knew anything, I would tell you. You know I would." There it was, alibi established, so smoothly he could pretend he didn't know exactly what he was doing.

"I know," she said. He blinked at her, then reached for his guitar.

"You'll come hear me play, won't you? I think it's about time for some music." He rested the instrument on his lap and picked a couple of strings, tuning as he did. The notes whined. She remembered that sound.

"Not tonight, I'm afraid."

"Well, then. I'm sure we'll have other chances to talk. Maybe after the unpleasantness is done."

"Maybe." She stood to see him out to the door.

"It's really good to see you, Enid," he said before leaving. "Sunshine in a storm. Oh—" He fumbled at the collar of his tunic for a moment and drew out a pendant on a string—a piece of sea glass, the one she'd given him, that she'd found the first time she'd seen the ocean. With him. "I still have it. Remember?"

She was amazed that he hadn't given it to someone else on the road. That he hadn't just lost it. "I do. You kept it."

Hers was sitting on a shelf at home, in the room she shared with Sam.

"It's one of my favorite things. Night, Enid."

When he was gone, Tomas ducked into the room. "That was unexpected."

Enid rubbed her face and sighed. "What are the odds? I can't even imagine!"

"You're not happy to see him?"

"I . . ." She paused. She honestly didn't know what she was thinking. What she ought to be thinking. "I'm curious about what he's been getting up to. He always had such a clear picture of himself and it wasn't so . . . domestic."

"Or he put on a good show of it before," Tomas observed, settling into the chair Dak had occupied.

Yeah, there was that. "That's a depressing thought. The show's what I liked about him."

She had never asked Tomas if he had a lover in every town, the way he'd so confidently told her that Dak did, back in the day. She didn't really want to know. Tomas had stayed with Plenty, back at Haven. Part of a legacy. The household had earned half a dozen banners during his adult life, and he'd fathered one of the resulting children. She also understood that he was the father of a boy at a household up north—they'd earned a banner, and the mother asked him, and he obliged. Enid didn't know the details. As far as Enid knew, he didn't have any kind of partnership like she and Sam did, or Olive and Berol, and he traveled too much to be close to his children —couldn't be said to be their father in any way but biological. A lover and a father were two different things. Her own biological father, Zen, was part of Plenty. He repaired windmills for most of the surrounding communities and traveled a lot. He hadn't been around much when she was growing up, and she hadn't really missed him—she had plenty of other people looking out for her. Folk like Tomas, in fact. But maybe she'd inherited her wanderlust from him.

With a household, a kid always had family. More than enough family sometimes, as Enid thought of her own crowded childhood and that overwhelming urge she'd felt sometimes to *flee*. She liked her own small cozy household just fine, and when Serenity's kid finally came, it would have four parents. And probably want to flee just like she did.

She took a long drink of cider and got out her notebook. "We need a timeline of what happened. Who saw what when. This is a tangle; we've got to keep it straight."

They worked backward from when Sero's body was discovered. They had holes to fill in, to get as close as they could to the definitive last time he'd been seen by witnesses. Earlier that morning, possibly.

Witnesses said Miran had been there that morning. She might have misremembered when she was last there, or might have been lying. She said he'd been doing work at Sirius household; that might be their starting point. From the time of death, Enid worked the timeline forward to the call for an investigation and her and Tomas's arrival. A full day had passed, near as Enid and Tomas could figure. There'd been a debate before Ariana had sent a courier to the regional committee. It had arrived two mornings ago. Which meant Pasadan had had four days to clean up evidence and hide witnesses. But no one had bothered checking for footprints and blood around the shed. Loose threads still waited to be pulled.

They needed to talk to Philos and Ariana again, find out how deep their argument ran. This business over Sero might just have been the latest bout in a long-running conflict. She also wanted to see Miran and the rest of Sirius household, and to find Miran's friend Kirk. He might be a reason to go check out the party after all. Or they could leave it till morning—the truth had waited this long.

"We've got our list to talk to in the morning, then," Tomas said, shutting his notebook.

"We do." She leaned back, already tired. "No one is happy about us being here. Not even Ariana. They all just keep saying that no one liked Sero, as if that explains everything. People are horrible," she said, even though she didn't mean it. Saying so was cathartic sometimes. Tomas quirked a smile.

"It's likely we won't have to push for more than a day or so, and guilt will pull someone out. They won't be able to take us poking around anymore."

"One can hope. But it'll depend on who they're more scared of. Us, or everyone else in town looking at them to keep quiet?"

He made a grunt of agreement. It was them against everyone else, like usual.

///

ENID FINALLY GOT her shower late that night. The water drained from a solar-heated cistern on the roof, and while it wasn't hot, its lingering warmth still cut through the day's sweat and stress. Five minutes of scrubbing with a washcloth and she felt almost new. She might even sleep, if she could keep from turning over the images of Sero's body and that smear of blood on the outside wall.

The way station, just a room behind the committee house, was made up of the washroom and four cots. She and Tomas settled into sleep. Dak still played outside, the music sounding vague and distant through the wall. Enid tried to ignore it.

The next morning during a breakfast of bread and tea in the meeting room, she and Tomas were going over their notes again when Philos, wearing his gray committee sash, arrived and stormed into the room to lean on the table where they sat. Enid still had a mouth full of biscuit.

"Well?" he demanded.

"Well what?" Enid asked, swallowing quickly, leaving an

annoying lump in her throat. Tomas leaned back in his chair, thumbs hitched on his belt, looking all casual like he wouldn't hurt a fly. The stance usually made people nervous—his hand was next to his pouch of tranquilizers now. Sure enough Philos kept glancing over at him.

"Finished yet?"

"No," she said. "We'll let you know when we're finished." She leafed through pages of her notebook, resting on the table in front of her—this was mostly for show. "We need to talk to Kirk, of the Bounty household. Can you tell me where I might find him?"

Philos looked sharply at her. "Why do you want to talk to him?"

"Same reason I want to talk to everyone. His name's come up a couple of times. Is there a problem?"

"He's my son. Bounty is my household."

"Not sure that necessarily follows," she said, amused. That was an interesting bit of information, but not necessarily relevant. "I don't think you should worry so much, sir."

The old man seemed to be gnawing at his own cheeks. Maybe he just had a nervous disposition. "I keep telling you you're going through a lot of trouble for nothing."

"That's for us to decide, I think. So. Since Kirk's your son, can you tell me where I might find him?"

She let him spend another moment trying to figure out how to get his son away from her attention. Finally, he gave up. "I'll go get him. I'll send him over here in the next hour—"

"How about I go with you, save the trouble? He won't have to leave whatever he's doing; I'll just talk to him right now." And Philos wouldn't have a chance to coach him.

He glared. She was getting used to that expression. Philos

marched out the door and headed in the direction of the town center. She quickly stood, brushing off crumbs and washing down a last gulp of tea.

Tomas said, "You go on. I'll check with the households Sero had been doing work for."

"Right."

Packing her notebook, she followed after the committee-man. He was rushing, moving at a fast shuffling walk that made his tunic flap at his sides. He seemed to want to get far enough ahead to be able to warn Kirk. As much as she might like to keep that from happening, she wasn't willing to race after him. Better to maintain some semblance of dignity.

Enid wasn't at all surprised to find that Philos's household was organized, attractive, comfortable—a place anyone would be happy to live in, and she imagined he was very proud of it. Philos seemed to pay attention to appearances. Several white-washed cottages, roofed with shakes and solar collectors, sat around a courtyard that marked where the blocks and streets from before the Fall must have been—the center block was left open and held a couple of fruit trees, a kitchen garden, and the ubiquitous chicken coop. Hens scratched in the dirt path surrounding the yard. A windmill and cistern were tucked back behind one of the cottages. A painted sign stood at the entrance; BOUNTY, it read, and was decorated with the same flowers and loops of ivy as the sign into Pasadan, likely made by the same person. Nice touch.

An open-air shed housed a forge, cold and quiet for now. The rhythmic clap-and-beat of a loom sounded from another cottage. Bounty farmed grain for trade but produced their own staples of cloth and metal. Nothing out of the ordinary jumped out at her.

"What's Kirk do?" Enid asked. Philos continued a hard-

and-fast pace to the larger cottage at the back of the household, probably the kitchen and sleeping quarters.

"Manages the household," he stated over his shoulder. "Building upkeep, taking care of water and heat. He also does our trading. He travels."

Philos let her into the cottage's common room. "Wait here," he ordered, then disappeared out the back. Gamely, she did so, hands clasped behind her, studying the wild roses in the vase on the table, the couple of banners hanging on the wall.

It wasn't long before two men came storming back through the back door as if in response to a terrified scream. But no, it was just her, gazing back calmly and with interest.

Kirk saw her, glared. "What do you want?"

He could be more polite, Enid thought.

"She wants to talk to you," his father declared.

"I want to talk to you," she repeated, more cheerfully. "Shouldn't take long. Would you like a seat?"

He remained standing, Philos beside him, the two of them together like a wall.

Enid said, "Philos, would you mind leaving us alone for a bit?" She knew he very well would mind. Why was he so very protective of his son? Did Kirk need protecting? When Philos didn't leave—when he clenched his fists at his sides like he was considering defying her—she wondered if she should have brought Tomas and his staff with her instead of leaving him to conduct the other interviews on their list.

But no, she stood her ground, kept her expression calm, and Philos ducked his gaze and left through the front door. Kirk still didn't sit down, but Enid did. Just to throw him off.

She said, "I saw someone with Miran watching Sero's pyre yesterday. Was that you?"

There was often that moment when someone hesitated,

deciding whether to tell the truth or lie. Deciding which one would cause them less trouble.

"Yeah," he said finally. He gave a decisive nod as if saying yes, this was the story he would settle on. "I was only there because she was. What's your concern with her? She hasn't done anything—"

"Never said she did. She's a friend?"

"Yeah."

"And why was she there?"

He shrugged, looked away. "I think she was just curious. I told her she should let it go. It's kind of morbid, you know?"

"How well did you know Sero?" she asked next.

"I didn't. I never spoke to him."

"Never?"

"I had no reason to."

Her turn to shrug. "You might have, if he'd ever done any work here or nearby. Pasadan isn't that big of a village."

He crossed his arms. "I never talked to him. I didn't know him at all. I mean, apart from rumors. People talked *about* him. They say he was bannerless."

"Yes, I know. He wasn't, though. That's just a rumor. Do you know if Miran talked to him?"

"Never. Why would she?"

"In fact, she did. He did some work for Sirius household. I understand she was his contact for that."

He didn't deny it this time, and he didn't look surprised.

She said, "We're trying to learn who the last people who saw Sero alive might have been. They might give us a better idea of what happened to him—"

"I heard he fell. He just fell." Kirk picked at the seam on his trousers.

"Do you know anyone who might have been at his house before he died?"

"No, no—"

"What were you doing, oh, five days ago? Where were you that morning?"

"I'd have to think about it a minute."

"Take your time."

He did. He paced, just a short little arc around that end of the table. He kept glancing at her, presumably watching for signs of impatience. She didn't show any, waiting calmly, still studying him like he was an interesting experiment.

"Five days . . . I was working here at home. Weeding the garden, getting the kitchen ready for canning. Summer chores, right? Anyone can tell you. Philos was here—he'll tell you I was here all day."

She imagined he would. "Bien, thanks. Please let me know if you remember any other details. Oh—and why did you want to see Sero's pyre?"

"I didn't, I told you. I was there with Miran."

"Because you're friends."

"Right."

"Thanks, Kirk." She turned to go, leaving him looking sour and distracted.

Philos was waiting for her directly outside. He might have been listening in the whole time. The image of him leaning in with his ear pressed to the wood amused her.

"Can I help you?" she asked him.

"You're not going to find what you're looking for."

She cocked her head, inquired quizzically. "What is it you think I'm looking for?"

"Someone to punish."

"Ah . . . that isn't even my favorite part of the job."

"What is?" he asked.

She leaned in. "Making people squirm. Have a good afternoon."

She strode off, aware of the man watching her leave—making sure she left.

Philos was hiding something.

///

"ENID!"

She was on the road back to the community house and stopped at the call. Dak was coming up the lane, because of course he wouldn't leave her alone. Complications, indeed.

"Hola, Dak," she said. "Sounds like you all had a wonderful time last night."

"We did. I'm sorry you missed it."

She hid a smile, because she felt rather like she'd been there the whole time.

"You know I've not had a hug from you yet?"

She had to think back, and sure enough they'd never come closer together than arm's reach last night. Being very careful with each other. She was still getting over the shock of seeing him at all. Did he really *want* a hug from her, in this uniform?

"Not while I'm on duty," she said. "It's not really appropriate."

"Ah. Yes."

She considered that he might actually make a good informant—everyone knew him. Everyone *liked* him. Assuming he didn't realize she was trying to turn him into an informant. "Can I ask you something? Just to get your perspective."

"Sure."

"Are Kirk and Miran in a relationship?"

"Well, yes, that's gone on for almost a year now."

Just friends—they'd both said that. Why not say more? Might not be important, but then again it might. "Any reason they might not be upfront about it?"

He chuckled. "They are a little squirrelly about it, aren't they? I think they're worried about pressure from their households. Bounty doesn't want Kirk to leave; Sirius couldn't survive without Miran; and if the two of them start talking about a banner together . . . which household gets the banner, and so on. I think they're trying to avoid the fuss and rumor."

Enid couldn't blame them; seemed to be a lot of both around here. "Might they try to skip the banner?"

He looked sharply at her. "No. They'd never do that. Being an investigator really does give you a devious mind, doesn't it?"

"I've seen some pretty devious things," she agreed. "Your imagination would be shocked. What do you think of Philos?"

"He worries a lot. Ariana, too. But that's why they're on the committee."

"It's a hard job. Lots to worry about. And why is Lee on the committee?"

"Ah, yes. The third seat rotates households every two years. It was his turn. He's doing the best he can, I think."

Poor man. Not really suited to decision making or standing up to either of the other two. They probably liked it that way.

"You like it here, then?" she asked him. "Will you take a turn on the committee when your chance comes up?" She had a hard time picturing Dak on any kind of committee. But people changed . . .

"Pasadan's a nice place, Enid. Not like some we've seen. You know the ones."

Yes, she knew: the villages and households they'd visited

without enough resources, in states of disrepair and neglect. No, Pasadan wasn't like that at all.

"Just perfect here, is it?"

"Well. I'm sure you'll find cracks if you pry hard enough. Ariana and Philos not getting along, for one."

"Why is that, you think?"

He studied her, a wry tilt to his lips. Here she was interrogating him, and he was trying to look amused about it. "Town's due for another banner. It can feed another mouth without stretching resources. And with Sero gone . . . well. That's yet another mouth, isn't it?" Not that a death automatically meant a new banner—or murder would be a lot more common, wouldn't it? The accounting of resources was more complicated than that. "Trouble is, whose household deserves the banner? Ariana's or Philos's?"

They were fighting over who got the next banner? That almost seemed too easy. "Draw straws, I say."

"Spoken by someone who never wanted a baby," he said.

Enid didn't mean to, but she thought of Olive and scowled. Would he be surprised to learn that her household had a banner? Looking hard at him, she said, "Are you giving me rumor or data? Do you actually talk to anyone about this sort of thing?"

His tone remained amused—the better to cut her with. "I hardly know this side of you, Enid. So hard, so terrible. You didn't used to be like this."

She laughed. She didn't mean to, but she couldn't help it. For him to make a pronouncement like that? For him to judge *anything*? "You never knew me, Dak. Not further than you wanted to see, anyway."

"Enid—"

"Are you going to tell me we shouldn't be here? That nothing wrong happened here? Someone died in a terrible accident, and you're all just innocent as lambs—"

"The town should be able to take care of it—"

"Yes. Yes, they should. But they're not. *You're* not. It's too hard, isn't it? And that's why we're here. Because it's *too hard*."

He stepped back. Conceded the point with a bow of his head.

"I'll talk to you later, Enid. Maybe after you've wrapped up here." He strolled off on whatever business he was on.

For now, at least, he'd stopped wandering. He had roots here and couldn't just take off when he didn't like the look of a place. Who'd have guessed?

//

ENID HID AWAY in the meeting room, where she wouldn't be bothered and wouldn't be stared at. She pulled out all the records and notes about Pasadan they'd brought with them from the archives. Everything that might be relevant, just to get a rough idea of how the place was doing. Back at Haven, Tomas had identified the trouble with research before a case—one never knew what might be relevant, and so *everything* looked relevant. They hadn't had much time to prepare; the notes were rough.

The town hadn't had any quota violations, not in a decade. This was usually how a town like Pasadan got in trouble—exceeding quotas, wasting resources, misappropriating excess. Cutting down all the trees in a forest when it only needed half, tilling twice as much ground as required, exhausting farmland that might be desperately needed in another five or ten years.

Not planning ahead, and not learning lessons of the past—this was the kind of trouble most towns got into, what committees and investigators tried to prevent.

Philos had been on the committee here for almost a decade—not unusual. Some towns rotated out committee members every couple of years. Some liked to keep at least one person on for longer, sometimes for life. It created institutional memory. But it also created inertia. Bad habits.

Tomas came in, knocking as he did so she wasn't startled. "You look very serious," he said.

"More so than usual?"

"You've always been serious. You like fixing things."

Hmm. She could be accused of worse. "Did you notice that in ten years Pasadan has never had a quota infraction?"

He pulled up a chair and melted into it, pulling off his boots with a sigh. They had planned on being back on the road to Haven by now. "Really. You think it means something?"

Towns and households usually had some kind of quota blip—usually by accident, not anyone's fault and not a big problem. An unexpected bumper crop or an enthusiastic season, the give-and-take as a place found its best balance. Folk —committees, investigators—looked for that kind of up and down. All of it normal for a dynamic system, as any system involving people was. The problems they looked for were large and purposeful—intentional rule breaking.

Pasadan's record was ideally, predictably normal. Enid showed Tomas the numbers. If she hadn't been looking for something to be wrong, she might not have noticed.

"So who's hiding what?" Tomas asked.

"It's that obvious once you shine a light on it, isn't it? Philos is the person least happy to have us here."

"He might just have an anxious disposition."

"Maybe he does. But it merits a look around. You find anything?" she asked.

"Couple of things. We should keep an eye on Ariana and Philos. I get the feeling this has brought a deeper conflict to the surface. Not saying it'll help figure out what happened to Sero, but it's something."

"Yeah. I talked to Kirk."

"What's he like?"

"Defensive. They're all so *defensive*. Philos barely let me alone with him."

"They don't want anyone poking around."

"Except Ariana," Enid said, pointing. "Ariana wants someone poking around. What else did you find?"

"I'm pretty sure Miran was the last one to see Sero alive, the morning he died."

"Really? But she would have seen him at the house. Or would she have gone to the shed? What did she see?"

"We'll talk to her again," he said. "Push harder next time."

"And then there's Dak." She shook her head, scowled. "He's thrown me off."

"Yeah?" Tomas said suggestively, eyebrow raised.

"I think maybe I was a little more torn up about Dak than I wanted to admit back then."

He had the nerve to laugh. He probably could have told her that years ago. She'd been too proud to ask.

Escape

Enid tried sneaking into the common room at Petula Dock to listen to the investigators talk to Fisher but was noticed and politely asked to leave them alone. Instead, she tried to track down what gossip she could in a town she didn't actually know. Everyone knew investigators had arrived. No one would say why, and their gazes flicked away from Enid when she pressed.

She wasn't an investigator. It wasn't any of her business, and she should let it go.

The sky was overcast, but the rain had stopped. Gulls sailed overhead, calling. The place smelled of rotting seaweed. Folk were out working while they had the chance. Near the docks, on a wide gravelly stretch of beach, a couple of men spread out nets, checking them over, making repairs when needed. The nets gave Enid an idea, and she asked for—and they gave her—some of the scraps of hemp twine they were using. Sitting on one of the docks with her feet dangling off the edge over the water, she knotted the twine into a sort of mini-net, a snug little bundle just big enough to hold the pieces of sea glass she'd found in the sand a few days ago. She made two, one for each piece, the white one and the green one. Next, she attached the pendants she'd made to long cords, to be worn around the neck. Might have been more elegant to drill holes in the glass. She knew it must be possible, but she didn't have the tools or ability, and didn't want to risk cracking the glass. So a rough woven setting it was. One for her and one for Dak.

Maybe not pretty; definitely not useful. She felt a little silly, like a kid painting rocks and calling it art. But, well — it meant something. The frosted glass from another time, and the sudden otherworldly feeling that she didn't belong anywhere. She put the green one over her neck, then hid it under her shirt. The feel of it against her breastbone was an anchor, reminding her to breathe.

She walked back to Petula, the other pendant stuffed in her pouch.

Not long after, Dak and Xander came up the hill. She waited for them. They both looked worried, holding themselves stiffly, leaning in as if in conversation.

Dak saw her and asked, "Enid, where are they now?" Didn't need to say who, just assumed she'd know what he was talking about.

"They were in talking to Fisher for a while," Enid said. "Don't know if they're still there. Do you know what it's about?"

Xander frowned. "Could be a couple of things. If my hunch is right . . . well. We'll find out soon enough."

He *knew*. There was something wrong in Fintown, and Xander knew what it was. Did everyone know?

First thought that came to her was the one that came to everybody when investigators showed up: a bannerless pregnancy. Someone had cut out their implant. Someone was hiding a baby. Enid realized the only true bannerless pregnancy she'd ever known of firsthand was the case in Haven a couple months ago, the one Tomas handled. And that one had turned out all right, because it had been an accident and Tomas awarded a banner retroactively and everything worked out fine. Not like some other stories.

Everyone talked about bannerless pregnancies. It was the most sensational—interesting—case anyone could gossip about. But how often did it really happen? She would have to file that question away and ask Tomas when she got back to Haven.

If she lived in Fintown, she'd know who was pregnant and who was supposed to be pregnant. Here, some households flew their banners from the masts of their ships, a proud display of their accomplishment. She'd recognize if anyone was missing—hiding because they were keeping a big pregnant belly secret. But Enid had only been here a couple of days. She just didn't know.

At dinner that night, all the talk was about the investigation.

"They wanted to talk to Stev," Fisher said. "Investigators usually do, just to make sure he's okay. I try not to get offended." She only seemed to be partly joking at that.

The implication was that in some households, someone like Stev might not be okay. Enid didn't like thinking about that.

Stev was clearing the table, taking plates to the basin, and stacking them carefully. He looked up when Fisher said his name. "They were nice. I took them out to count chickens." He beamed. Smiling, Fisher handed him the next plate.

"And how many chickens are there?"

"Thirteen," Stev said.

"Excellent work," Fisher said.

"But what did they really want to talk about?" Xander asked.

"Bonito."

Nods and murmurs of understanding passed around the table. Nobody seemed surprised.

Enid blinked and looked around, trying to decode the meaning behind the one word. "What?"

"It's a household up the hill a bit. Been a problem for a while," Fisher said. "Their youngest walking around with bruises, keeping to themselves in a way that's strange. Rumors of breaking quotas and hoarding, but nothing anyone can prove."

"Probably good someone's stepping in," Raul said.

Xander shook his head. "Shouldn't have been necessary. Town ought to take care of itself. Committee sees something like that—like that black eye Reni had last month—and they ought to do something."

"Then do we know who requested the investigation?" someone else asked.

"No, they're keeping it confidential. Can't say I blame them."

Who would the town resent more: the household that did something wrong, the investigators called in to judge them —or the person who brought all the worry down in the first place? Should be the first, Enid thought. Shouldn't it?

Fisher said, "It's hard, having to take to task people you see every day. People you have to live with. No one wants to be disruptive. As much as we don't want to say it, it's probably a good thing we have investigators. Let someone else be the villain, hmm?"

Hild, the youngest of them, frowned. "But where do they

even come from? Who would even want to be an investigator? Everybody hates them."

Enid spoke up. "A couple of my household cousins are investigators. They do it to help."

Everyone turned their attention to her; she told herself to straighten under the scrutiny, rather than slouch. She was proud of Tomas. She'd tell anyone she was.

"Is that how they get to be investigators? It's all people in the same households?"

"No—it's not that easy. They have to be recommended for it by committees from a couple of different towns. There's a long apprenticeship. They travel a lot—I think some of them sign up for it for the travel."

"Easier to learn to play guitar," Dak said wryly, and everyone chuckled, just like they were supposed to.

"Nala was asking about quotas. If we think they're fair, if anyone's been regularly exceeding them. That's what they're going to get pinned on, I bet. Not the bruises, but the quotas."

"Well. Be interesting to see how it comes out," Raul said.

"What'll happen?" Hild asked, her voice small.

No one answered. Instead, they all looked to Fisher to make the pronouncement, to decide how much the young girl should know. To Enid, the conversation was familiar, commonplace. No one back at Plenty danced around these topics, and she found this talk fascinating. She wished she could ask Tomas or Peri about it. She tucked it away with the other stories she planned on telling when she got home. Dak sat back in his chair, hand on his chin, concentrating on the talk as much as she was but likely for different reasons.

"Maybe just restrictions," Fisher said. "What and when they can trade, quota reduction. No banner. Worst case, the whole house'll be broken up and everyone'll have to leave, find other households to join."

"Place like Bonito, would that be a bad thing?" Raul said with a huff, looking into his food.

Fisher frowned. "I'm guessing it won't come to that. I'm hoping the investigators will make it easier for Reni and anyone else who wants to leave to do so. It's what I'd do."

"They couldn't just leave if they want?" Hild asked.

"It's not so easy when you've put a bunch of work into a household, and the work and the credits stay there," Fisher said. "Sometimes if you want to leave, you have to start all over again. Find folk to help if you can. It's not so easy."

She spoke like someone who knew.

By now the table was clear, and Fisher stood and clapped her hands. "Dak promised to play tonight. Let's say we all go listen and see if we can cheer twice as loud as anyone else?"

"And maybe pick up more gossip while we're there," Xander said.

Yeah, Enid thought. There'd likely be plenty of gossip. The thought of it, the implications of it, made her stomach clench. She wasn't sure she wanted to know what sort of tragedy could disrupt such a nice place as Fintown.

///

INVESTIGATORS NALA AND Holt weren't at the party. Probably for the best, as the mood was already subdued. A couple of brown uniforms in the mix, the party would never even start. Even if they didn't wear their uniforms, they'd still be strangers and everyone would know. As it was, as Xander guessed, lots of gossip passed around. Other heads of households coming to Fisher to compare notes on what the investigators had asked her about, what they seemed to be looking for.

The community house had a covered patio where people gathered. Candles and lamps lit up the space as the sun set over the ocean, and a fire burned in an iron brazier for warmth. Someone had brought a cask of cider, another household brought honey cookies.

Dak sat on a chair at the front of the space, a handful of kids surrounding him as he explained how the guitar worked. He let them pluck the instrument's strings, showed them how they made different notes. Someone on the Coast Road must know how to make guitars and other instruments; Dak's shining black piece wasn't a survivor from before the Fall. Whoever it was had to have learned the skill out of pure love. Or just enough people wanted guitars to make it worthwhile.

Enid sidled up next to Xander. "Anyone from Bonito here?"

"Yeah," he said, nodding to a clump of the older people who had their heads together, gossiping. "That's Jada at the end. She's the only one, though. She's not the head of the house, but I'm wondering if she's here to try to suss out what folk are saying. See if there's anyone who might speak in favor of Bonito."

"I get the feeling the answer is no."

He huffed a humorless chuckle. "It shouldn't have taken investigators to fix this. Our committee should have been able to handle it on its own." He spoke softly, so only she could hear. She wondered if he'd have said such a thing to anyone from Fintown.

"But that's why it's good we have investigators. When a place can't fix things itself."

"I think you're the only one I've ever heard say anything good about investigators."

She blushed, looked away. Growing up with Tomas had biased her, clearly. She would be quiet about it from now on. After all, this wasn't her town, her household, or her problem.

Dak played for a long time that night—he had a familiar and enthusiastic audience who seemed glad to have him there. Folk shouted requests. Even when the very young and very old drifted off to bed, a good-sized group kept the fire up and passed around more cider. The excuse to celebrate something, anything, seemed welcome . . . because that tension lingered; just a couple of buildings away, at the town's way station, the investigators lurked.

Enid sat in the back of the gathering, full up on drink and food, wrapped in a blanket because a breeze was coming in off the water. Xander had moved up front, joining Dak on some of the songs with the comfort of practice. An old friend of Dak's, then. She wondered where Dak had been born, and what had set him wandering.

Dak had a song he didn't often sing for crowds, but saved for late nights around dying fires, when only the restless and bleary-eyed stuck around to listen. Enid had only heard it a couple of times, but she remembered it and sat up when he played it now. The chorus was about dust in the wind, and how everything would eventually blow away and come to naught. The melody was sad and haunting, a rain of notes plucked on the strings until they faded out, just a lingering vibration through the wood of the guitar. The sound seemed to carry, even after the song ended.

"That was really sad," one of the half dozen left on the patio said, and the words seemed rude somehow. Like after that they should have all just vanished without a word, melting into the night.

"I learned it from an old man when I was just a little kid. He said it came from a place called Kansas."

Enid said, "I've seen Kansas on a map." A crinkled atlas in the Haven library had the continent marked up into regions that didn't mean much these days. "It's over a thousand miles east of here."

"Maybe we'll see it someday."

She shook her head. "There's nothing but mountains and deserts between here and there. It'd take months." And once you left the Coast Road, you couldn't be sure of anything.

"We don't even know if there's anyone left out there," Xander added.

"I bet there are," Dak said. "Folk find a way. You'd be surprised."

"Seems kind of a waste to me," one of the others said. "All that effort getting there, and what would you have to show for it?"

"Some things worth doing just to do them," Dak said, patting the body of the guitar so it gave off a resonant echo. He strummed up another song, about lemon trees and love gone wrong.

When Dak drank a long cup of water and started packing his guitar in its case, Enid realized she didn't want him to stop. Because then it would be time to go to bed, and she didn't know where she was sleeping—or with whom; she wanted to sleep with Dak, but she didn't want to have to compete to do so, and she had a feeling she was the only one who looked on this as a competition. It was all so much simpler when she and Dak were alone on the road together. She was starting to think that maybe she wanted to go home, and that disappointed her. She had thought she'd be traveling for *years*.

And then Xander left, and Dak was at her side, running his thumb on her cheek and leaning in for a good long kiss. Her resolve to be sullen about the whole thing collapsed. She wrapped her arms around him, content.

"Hey," she said after a moment, pulling away only enough to reach into her pouch. "I made something. Just, you know. A thing." She drew out the second pendant, the white one, and offered it in her cupped hand. She shrugged, wanting to apologize. For what, she didn't know. For being weird and maudlin. Scared, maybe. She had no idea what he was going to say.

He smiled. "Oh, nice." He picked it up, smoothed out the cord. Held the glass up to the light. "This is what you found on the beach the other day, yeah?"

"Yeah."

"I love it." He pulled the cord over his neck, let the glass hang, and beamed at her.

She sighed, and he wrapped an arm around her shoulder and pulled her close.

They went for a walk; he had a place picked out, a sheltered pocket of sea grass and weathered boulders, and they sprawled on the blanket she'd brought, then stripped and tumbled together until they lay back, cuddled for warmth, and looked at the stars. The sea glass sparked on his bare chest, the frosted white almost glowing with its own light.

"I'm thinking it's time to get back on the road," Dak said. Already gazing at the horizon like he could see past the next hill.

"But . . ." She didn't have a good reason to stay. In fact, she had good reasons to leave. But she liked Fintown. "I mean,

I'm sure everyone would love to hear you play a couple more nights at least."

"Enid, if there's trouble, I don't want to be here."

She sat up on an elbow, gazing down at him, his long hair fanned around him, his eyes half-lidded, half-asleep. "What kind of trouble do you think there's going to be?"

"I know you have investigators in your household back home, and you're from Haven, where everything is perfect. You don't really understand what can happen on the rest of the road."

That was it, was it? She was sheltered. She was naive. "Seriously, Dak. What do you think is going to happen?"

"I don't know. I just don't want to be in the way when it does."

"But I want to see how it turns out."

He gave her that look again, the pitying one, like she was a child and couldn't possibly understand. "I'm not sure you do, really."

"But . . ." She realized she didn't have anything else to say, that she wasn't going to convince him of anything. He brushed her cheek, smiling like he thought he'd won something. She sank into his arms because her body wanted it.

He was right, after all. What happened in Fintown was none of their business, really. Dak could do whatever he wanted, and it wasn't as if she hadn't accompanied him by her own choice. She could go her own way whenever she chose.

She was annoyed at herself for being so annoyed by all this. But she couldn't seem to convince her emotions to just *stop*. Alas.

ENID AND DAK packed up the next morning. She liked Fisher and thought she could learn a lot from her. She wanted to go sailing with Xander again. Count chickens with Stev. Spend a whole day watching ocean waves shush in endlessly from the horizon.

"You're welcome back anytime," Fisher said. They gave each other a long, heartfelt hug, right after she put handfuls of fish jerky, boiled eggs, and flatbread in Enid's pack. Enid's, not Dak's. Fisher was talking to *her*. And Enid felt welcome. She could always come back, and she thought that yes, maybe she would.

Dak and Xander said their farewells privately, for which Enid was grateful. She'd rather not face that particular mess of emotions in her gut right now. But before that, Xander sought her out.

"I'm very glad to have met you, Enid," he said.

She smiled. "Me too. I really liked sailing."

"You two look out for each other, yeah?"

"Yeah."

Enid had time to run out and find Nala and Holt. They were at the way station, eating breakfast. She knocked shyly at the open door, and they invited her in.

All in a burst she said, "After you leave here, if you see To-mas, tell him I'm okay? I don't know if he—or my household —is worried about me. But. Well."

"I'm sure he'll be glad to hear news about you," Holt said. "Even if we don't see him, we can pass on a message."

"Thanks."

"Take care of yourself," he said.

Then, late in the morning, Enid and Dak hiked back to the main road and continued south, and inland.

After another week of walking, the Coast Road ended. Just trickled out to one southern outpost, a lone household called Desolata at the edge of baked desert, home to a briny inland sea that shrank a little more every year. Farther north got too much rain; here, there hadn't been any rain at all in years. Somehow, the household survived.

The folk here took in Enid and Dak for stories. Dak didn't even need to sing; they just wanted news of how the harvests were going and the number of storms that had hit the coast over the last year.

The people here produced salt. Scraped it off the flats and sent it north once a year with a trading party that brought cloth, herbs, cider, and foodstuffs they couldn't provide for themselves, which was pretty much everything. Enid asked them why they didn't leave. They could go north, buy into another town, go to a more prosperous household.

"This is our home," said Vega, a sun-toughened old woman with grizzled gray hair and arthritic hands; she grinned warmly.

They didn't have any banners hanging on the wall of their common house. Not a single one, which struck Enid as incredibly sad. They barely took care of themselves; they certainly didn't have enough to feed another mouth. But the household had been here for decades, they said. It seemed that every few years someone wandered in, wanting to see the edge of the world, decided they liked the quiet, and stayed. The place just suited some people. Even bannerless, Desolata would always be populated.

South of that was more desert, an alkaline wasteland. Stories said there used to be cities even here, and even farther south. Paved roads and power lines and all the rest. Enid and Dak wandered along mesas and gullies and found isolated slabs of concrete, the rusted struts of a steel tower, a set of foundations half covered with sand dunes. Like everywhere else, these places lost their people, and without power or anyone maintaining them, the buildings fell and were swallowed up by drought and the expanding desert.

Vega told them she suspected there were still people farther on, scattered places where they hunted, scavenged, and maybe survived. Maybe. No one felt inclined to travel on to see. You couldn't carry enough water to keep going that far.

After spending a couple of days at Desolata, sharing their stories in exchange for the roof, Enid and Dak turned around and started back north. Neither one said a word about continuing on into the desert or heading east to try to find Kansas.

Northward, the desert gave way to scrubby plains, then the rocky grasslands near the coast. They came back to the turnoff to Fintown. Enid considered: they could just pop in. Say hello to everyone. Find out what happened with the investigation. Dak didn't want to. It'd be a couple more days before they reached the next town, and they were low on foodstuffs. But still he didn't want to go.

"Not even to see Xander?" she said, her tone biting, but she didn't really care.

"What's that supposed to mean?" He stopped, turning on her.

Any other time, he would have laughed her off. Told her she was being silly, toss off some flippant excuse. Nerves were fraying, and wasn't that an interesting sensation? She could march away from him right now in anger. She'd regret it by nightfall, but even knowing that, she'd still do it.

She took a deep breath and explained herself. "I'm frustrated. Rain's coming, and we have friends not two hours' walk away." She pointed to gray-green clouds on the horizon. Not close enough to thunder at them yet, but the storm was no doubt causing havoc at sea. It might move to shore; it might blow out. But sometime in the next week, there would be rain.

"We'll be fine," he said. "I don't want to impose on Xander and Fisher."

"You don't want to be around investigators," she stated. "Are you hiding something?"

He was the one who marched off then. Astonished, she watched for a whole round of breaths, giving him a head start. He never looked back. Too stubborn to care if he left her behind.

"You are!" She ran after him. "What was it? What happened?"

His steps fell hard, pounding the earth. She matched his stride and studied him, waiting. Imagining the worst. Had investigators broken up his household? Had he been accused of something and kicked out? Was that why he wandered? Was he bannerless?

He was biting his lip, as if trying to hold back words, but she just kept watching, wouldn't look away and wouldn't leave. She wanted to beg him to say something, but suspected that would only drive him further into uncharacteristic silence. Here was a story the bard didn't want to tell, which made her want to hear it more. So she was patient.

Finally he said, "I was nine. Investigators came to the household. Two of them, like usual. Talked to everyone separately. Came to me last, and asked if Cole—he was the head of the house and my father—had ever hit me. Just like that."

More walking, the only sound their boots scratching on dirt, until Enid asked, "What did you tell them?"

"Nothing. I didn't say anything. They must have asked for an hour and I froze. What was I supposed to say? Mom had broken her arm a couple of weeks before and apparently Cole did it to her, but I didn't see it happen so I didn't really know. And he never hit me. Got close a couple of times, but never did. I didn't want to believe he'd done it to my mother. But they kept asking and asking, and I sat there with my mouth all stitched up.

"They broke up the household. Decided we couldn't be fixed, or they couldn't just send him away, so they broke us up and scattered us. Odd thing—I didn't want him to be sent away. I think . . . I think he wasn't a good guy, you know? But I didn't want him to go. Haven't seen the man in a dozen years, and I still don't know what happened to him."

"But you've been looking," she said.

"They put Mom and me in a new household fifty miles away. The folk there played a lot of music, and I picked it up. The guitar was just a distraction at first. Guess I needed a lot of distracting."

"I'm sorry that happened to you," Enid said, which felt inadequate but she couldn't think of anything better.

"Didn't have to happen at all, the way I see it. The investigators interfered. They go where they're not wanted and break things, Enid. That's what they do."

Yeah, things that were already broken, she wanted to say. Someone must have called investigators to his house—his mother, she wondered. And maybe she hadn't told Dak that she was the one who'd summoned them, to protect him. To keep a child out of such serious business. Enid almost suggested this to him, but for once, she stopped prodding.

"I'm sorry," she said again.

"I told you, you don't understand. You don't understand any of it." He glared ahead and kept marching harder than he ought, if they were going to keep walking all day.

Maybe he was right. Maybe she didn't understand.

//

AUNTIE KATH HAD kept journals. Four hardcover notebooks, each eight inches or so long with old, cracking paper and writing in faded black ink and smeared pencil. They were carefully wrapped and stored in oilcloth to protect them, in a waterproof, lined, and sealed box in Haven's clinic archives, along with a dozen other handwritten diaries and journals and even loose sheets of paper that had been deemed important enough to save. Worth spending resources on, because yes, this was something they should remember. The diaries had all been copied out a number of times and taken to the couple of other formal archives that had been established on the Coast Road, but Haven had the originals, and Enid had spent the previous year begging and pleading and training to handle archive materials, proving herself worthy of the privilege. Mostly, she'd wanted to see what Auntie Kath was leaving out of the stories she told, what might fill in those blanks when she'd paused . . . since she wasn't around to ask anymore.

Kath had written most of it before and during the Fall, when she'd been a teenager. She'd said that back then lots of people kept journals and diaries of one kind or another, and that most of it was meaningless drivel. Rambling about life and love and how hard things were, even when they weren't. What you did and what you ate. She said she'd started the thing because she didn't have anyone to talk to—which wasn't true, she had friends, had lots of people to talk to. Right up until she didn't.

Many of these journals were recorded electronically, which meant they were effectively gone now. Maybe someday the circuits and servers and things they'd been stored on could be recovered. But probably not. People had so many more important things to recover, like surgery and batteries. Still, the Haven library kept a few boxy computers and disks stored away, just in case. Mysterious plastic boxes with slots and wires and dead lights. Screens that stayed dark. Mysterious and a little bit sad.

Fortunately, Auntie Kath's journals were on paper, books with pictures of flowers, forest scenes, and fairies on the covers. "Fairies weren't ever real," Kath had felt the need to explain of the pretty, faded paintings of lithe girls with sparkling wings and blue and purple hair, when Enid had first seen the archives, years ago. Enid knew that but didn't argue with Kath.

When the first flu epidemic hit, seventeen-year-old Kath had fled. Her parents died, her older brother was away at college on the other side of the country and unreachable—she never did learn what happened to him. There'd been one last panicked phone call with him before networks went down and power went out, where they assured each other of their love, her brother telling her that she should try to stay put, that he would get to her somehow. But that had been a very long time ago. She didn't stay put but went with her mother's friend, a doctor who worked at the clinic that would eventually become the core of Haven. And she kept up the journal, though her handwriting became tiny, every line carefully pressed together to conserve space, because she could foresee a time when paper would become scarce.

That first epidemic was bad enough that it affected everything from emergency services to travel to utilities. In just a few weeks, there simply weren't enough people healthy and able to work to keep infrastructure moving. Schools shut down, stores emptied and didn't have enough supplies or people to restock them, the economy stalled. And then storms hit. Floods, destructive winds, tornados. One that first year, another the next. Two the year after, and it hardly mattered when they went three years before the next. There was no one to respond to emergencies, to shore up sea walls, to rescue the injured. Buildings collapsed and no one was there to pick up the pieces. The coasts got the worst of it, but the interior of the continent wasn't immune, when people who could flee packed up and went inland, burdening *their* resources. A ripple effect, where the ripples bounced back and forth, multiplying and interfering, amplifying outcomes that were already terrible. The still surface of the pond became wracked with turbulence. Any one of the disasters in isolation would not have broken the world. People could survive epidemics, rebuild after storms. But all of it together? Each disaster coming on the heels of the previous, on and on? It had been too much.

Enid never quite figured out the scale of it all. Kath was a good journalist: she copied numbers and data from news reports, and Enid corroborated the information against newspapers and magazines also carefully stored in the archives. Death tolls in the thousands, just from the storms. Deaths from the epidemics were in the hundreds of thousands. Enid didn't believe there'd ever been so many people in all the world. She couldn't even imagine the world itself: hundreds of countries and billions of people. No one she heard of had ever traveled more than a thousand miles from Haven, and that was mostly story and rumor. There were maps; there were atlases. There were pictures showing fantastical shell-shaped buildings on the other side of the world, massive bridges, and skyscrapers — but they all fell, because they needed constant upkeep, and with no one to make those constant little repairs, that fragile world couldn't stay standing.

Studying what had happened, learning a history that didn't much help grow food or build roads, Enid wasn't really sure what she was looking for. It was another way of getting out, maybe. If she couldn't travel from place to place, she would travel through time. If Auntie Kath wasn't around to remember anymore, someone else would have to do it for her, at least a little. No matter how much she traveled, how much she read, or how many places she saw, it would never be enough to satisfy her, none of it.

Two months after Enid got her implant, Auntie Kath died. She'd been sitting on the porch at the clinic all afternoon. People walked to and fro like they always did, raised their hands, and called hello like they always did, and if Auntie Kath didn't wave back, well, she must have been napping.

Only at twilight did Peri come out on the porch to check on her. She touched the old woman's neck and cried. They all did.

There at her pyre, when it was so clear that the body that had held Auntie Kath simply wasn't her anymore, people spoke of a great woman earning her rest. As if death were a resource that had to be earned, that could ever be used up or wasted.

Interrogations

Enid's first case as lead had been relatively simple. A house-hold had been discovered hoarding wheat—two extra fields sown in secret, over their quota, when they should have lain fallow. The two heads of the house declared that they were right to work the land and risk leaching it of its future ability to grow food; they were right to keep it secret, to lie to their committee. Even as they listed off every exact infraction they had committed, they insisted that they were right. To Enid, that had seemed the worst violation of all. You had a problem with quotas, field rotation, any of it—you petitioned your committee. You worked with the committee; you didn't go haring off on your own. Not when a whole community depended on you for food. Enid had seen what real hunger looked like.

Everyone thinking they knew best and going off with their own plans with no mind to anyone else was what had gotten the world to the Fall. What had kept people from doing anything about it until it was too late.

"Did you think of anyone else?" Enid had asked the folk

of this household. "Did you think of the next generation that'll have to work this land and wonder why they're getting half the yield they should? Or the ones who'll starve when the land gives up because you"—she had pointed at them, with two stiff fingers—"couldn't be bothered to take care of it?"

They hadn't answered. She hadn't expected them to. She'd just been angry. That had been her mentor Nan's major criticism of her work. Not just her, but Tomas, too—in fact, everyone—said the same thing: You're too angry, Enid. You take it personally, and you can't do that. Be an arbiter. Be stone. Your anger won't touch them, so be stone.

When that case concluded, the investigators had the regional committee move new folk in to run the household, and the two culprits were banned from having a vote in local committee matters and from being eligible for a banner for a decade. This effectively meant they'd never earn a banner at all. If they thought the extra grain they harvested by breaking quota would get them a banner, they were wrong. Instead, they were shamed and shunned.

Enid hadn't gotten much better at reining in her anger in the few years since. She always seemed to approach her investigations with a sense of . . . disbelief.

"It's no good to ask what they thought they were doing," Nan told her. "They still think they have the right. The consequences are too far ahead for them to think about. They're sure the future will take care of itself."

"If it could, we wouldn't need any of this," she'd muttered, tugging at the hem of her brown tunic and scowling up the road as they walked away from the case.

"Enid. You're trying to save a world that went away a long time ago."

No, she wasn't. That old world, everything from before the

Fall, might as well be a made-up place in a story. Long ago and far away. She was trying to save *this* world. She was trying to save everything. "Enid. It's not your job to save everything. Just do this one little thing, yes? Then do the next little thing. It's all right." Funny, how she could still hear Nan's voice chiding her.

///

NEEDING TO FIND Ariana, Enid tried to guess the committee-woman's schedule, where she might likely be this time of day. Probably at her household, Newhome. Enid could go over there and maybe interrupt her and Dak gossiping about the investigation. Enid wasn't above listening at doorways herself.

Then she got lucky, and the woman herself brought a crock of stew and cornbread to the meeting room for lunch, while they were still going over Pasadan's records.

"Hello!" she announced after knocking, bustling with what seemed an excessive amount of energy. "I saw you were here and thought you might be hungry, and we had plenty to spare if you'd like some."

Tomas welcomed her in. "Thanks. I can smell it from here." They set out bowls and spoons, and yes, the stew smelled wonderful. Full of herbs, onions, vegetables, it had probably been simmering all morning.

"Would you like to join us?" Enid asked, casually enough. "I have a few more questions for you, if you don't mind. It should only take a minute or so." Her politeness felt down-right aggressive—to match Ariana's own. The woman didn't even flinch; she smiled and settled into the chair like she'd been waiting for the invitation.

"Of course, I'll help however I can."

She's the one who wants us here, Enid remembered. She poured them all cups of lemonade, smiling all the while.

"What do you need to know?" she asked.

"I'm just curious, mostly," Enid said, pleasantly enough. This was just a conversation. "We come into a place like this as strangers—it's hard sometimes to get the feel of a town right off. Every place has its own quirks. I suppose I'm just looking for a little insight."

"Pasadan's not really any different from any other place, I suppose." Ariana shrugged. "We're proud of our households; we take care of our families. There's not much more to be said than that."

"How long have you been on the committee?"

"Only a couple of years."

"You liking it?" Tomas asked. He'd been focused on eating. Easy to forget about him, and Ariana blinked as if surprised that he'd spoken.

"I do. I like helping. I want to fix problems before they start, if I can."

"But some problems are a little harder than others," Enid said.

The woman lowered her gaze for just a moment. "I think we do well enough. Under usual circumstances."

"And the rest of the committee? What do they think?"

"I'm sure they feel the same way," she said.

Enid still wasn't even sure how Ariana felt. Not really. "So you and Philos aren't usually so at odds with each other?"

Ariana paused to pour herself a cup of water from a nearby pitcher. Enid let her have the moment to think, but was considering how she might press. Get the woman to make an accusation.

"We do all right," she said. "Pasadan is stable, isn't it? We get along well enough to keep everything running."

"Except that you called us here to investigate a murder."

"I didn't think it was a murder," she said softly.

Enid leaned in, and Tomas rested a hand on her arm. Just a brief touch, then he pulled back. Reminding her to be patient.

"Then why did you send for us?"

"I . . . I disagreed with Philos." She looked ceiling-ward and sighed. "Philos does not see the town's committee as a collaboration between equals. He expects Lee and me to . . . defer. I was tired of it."

"If he's so hard to get along with, why doesn't anyone vote for a change?" Enid said.

"He's . . . popular." She gazed steadily across the table. "He's . . . quite political and makes sure that people will support him. Convinces everyone they need him." Her puckered smirk told exactly what she thought of that.

"Makes it hard to stand up to him, I imagine."

"Someone has to," she said.

"Do you know why he's so set against having Sero's death investigated?"

She knew—Enid knew that she knew. The way her expression didn't so much as flicker, the way she straightened and spoke her words carefully. "I imagine . . . he doesn't like having investigators around. You challenge his authority."

A simple, straightforward answer. "And do we challenge *your* authority?"

Her smile tightened. "I'm not sure I have any, not really."

Deflecting attention. Enid took a chance. "Do you remember where you were, what you were doing, that morning four days ago—or rather five days ago, now?"

Finally, the woman looked startled. Her hands clenched over each other. "You can't think I had anything to do with Sero. I'm the one who wanted an investigation."

Enid's voice was bland. "Which might be a very good way of deflecting attention from one's self. If you had something to hide."

"No, I'm not hiding anything. I was just as shocked as anyone when the body was found. I didn't do anything—"

"Not saying you did. It's just a routine question. Helps us get a picture of what else was happening. So where were you?" Tomas had taken out his notebook, as if recording her testimony.

Ariana nodded. "All right. Okay. I was at home, working. Baking, I think. Ask anyone from my house. Tull, or . . . or Dak. We were all there when Arbor came to get Tull."

"Dak was at the house that morning, too?" Enid narrowed her eyes. Dak had said he was away, that he didn't get home until the next day.

"Yes . . . I think so." She seemed to notice her clenched hands then, and smoothed them onto her lap and sighed. "Maybe I was wrong about the whole thing. Maybe I overreacted, and Philos is right about this being an accident, an unfortunate accident—"

"Yes, you said a moment ago you thought it might be. But you still called for an investigation, and I want to know why. It can't be just to annoy Philos. Because if that's really the reason you called us, there'll be consequences. And not for Philos." Despite Tomas's warning, Enid didn't try so much to tamp down on her own growing anger. Let Ariana be frightened.

The committeewoman stared back at her and breathed, "You wouldn't. You can't. I didn't do anything wrong."

"False reporting? Wasting our time?" Waste, one of the worst things she could accuse anyone of, and Ariana drew back as if Enid had raised a fist at her. "And all for the sake of simply making a man's life difficult?"

"No, that wasn't it; there's more to it than that—"

"Then tell me what it is. Tell me why you really called us here."

Stricken, eyes wide, she might not have been pressed up against a wall, but she looked like it. Enid thought the woman might flee, and planned what she would have to do to leap out of her chair and cross the room to block the doorway. There was a secret here; Ariana knew it—she just didn't want to have to be the one to expose it. Yet here they all were. Enid and Tomas stayed quiet, letting the silence press on her until she sagged.

"I think he's violating quotas. I—I don't have proof, just that too many of his folk are gone off doing some kind of work that the rest of us can't explain, and they're trading too much. They *have* too much."

"Philos is violating quotas," Enid said, just to make sure.

"Yes," she said. As if confessing the infraction herself. She had wanted to throw the investigators in the middle of the town and step back, Enid suspected. Now here she was caught up in it herself.

Proof in these cases was sometimes tricky. If the household bypassed the checks, the counts, and committee monitoring entirely, no one would ever know. Since Philos was on the committee—controlled the committee—he'd be able to bypass monitoring easily. But there were signs. There was always evidence to find, if you knew what to look for.

Ariana continued. "He's going to request a banner and use

Bounty's productivity to back him up. But it's a false productivity, based on breaking quota. He doesn't deserve it! Especially when he's purposefully blocking other households' requests for banners. It's not *fair*—"

"And you felt you didn't have enough support to bring a complaint against him to regional on that score?"

"Can't bring a complaint just because you have a grudge against someone."

"So you needed a reason. An excuse."

"Yes, I suppose you can look at it—" She stopped, bit her lip as the implication dawned on her.

Tomas said, "You want the banner for your own household? For yourself?"

"Of course—but only if that's what the committee decides, if the decision is *fair*. But this doesn't have anything to do with your investigation—"

"Except you used Sero's death as an excuse," Enid said. "Brought us here and now you're trying to point us somewhere else, when you could have just reported your suspicions. We could bar your household from earning a banner for years, based on false reporting."

"Except . . . except you think Sero really was murdered."

She saw investigators as a tool—which they were, Enid had to give her that. But they weren't a tool someone like Ariana could just *use*.

"Yes. And don't you dare be glad of it," Enid said.

"Thank you, Ariana," Tomas said, with a professional calm that Enid couldn't quite muster. "You can go now. Thank you for the lunch."

The woman stood and gave the barest bow, jaw set and lips pursed, before calmly walking out. Enid grabbed a piece of cornbread and started tearing it to pieces. Some of it ended up in her mouth. Patiently, Tomas sat back and let her be frustrated.

"Would she really have done it?" she finally exclaimed. "Killed someone just to draw in investigators so she wouldn't be accused of holding a grudge?" The one person in town without a household, who wouldn't be missed even. It seemed ludicrous. Which was why Enid couldn't discount the idea out of hand. "What a terrible thought."

"Should we go to her household and look for bloodstains on clothes?"

"They've had plenty of time to wash everything," she said. "You know—Dak told me he was gone that day. Traveling back from the market at Porto, didn't get back to town until the next day when everything had already happened." So was Dak just scared, or was he hiding something as well?

"They should have worked a little harder to keep their stories straight," he said. "So what do we do about this quota question?"

"Investigate, I suppose," she said. "What a mess."

"They usually are, by the time we get called in to clean up."

She finally abandoned the cornbread and frowned at the crumbs she had scattered over much of the table. "I feel like I'm messing this up. My first lead on a murder, and I'm screwing up. You'd tell me if I was screwing up, yeah?"

"Enid. You're not screwing up."

"But you'd tell me."

"Yes, I would tell you," he said with some exasperation, and she felt suddenly like a child.

And what would happen if they didn't figure this out? A villain wins. Some of the perceived authority of the investigators gets chipped away. People here might keep telling her

Sero's death wasn't important, but that wasn't true. The stakes were real.

Tomas didn't give her more calm reassurances, which meant he was worried, too.

"I think I'm going to take a walk," Enid said, cleaning up the crumbs and finishing off her drink. If Philos and Bounty were violating quotas, there'd be evidence. You just had to know what to look for.

Tomas nodded. "Good hunting."

///

ENID NEEDED TO look at the whole of Pasadan as an outsider, with fresh eyes.

Taking the whole afternoon to do it, she walked a circuit not just of Pasadan proper, but of the outlying households, including a creek and a grain mill, a couple of orchards, and miles of farmland growing barley and corn. Pasadan even had a quarry, and a household whose main occupation was making bags of concrete mix they traded up and down the Coast Road. She walked out along the hillside they'd cut into for their limestone, and the gash in the rolling hills made her stomach turn a little. Maybe they all needed concrete, but rock would never grow back and that exposed wound in the land would take years to heal. A half-dozen people worked, some of them digging into the rock with pickaxes, a couple of others carrying broken rock in wheelbarrows to a building where some kind of machinery wheezed and pounded, smashing the rock to powder. They all wore cloth masks over their faces. A chalk-smelling dust seemed to hang in the air around the site. It was all very loud and off-putting.

Pasadan was prosperous. The questions she had to answer:

Was it more prosperous than the records said they should be? Were they using more resources than they had a right to? She almost preferred the murder investigation. The town's general anxiety about an investigation might have nothing to do with Sero's death. The way to untie a knot might very well be finding the other end of the string Ariana had given her.

Hiding an entire cultivated field of grain was easier than one might expect. It really only required a couple of specific quirks of geography, or a willingness to travel far off a town's beaten path, into wilderness. Some kind of ravine that could be camouflaged, or some other loud and busy activity distracting from anything unusual.

In her first case, the perpetrators had planted a stand of cottonwoods to disguise the gully they'd used to grow extra oats. From a distance, the place looked like an ordinary copse of trees. But the blind also proved that they knew very well they were doing something wrong. They couldn't claim ignorance.

Enid searched for those signs here. Which brought her back to the quarry, and the grinding racket and chalky smell that made one want to circle wide around the place. A distraction. A place one wouldn't look because you assumed you knew what was going on there.

She went straight through the site, ignoring the workers who paused to watch her. Followed the rock cut along the hillside until she left the quarry behind, and the hill turned into exactly the kind of gully she was looking for. Tall meadow grasses gave way to stalks of cultivated barley. From a distance, you couldn't tell the difference. You'd have to walk right up to the field in order to learn what exactly was growing here.

A ton of work, cultivating an awkward out-of-the-way field

like this, just to avoid drawing attention. Much easier to petition for a higher quota . . . except a petition could be denied.

So, someone in Pasadan—Philos, according to Ariana—
was growing grain outside their quota. Likely using it for trade
in small quantities to avoid raising suspicions. But they could
acquire extra cloth, foodstuffs, incidentals. Lumber for fencing
and paint for pretty signs. None of it by itself was suspicious
—lots of places had pretty signs. But all of it together made a
picture.

Now she and Tomas had two investigations to conduct.

///

"MIGHT SERO HAVE known?" Enid asked Tomas. She'd pulled
some stalks of grain from the hidden field—just a couple of
weeks from harvest, if she judged it right—to show to him.
"Might he have threatened to report it? Might that be a motive
to hurt him?"

"Except he didn't talk to anyone," Tomas said. "That's
what everyone says. Wasn't like he'd be motivated to report it."

"Maybe. But . . . Tomas—if the extra grain was to try to
get a banner quicker, then everyone in town who wanted a
banner might have a motive."

"For violating quota. But not for killing Sero. We're only
speculating that he knew, that the two cases are at all connected."

"If he knew, would he have told anyone?"

He thought for a moment, until a connection lit in his eyes.
"Miran. If she was the last person to speak with him, he might
have told her something."

"Let's talk to her again," Enid said.

They decided to bring Miran to the community house, to the meeting room they'd made their own for the investigation. Their own territory. Since Enid had talked with her before, she went to Sirius household to get the young woman. It would rile folk, seeing an investigator escorting one of their own, and word of that would spread just as fast as word of their arrival at Pasadan had. That they were focusing attention on such a young and demure thing—people would read that badly, and Enid was almost glad for it.

Back at Sirius household, the wash had been taken in and the chickens were safe in their coop. Enid heard voices from what must have been a kitchen but didn't see any sign of Miran. Instead, an older woman was working in a standard kitchen garden, picking herbs—chives, looked like.

"Hola," Enid called.

"Oh!" The woman looked up, first startled, then fearful—her hands clutched tightly, crushing a bundle of chives—then she quickly calmed herself. "Hi. Can I help you?"

"Just wondering if I could speak to Miran. Is she here?"

"I think she's busy—one of the dogs got into some brambles; she's cleaning him up. But it should only take her a minute. I'll go get her—"

"Before you go, can I ask you a couple of questions?"

The woman had that round-eyed startled look again. The one so many people got with investigators.

"Yeah, of course."

"What's your name?"

"Fern. I'm Fern."

"You head of household here?"

"One of 'em, yeah. We're pretty informal here." She flashed a smile. She seemed to just remember the chives in her hand and went to drop them in a basket on the ground.

The woman reminded Enid of Olive—smiling, considerate, unable to pass a puppy or goat on the road without stopping to coo over it. At least, how Olive used to be before the miscarriage.

"Can you tell me about Sero?" Enid asked. "Did you talk to him much?"

"Oh, no, not really. But . . . well. I worried about him. It's just not right, him out there all by himself. Maybe no one else worried, but I did. Doesn't look good for the town, you know, having one person cut off like that. Like an outcast. It's just so sad what happened, and maybe it wouldn't have if he'd had someone. You know?"

Fern must have been in her early fifties, with a worn, pale face and a long graying braid resting over her shoulder. Matronly. Enid wondered if she'd ever had a baby.

"But you never spoke to Sero?"

"I sent Miran there with food. To thank him for all his good work. I thought, well, if we reached out to him enough, he'll come to us—ask to be part of Sirius. We had the space for it."

Enid grew frustrated. "You thought he could be part of your household, but you never went to talk to him yourself." She stated it, just to be clear.

"Well, I never really had time. And Miran did, quite often, I think. I didn't want to force him with too many of us going at him. Scare him off, you know? Like how some dogs are."

Yes. Because Sero was exactly like a dog. "Can you think of anyone who might have had a grudge against him? Maybe didn't think much of him living like an outcast?" Enid wondered, if Fern had been of a different disposition, might she have thought of a different solution for the "problem" of a loner than setting out food for him like he was a stray?

The woman's eyes clouded for a moment, as if she caught a hint of Enid's implication but just missed grasping it entirely. "Enough of a grudge to hurt him? Oh, no. No. I can't even imagine." Her hand went to her heart, a guarding gesture. Purely symbolic. Olive would have left Sero alone, as the man seemed to have wished. Enid was sure of it.

"Thank you, Fern. Maybe you could call Miran for me now?"

Fern disappeared into the kitchen, and Miran rushed out a moment later.

"What? What is it?" She saw Enid and pulled up short, stricken.

"Miran. Could you come with me? My partner and I would like to speak with you somewhere a little more private."

"But I haven't done anything." Her voice was tight.

"Yes, I know. It's just we've got our office set up in the committee house. You don't have to go, but it would be really helpful if you came and spoke with us."

Enid always gave people an out. Always told them they didn't have to go with her. But somehow, they always did.

///

THE WALK BACK, Miran seemed to struggle to keep from crying. Hunched in on herself, shoulders slumped, arms in tight, she looked as cowed as a person possibly could. Enid stayed more than an arm's length away from her. Escort, not captor.

Enid spotted Dak walking across town. Or they spotted each other. He was too far away to call out but raised his hand in greeting. His smile seemed to waver a bit when he spotted Miran with her. Enid tried not to read too much into that. Tried not to spin ways that Dak might be involved with this whole mess. Either he'd lied about being in town when Sero died, or Ariana had.

She answered his wave with a nod and kept going.

"Lived in Pasadan your whole life, then?" Enid asked. A casual question, but it would sound like part of an interrogation. Couldn't be helped.

"Yeah, I was born here. Fern's my mother."

"I don't suppose there's ever been an investigation in Pasadan in your lifetime. You ever even seen one of the uniforms?"

"Yeah," she said, nodding quickly. "I've been to the fall market in Haven a couple of times. Seen investigators walking around and things. I heard a lot of investigators live in Haven."

"I live there," she said. "In a household called Serenity."

"You do? I mean, that's nice. I guess."

"It is," she said, smiling. "I think Haven has the best fall market, but I'm biased."

"No, I think you're right. Not that I've seen that many."

And just like that, they were at the committee house. Tomas was at the doorway, looking particularly stern and enforcer-like. Miran hung back, and Enid gently urged her forward. "Let's go in, yeah?"

"Hello, Miran," Tomas said kindly. "Would you like to sit down? Can I get you a glass of water or something else to drink?"

"No, thank you," she said, achingly polite, and made her way to the chair Tomas had out waiting for her. Enid joined her, taking a second chair. Tomas remained in the doorway, leaning with his arms crossed, casual-like.

Enid turned back to Miran, pausing a moment to gather her thoughts, to study the woman in front of her. Nervous wasn't the same as guilty. She was pretty certain Miran hadn't hurt Sero—she didn't exactly have the physical stature of someone who could knock over a sturdy man eight inches taller than she was. And her feet weren't big enough to have made those prints in the ground outside the shed. But she might have seen something. And if she was protecting someone — that was a thread to follow.

"I have a few more questions for you about what happened to Sero. Is that all right?"

She nodded, hugging herself even more tightly. She seemed to shrink even more, if possible. Enid would have to step cautiously.

"A witness saw you at his house the morning he died."

Her eyes widened; she glanced away quickly. "Who said that?"

"Were you there? Did you talk to him?"

"I didn't do anything —"

"Not saying you did. I'm just asking if you were at his house, and if you were, what you talked about."

"We hardly talked at all. I was hardly there —"

"And?" The girl must have been having trouble gathering scattered thoughts. Enid wanted to press, to see what fell out of the confusion before she could get her story straight.

"Fern kept asking me to go there; I'm the youngest, so I get the chores no one else wants. It's not like anyone else was too busy; it's just I'm the youngest . . ."

"Why did she ask you to go?"

"She liked his work. She kept asking him to do work. And then when we had extra food, baked an extra pot pie or curry or whatever, she'd send me over with it for him. I was just a messenger; that's all it was."

Such a simple, commonplace job should not have inspired so much anxiety, but Miran was twisted up, hugging herself, eyes red.

"Are you sure there isn't more to it?" Enid asked gently.

Miran bit her lips, took a long, shaking breath. And she said, "I think she was going to ask him to join the house, to join Sirius—she felt sorry for him, being out there alone. But none of the rest of us wanted him. We didn't want him but she kept pushing, and I even think it made him uncomfortable. But Fern wouldn't know that because I was the one who had to stand there, and he couldn't even say thank you, he stuttered so badly—"

"Miran! Miran!" a voice from outside shouted. Kirk.

The woman jolted, her whole body clenching, and she looked to the doorway. Tomas had straightened, preparing.

"Where is she? Where is she!" Kirk himself appeared at the doorway, very nearly slavering in fury. He seemed to have every intention of storming in, but Tomas put out his arm and caught him.

Kirk saw Enid and addressed her, spitting words. "What are you doing? You can't keep her. She didn't do anything. What's wrong with you people!"

"Kirk, wait outside, please?" Enid said. "I'm almost finished here, then I'll speak with you."

"No! Miran—come on, come out of there. You don't have to stay; you don't have to talk to them."

He lunged, even against Tomas's presence. The enforcer had to hold on to him, arm across his chest like a bar, feet braced.

Miran stood. "Kirk, no, it's all right—"

The sight of Enid had drawn him in, but the sound of Miran's voice drove him into a frenzy. The boy twisted, snarling, wrenching one arm of out Tomas's grip, half falling, then swinging upward with that suddenly free fist, right toward the enforcer's gut. Miran screamed and started to leap into the fray, but Enid stepped in and gripped her arm—torn, because she also wanted to help Tomas by knocking that boy to the floor. She could only do one or the other, so she held on to Miran, who couldn't possibly save Kirk from himself no matter how much she wanted to—and Tomas could take care of himself.

Kirk swung a punch up, and Tomas stepped out of the way, slapped a tranquilizer patch on the flailing wrist, then grabbed Kirk's elbow and twisted. On his knees now, gasping for breath, Kirk stared at his arm as if it had been stabbed. Enid could just about watch the tranquilizer taking hold, melting his limbs, his eyes gleaming briefly as he realized what had happened, then going soft as he ceased caring. He tried to stand, but only managed a couple of stumbling steps. Tomas let him sink to the floor on his own. Blinking a couple of times, Kirk looked back as if to protest, then finally laid himself flat on the ground, unconscious.

Enid had only seen Tomas tranq someone a couple of times before, but she always admired his deftness. She let Miran go, and the girl gave a yelp and fell to the floor next to Kirk, stroking his hair, murmuring.

"Will he be okay?" she pleaded with Enid. The tears had started and her cheeks were streaked with them now.

"He'll wake up in half an hour or so," she said. "He just needs a moment to collect himself, yeah?"

"Yeah," she agreed, and sniffed loudly. She didn't leave his side.

Tomas came to join her. "I believe those two are together, yes?"

"Yes," Enid said. "Yes, they are."

BECAUSE SHE HAD just about lost patience with the entire town of Pasadan, Enid stood Miran up and checked the girl's implant. Still in place. That was good—she and Kirk hadn't gone so far as to plan on sneaking off together to have a bannerless baby. But when this many people had gotten together to hide something, consciously or not, she had to ask the question . . . and was relieved that she didn't have to add that to her list of suspicions.

Miran didn't seem to notice Enid surreptitiously pressing fingers to her upper arm as she helped the girl to her feet, and then assisted Kirk to a sitting position against the wall. They made the boy as comfortable as they could, a blanket tucked over his legs and a cup of water waiting for him when he opened his eyes.

"Is he going to be all right?" Miran kept asking that. Enid and Tomas had stopped trying to reassure her.

"Miran, you have any idea why he was so furious about us talking to you?"

She shook her head, pressed her lips together. "He gets emotional. Really emotional. Like everything's a matter of life or death. It's exhausting sometimes." But the way she said this hinted that she also rather liked it. This was a man who would seduce his beloved with a truly flattering passion. Enid knew how that went, and she blushed because the man who'd first poured that kind of passion on her was less than a quarter mile away.

"Have the two of you talked about earning a banner together?"

Miran looked at her, startled. Then settled, because of course Enid would guess—investigators were omniscient, weren't they? Enid stifled a grin.

"He promised he'd earn me a banner. Not that I wanted one. I mean, someday, sure, but not right now. I've got to earn it. I've got to work for it, or we work for it together. You know how it goes. You make a household, then you get a banner — not the other way around, like Kirk talked about it."

"Yes, I know."

"But he wanted me to promise. He wanted me to promise that I'd wait for him, that when we got a banner, it would be ours."

Kirk wanted a baby, and he wanted it with Miran. That might have been enough to put him in a panic. Or there might be more to it.

Like, if Philos was breaking quotas, his household — Kirk's household — might never earn a banner again. The man was trying to stake a claim. Make plans as some kind of bulwark against tragedy. As if simply making a plan meant that it must, *must* happen, just like that.

"Wha . . . what." Kirk started to come around, a hand twitching, head lifting. Eyes not quite opening, but head turning as if he were searching for something anyway. "Mir — Miran!"

"Kirk!" She gripped his shoulder and murmured. "It's all right, you're fine. Don't move just yet. Just rest, yeah?"

Enid expected him to ask what happened, and then to get surly. To try to pick up the fight where he left off, only sluggish and drunk on tranquilizers, which would be amusing to everyone but Kirk. But he did as Miran asked. Let the wall hold up his weight and reached for her hand as his eyes finally opened and looked out, unfocused.

"I messed up, di'n't I," he stated, and sighed.

"Yeah," she agreed. "What got you all riled up?"

His face screwed up — the previous rage tempered, with no

outlet. Enid held her breath, waiting quietly for Miran to continue questioning—Kirk would give her answers he wouldn't give anyone else. But instead of talking, the man looked like he might cry. Not so much unhappy as . . . lost. Defeated. And he wasn't going to talk, not even to Miran.

"Kirk," Miran whispered, prompting, and Enid decided that whatever Kirk knew, and whatever Sero knew, neither of them had told Miran.

"Enid," Tomas spoke warningly, straightening to block the door.

Someone was coming. Enid could guess who and heard Philos before seeing him.

"What have you done with him! Where is Kirk? What have you done!"

How had he found out? Everyone who'd seen Kirk's outburst was here. Ah, but a town like this—someone might have seen Kirk rushing up and gone to tell Philos. Philos himself might have been looking for Kirk and finding him nowhere else realized his son had come here.

Might then have been concerned about what Kirk was telling the investigators about . . . about whatever it was he was hiding. Whatever his whole household, or the whole town, was hiding. The old man approached, a ragged creature, hands clenched like claws.

"I've got this," Enid said, taking up a position at the doorway, Tomas standing at her shoulder.

"I've got another patch ready if we need it."

"You almost sound eager."

"Be a pleasure to take that man down a notch."

Then the man was upon them. He stopped, paused a moment. Maybe realizing he was facing down two investigators, official and frowning in their uniforms.

"Where is my son? What are you going to do with him? I'll lodge a protest—whatever is happening, I'll go to Haven myself and demand the regional committee reprimand you both. You can't overstep yourselves like this—"

"We've not overstepped anything." Enid stopped him before the speech could go any longer. "Your son attacked Tomas. Tomas subdued him—well within his rights."

"What are you accusing him of?"

"Assault, for the moment. But I'm prepared to forget it if I can understand what's really going on here. Can you help me understand that, Philos? What's really going on?"

His mouth worked for a moment before he said, "That's what you're here to tell me. I thought that was how this worked."

Properly, he should have told her about the conflicts on the committee and the extra field of grain the minute she and Tomas walked into town. Properly, he ought to be working for the well-being of the whole community. But he'd gone defensive. Placed himself on the other side of a divide from her. She'd forced him to a place where he could only argue.

She had to build the wall behind him before she could back him into it.

"Extra fields," she said. "Grain fields exceeding the town's quotas. Whose fields are those? Who have you been protecting?"

From the floor, Kirk leaned up and muttered, "I didn't say anything, Philos. I didn't tell them anything."

Miran gazed open-mouthed at Kirk, then at Philos. "What? What's going on here?"

Philos kept on. "I don't know what you're talking about! You don't have authority here!"

She considered him, keeping her expression still. Investi-

gators' manners, their faces, were as much a part of the uniform as the color they wore. Calmly she said, "You're right. If
you don't want us here, we don't have to stay. We only have the
authority you let us have. But if we leave, if you reject us, you
give up the right to trade with any other town on the Coast
Road. Anything you need supplied by anyone else? Gone.
None of you will ever be able to settle anywhere else. No one
else will have you. Once we get the word out, Pasadan is on its
own. Outcast, from the whole of civilization. Is that what you
want?"

He didn't say anything. Nobody said anything.

Cut off from the Coast Road—that could kill a town like
this, just a little too small to get all it needed on its own, that
depended on markets and trade for the things that made life
easier. Enid had the power to make that happen. Such a simple
thing to say the word, to enact such a shunning. She took the
uniform she wore seriously indeed, because people were right
to fear it.

Whatever he was hiding, Philos wouldn't go so far as to
wish death on his town. So he remained silent. With a final
glare at them all, even Kirk and Miran, he turned and stalked
out.

Miran slumped as if exhausted.

Enid touched the young woman's arm. "Take Kirk home,
why don't you? We still have an investigation to finish. You
know very well that the sooner those answers come, the sooner
we'll leave and all this will be done. But I won't leave till I know
what happened. Spread that word. If anyone knows anything,
they'll do best to come to me quick. Right?"

They avoided her gaze as if it would allow them to avoid
the subject at hand. She had cornered them well and good, and
they didn't like it.

"Come on," Miran murmured gently, happy enough to be taking care of Kirk. "Let's go."

The boy still looked like he was about to cry. He hunched his shoulders and leaned into Miran's touch, his face turned from them all.

Enid turned to find Tomas propped up in the doorway, looking tired and suddenly old. Like he'd had just enough of this and didn't find any of it fun anymore. She could agree with that.

"Well," she said brightly, hoping to distract them both. "That was a whole lot of interesting."

"Were we finished with her?" he said. "Before the 'interesting' arrived?"

She thought about it, tracing back the events of the last few moments, the conversation with Miran, who'd been talking when Kirk barged in. What had she been saying . . . about Fern wanting Sero to join their household. Not that Sero would ever have agreed to that, based on what they'd learned about him. Miran shouldn't have worried. But yes, she had seemed worried. Was that thread worth following? Enid suspected not. She was just a girl caught in the middle of it all.

"I think so," Enid said. "She just happened to be the one to talk to Sero more than anyone else by virtue of her household feeling bad for him. Strange how people get mixed up in these things."

"Yeah," Tomas said. "I wonder, though."

She made an inquiring noise, and he shook his head, dismissing his own thought. Tomas rubbed his shoulder, kneading muscles like he had strained something.

"You all right?" Enid asked.

"Yeah. Think I may finally be too old for this. What would you say if I took up basket weaving instead?"

He was fifteen years older than she was. Not as much older as he used to seem. Not old at all, really. "Whatever makes you happy, but I say you're still the best enforcer on the road. Beautiful takedown with the boy, there."

He rolled his eyes like he wasn't convinced. "Thanks, I think. Not sure it's a skill one should be particularly proud of."

"The hard and necessary work that must be done."

"Ah, yes," he murmured. He did look tired. Pale, as if the fight, however brief and however much he had had the upper hand, had taken something out of him.

"Sit. I'll get us dinner," she said, patting his shoulder and going to find Ariana.

///

THE SUN WAS setting by the time the drama with Kirk had dispersed, and Enid was ready to be done for the day. If she asked at Newhome in time, there'd be a couple of extra servings of supper for odd travelers and guests. Tonight was a chicken salad with chunks of fresh bread. The cook gave her a basket to carry the meal in, and Enid thanked him.

Halfway back to the committee house, Philos found her.

She had a moment of fear—an actual spike of anxiety—because her hands were full and the man was still angry. Prone to doing something rash. As he'd done with Sero, maybe? She wouldn't be able to easily defend herself. But she stood her ground, even while holding the basket, and faced him.

"Hola," she said, just to let him know she saw him coming from behind the outbuilding at the edge of the household.

"May I walk with you, Inspector Enid?"

This was very formal, which instantly made her suspicious of him. *More* suspicious. "Yes, Philos."

"We're a good town here. We have enough. Not too much. Every mouth gets fed; everyone has a place."

"Now that Sero is gone, at least," she said.

"We have room here," he continued, undaunted. "If you ever get tired of your work. If you ever feel that you need a quieter life." He looked her up and down appraisingly. "How old are you? Thirty?"

Wryly she said, "A bit younger. I've had some hard miles."

He smiled politely. "I really don't know anything about you. What you're like when you're not doing this. What you want. But I suppose . . . if you wanted a banner, you'd need to think about it soon, yes?"

Philos didn't need to know about Serenity's banner hanging on the wall back home. The one that didn't have a name on it yet. Even if she hadn't had that banner, she would have thought this was appallingly brash. She was almost impressed with him.

If she really wanted to have a baby herself, Olive would give her that chance. But Olive wanted to be the one to carry the child, to give birth. She was the one who yearned for it. Enid . . . she suspected she'd wanted the banner for the accomplishment of earning a banner and not for the baby. For the status. And that didn't feel quite right.

Philos didn't need to know any of that. Let him make his assumptions.

"I guess I would," she said, conversationally. "I've been a bit too busy to think of it. Pasadan gets all the banners it wants, I suppose?" She hadn't seen any pregnant women in town. That didn't mean anything, of course, and she thought of Olive again. She wanted to go home.

"We do all right. We hope to keep it that way. I'll do what

I can to keep it that way. But right now, that outcome is up to you, isn't it?"

"I suppose it is." They'd arrived back at the committee house. "Well. I'll be thinking a little more clearly after I've had something to eat, I'm sure."

"Thank you for your time, Investigator." He actually bowed himself away, and she wanted to kick his ass as he turned.

She waited until he was gone before entering the front room and setting the basket on the table. Teeth bared she said, "Philos just tried to bribe me. Let the whole thing go, and he'll get me a banner."

"Really?" Tomas said, with the hint of a chuckle. Like his prey had just landed in a trap. "That's a hell of a bribe."

"Tomorrow, I want to look at Bounty again. See what they've got tucked away in hiding."

Hunter-Gatherers

They bypassed Fintown and whatever trouble had settled there with the arrival of the investigators. Enid would have to remember to ask Tomas what had happened. Investigators all talked to one another; he would know. For now, they kept moving.

It rained. Off and on for the next two weeks, rain fell. Not a lot, but the misting, annoying drizzle still managed to turn the world wet and muggy. They traveled, until the landscape became green and forested.

Against Dak's usual habits this time of year, they took side roads, exploring several byways off the main route, discovering households that made their way off the main part of the Coast Road. They became enamored of their roles as messengers, exotic travelers bearing news from the wider world.

Travelers weren't taken for granted on the fringes.

Households on the frontiers made small livings with farming, foraging, and scavenging. A woman at one household made medicines, heady-smelling ointments and tinctures to soothe aching joints and sore throats. Her workroom smelled marvelous, as if every possible smell came together—sweet and bitter, musky and spicy—into a cohesive whole that made Enid feel pleasantly lightheaded after just a couple of breaths. Her name was Dream, and she said most of the ingredients grew wild. Her mother taught her to gather and prepare them. Her household had been doing it since the Fall, and they traded for cloth and tools with nearby households and travelers.

She offered Dak a wound salve to try for a bruise he'd acquired, stumbling over fallen branches. Dak smelled it. "I know this—I've seen this before! Or something like it. You think your goods might get traded farther out on the Coast Road?"

She shrugged. "I've got one lady takes almost all I make. Trades it to a market out east. Brings me back empty jars and things. She trades on the whole Coast Road, so yeah."

Dak grinned at this, and Enid marveled that even if this woman and her household had lived in this spot for decades, what she made had traveled all over the world. All over *their* world, at least.

Dream's household had banners, a half dozen hanging from string at the front door. The oldest, sun-faded and dusty, must have been decades old. One of the first, from when the system started. The newest was still bright. Enid had seen a teenage boy chopping wood out in a gully on their way in; it must have been his.

Enid and Dak passed through these small places, brought what news they could, trading stories and small chores for food and a roof, for messages carried. Enid collected a batch of folded letters and dropped them off at a way station at the next crossroads.

Then, the households ran out. All the settlements ran out.

All that was left was shrouded, muggy wilderness—and then the ruins came into view. The bones of the old city, a concrete scar slowly melting, turning overgrown, becoming something else.

As they had when walking south, they stopped and looked. As if the place were a magnet with some kind of physical pull. They couldn't *not* stop. The sight was eerie. A ghost, but one they could watch physically fade, getting weaker.

"You want to get a closer look?" Enid asked.

Dak didn't say anything. Adjusted the strap of his guitar case, a moment of fidgeting. He didn't say yes, but he didn't say no. So Enid started walking. Left the road and cut overland, kicking through grass toward the gap between the couple of hills that stood between her and the ancient city.

"Enid . . ." Dak called, then followed her.

They took the rest of the day to approach the city. The shape of it came in and out of view as they walked past hills, along creek beds, and through stretches of woods. Quickly, surprisingly, they came upon other signs of the pre-Fall world. A stretch of asphalt that hadn't yet been swallowed by grass. A white square of concrete pavement.

Enid's foot would hit a solid, echoing step, and she'd look up and around and suddenly see the shape of it: a long, straight dip in a meadow that must have been a road a hundred years before. The land was sunken, the grass a slightly darker color —that was all that marked the place. But there must have been more: buildings lining the road, the rusted shells of cars, signs and lights and all the rest. If she pulled back the overgrowth, dug into mounds of scrub oak, and cut through mats of clinging vines, she would find more evidence of what this place had been. More remains.

The vegetation suddenly seemed alien, a cloak hiding something ominous.

"What do you suppose it was like?" she asked, her voice sounding flat in the muggy air. They hadn't spoken in a long time, walking silently, somber, as if watching a funeral pyre.

"Doesn't really matter," Dak said. "But I would have liked to hear their music."

A sudden crashing in the underbrush ahead startled her. Startled them both—she reached out, heart racing, and his hand was right there to grab hers.

Cattle. Two feral cows with scraggy ruddy coats and beady eyes lumbered across the one-time road and into the next collection of shadows. She barely got a look at them, their brick-like faces braying and thick legs kicking.

She and Dak both laughed and came together in an awkward hug, bleeding out adrenaline. Looking around one more time, wondering what else was out there and if they ought to be worried.

"What happens if we see people?" she asked.

"We probably won't see anyone," Dak said. "They'll be scared of us. If there's even anyone here anymore. I don't see how anyone can live in this wild."

It was certainly different out here than what they were used to, even with all the traveling they did.

Enid didn't think anyone would be scared of the two of them—they weren't much to look at. A couple of kids with bulky packs and blankets tied over their shoulders, not to mention Dak's guitar. They weren't a threat—they were targets. She started studying the undergrowth, pulling up fallen branches, and testing them until she found one that was about a foot shorter than she was, that she could easily fit her hands around but still looked sturdy enough to cause damage if she swung it. After stripping twigs and leaves from it, it had the look of a decent walking stick. While she worked, Dak watched impatiently.

"You look like an investigator with that thing," he said.

"Bien," she answered. "*Now* folk'll be scared of us." If they needed it. Maybe they wouldn't need it.

Dak shook his head and went on, not waiting to see if she caught up or not. She got the feeling he was getting frustrated with her. Maybe she ought to suggest turning around? Maybe she ought to ask him if he was unhappy. Or *why* he was unhappy, rather. She wondered what he was thinking and couldn't bring herself to ask, because it would sound like whining. Because she might not like the answer.

She studied the angular, artificial shadows ahead. She wanted to see them up close; that was what she focused on.

///

FARTHER ON, ENID put her hands on the bones of one of those ancient structures. A spine of steel emerged from underbrush, thick enough she could put her arms around it, red and rusting, chipped concrete sloughing off it, spotted with fuzzy green moss. Plates of rusty-brown fungus grew out from the base —nothing they could harvest. The growths ate into the concrete, causing the remains of the structure to melt away almost as they watched.

So began a forest of metal, flat surfaces that had edges covered in vines, trees leaning off balconies that seemed to be freestanding, but on closer look it seemed that the walls around them were gone, and only steel frames held them up. Sloping hills of refuse might have been left by giant moles. Enid studied it all, trying to imagine what had been here before . . . and failing. She'd seen pictures of what this had looked like; what she couldn't see was the transition, how the world in those images had turned into this.

Auntie Kath would know.

"Well, this is it," Dak said, holding his arms out in presentation. "The ruins."

"Yeah," she breathed. Her heart raced; she smiled. There was a strange kind of echoing—birdsong sounded louder here. "Let's keep going."

The gaps between steel and concrete had obviously been streets. Some walls still stood—holes indicated where windows and doors had been. Strange, that some parts were so identifiable, yet also ghostly, no longer serving any kind of purpose.

She thought they had come to the end of the city when they reached a wide stretch of broken asphalt, with trees and scrub rooted in decaying black rubble. No buildings, nothing else—but in the middle of this space, more steel, carpets of broken glass crunching under their boots, beaten by weather over the decades. Enid crouched, cleared away some moss and grass, and the pebbles of glass flashed in the light. They walked farther, circling a steel boundary with struts and buckled walls. This had been a single building once, able to encompass some of the towns they'd been to. What did anyone even do with a structure so large?

Even after this, the ruined city continued. For miles, it went on.

Enid hoped to find artifacts. Tools to salvage or a toy or a piece of cutlery to show what life had looked like before the Fall. Maybe even a book—how marvelous would it be to find a book that no one from Haven had seen before. But no, all that had vanished long ago. Already salvaged, buried, or rotted away. So many things just rotted away if no one was there to take care of them.

In the last days, there hadn't been enough people to take care of much of anything.

Enid didn't worry about getting hurt—anything that might have fallen or broken off had done so a long time ago. She stood still and tried to take it in, the strange view, the rich smell of vegetation cut through with the musty odor of wet rock or concrete, only slightly unpleasant, only barely identifiable.

In the distance, the scrape of gravel.

"Shh," she hissed to Dak. He was already standing still, quiet. She gripped her walking stick two-handed.

"Enid, we should go, come on . . ." He started back the way they'd come.

"No, wait a sec." She continued on a few steps, listened harder—and heard voices. She couldn't make out words, but she definitely heard two people speaking, calling out curt instructions to each other.

Behind her, Dak looked ready to run, if only he could be sure she'd follow. But she wouldn't.

"Dak," she hissed. "Play something."

"What?"

"Get your guitar out. Play something. We'll pretend we're having our own little party and draw them out."

"Enid, that's a terrible idea."

"I want to see them."

"You'll do more than that if they find us!"

The voices drew closer. "Was that . . . heard somethin' . . ."

Too late, Enid and Dak had already been discovered. They'd have a confrontation on their hands—unless they could make themselves interesting. Enid said again, "Play something!"

Dak found the corner of a fallen slab to sit on and pulled

his guitar out of its cover. Enid stood nearby, leaning on her staff and keeping watch for whatever came around that corner up ahead.

Two figures, short and wiry, all joints and whip-like muscles. It took Enid a moment or two to realize it was a man and a woman—they both had rough dark hair, long and tied back with leather cords. Their clothes were a hodgepodge, wraps of leather and worn cloth held together with twisted rope, stitched and mended moccasins. Their skin was brown, sunbaked, and their gazes were wary.

Enid stayed very still, watching them enough so they knew they were watched. She tried to keep her gaze soft, interested but not too intent.

Dak focused on the guitar, and only slowly did he start playing notes, sliding gradually into music like the first drops of rain before a steady, calming drizzle. A light song, the notes were clear and simple, arranged in a rolling melody that repeated, shifted into a variation, then went back to the beginning. A simple exercise for Dak, but he let the song flow. Didn't sing. The plucked strings were enough here.

The folk from the ruins stood still, listening for a long time. The notes seemed to hang in the air. Eventually, on Dak's third song, they approached. The man had an unstrung bow and a quiver of arrows on his back. The woman had a metal pipe as long as her leg—clearly a weapon. For the moment she held it like a walking stick. Right now, they weren't a threat. They did give Enid's staff a look up and down. There was something equitable about the way they sized each other up, like they were deciding that yes, they were on the same footing and there'd be no trouble. An agreement that all would be well as long as they kept a certain distance between them—for politeness's sake.

The third song finished and Dak paused. Their turn, now.

"Names?" the woman asked in a tired, broken voice. Like she was getting over a cough. "You've names?"

"Enid," she said, hand on her heart. "This is Dak."

"Star," the woman replied, and pointed to her partner. "Rook."

Enid nodded, accepting. Thrilled, really. She felt like she'd come to the end of the world and found it welcoming.

"Where you foot it from?" Rook asked next.

Enid started to say, "The Coast Road—" but Dak jumped in. "Just traveling. We've been all over."

They nodded; they seemed to be familiar with the nomadic life.

"You been around," Rook said next. "Any sign of storms coming up?"

"Rain south of here. Nothing too bad," Enid said. They had a clipped way of speaking, and she found herself adopting the short tones. A careful way of speaking to people you weren't sure of.

The man pointed out, a vague direction north. "Some wind coming up. Seasons changing. Best to watch out."

"Yeah," she agreed. The big typhoons would scour out a place like this. These folk must have had a strategy to keep safe. A place to shelter.

"Why don't ya come and sit by the fire. Rest a bit. Can ya? Maybe do some more of that?" He waved a hand at the guitar.

Enid looked at Dak, leaving the decision to him. But he had a hard time turning down a request for music.

"Sure, bien," he said, as she expected.

They followed the pair of hunters farther into the ruins.

THIS WASN'T THE Coast Road anymore, but trade still worked. Music for space to rest. There was some reassurance in that.

The folk here had a camp of sorts. It wasn't any more than a camp—lean-tos made of fallen branches, tents made of cowhide, ramshackle bolt holes built into the ruins; and all of it looked like it fell down and had to be rebuilt every time a storm passed through. They had scavenged tools, ax heads that they kept sharp, hammers that were worn almost round. They had plenty of fire, with wood and cow dung for fuel. The wild cattle seemed to be how they made their living—they hunted for meat and leather, foraged for the rest. Bladders and barrels of rainwater sat protected under overhangs. They defended their territory, because apparently several nearby settlements made raids back and forth. Lots of skinny children running around. *Lots* of children. It shocked Enid, and she looked for where the banners would hang, on a wall or a line or a pole, but there weren't any banners. No implants.

Star introduced them. The settlement was made up of three family groups, what Enid had to think of as a household. Three mothers and their children, with several other adults who came and went—someone was always out hunting, while some stayed to look after the camp.

All of them were wary as Enid and Dak approached. They didn't smile, only nodded politely.

Dak found a perch near the main campfire, which had a spit made of scavenged metal over it, empty at the moment. He started playing—seemed the best way to set everyone at ease. Enid kept close to him. Standing watch over him, she thought of it. As if these people would knock Dak over the head and steal him away if she didn't protect him.

He played, sang softly, counterpoint to the guitar's chords.

The children came out of hiding, gathering close. Seven of them, including the baby one of the women bounced on her hip. A couple of older ones, fifteen maybe, just as lanky as the rest and holding spears and worn knives. Hard to call the older ones kids — they dressed like the adults, looked like the adults. Soon as they could hold a knife, they likely started hunting with the others.

The children quieted and listened, rapt. They crept closer — they might not even have realized they were doing it. One of the mothers brought some seasoned dried beef to share. Enid accepted gratefully, knowing how much it likely cost her.

Dak was such a good sport. He got over some of his discomfort. He smiled at the kids, held the guitar out for them to touch, showed them how to strum the strings, to make the sounds that reverberated. Not so different from every Coast Road market he ever played at. The kids loved it, laughing. They all had to try it. Enid was glad because she had nearly convinced herself that the kids wouldn't know how to laugh.

They were offered food, wild onions that had been roasted in the coals. They tasted smoky, juicy, and good. Enid offered some of their fish jerky, which was gratefully accepted, though she got the impression that they weren't used to the idea of drying fish — one of them asked where the fish came from, how they prepared it, and Enid was glad she'd paid enough attention to be able to answer. One of the women broke pieces off the fish, distributing them among the children. The kids grabbed them and clamored for more. She hissed at them to be quiet.

This was what it looked like when folk didn't have enough to feed all the mouths they had, when they couldn't keep everybody safe. But they kept on anyway, just like this.

The conversation took a weird turn when one of the mothers, Bel, asked, "Kids yet?"

At first, Enid didn't know what she was talking about. Only when Bel nodded knowingly at her, then Dak, did she figure it out: Did she and Dak have any kids? Was she expecting? Bel looked at her like she ought to at least be pregnant.

"What? No—" Enid thought better of trying to explain the implant or banners or any of it. Seemed like trying to explain fish to someone in a desert. "Just no," she said softly.

"When a baby comes, you'll need to find a place to shelter."

When, not if. *It's supposed to happen the other way around,* Enid thought. *Shelter, then baby.* She looked to Dak for his reaction, but his head was bent over his instrument, playing with focus.

At dusk, the women banked the fire and sent everyone to sleep. Enid and Dak found shelter in a sunken space where a building had once been. They didn't make love but clung to each other, anxious and needing comfort.

///

THE SKY GREW light. The voices of folk just waking up moved around the camp. Enid shook Dak awake. She wasn't sure she'd slept at all, but spent the night in a half-waking twilight dream, her muscles bunched up and waiting for thunder.

"What—what is it?" He wasn't a morning person, and the late nights of music never helped.

"Nothing. Just wanted to let you know I'm taking a walk; I'll be back in a couple of hours." She patted his shoulder and went to get her staff.

"Enid. Wait a minute. Just—" He rushed, throwing off the blanket, shoving his feet into boots. Hurriedly putting his things in the concrete cubbyhole they'd claimed as theirs while they stayed here — except for his guitar, which he slung over his shoulder. He'd never leave that behind.

She was already walking but paused when he called, waiting for him to catch up. Likely, he didn't want to be left alone. She didn't mind if he followed. But she was on her own trek.

Sheltered campfires were being nursed back to life and kids sent out for fuel to keep them going. Enid passed them by and picked what had been the widest road and followed it, weaving around broken slabs of concrete and fallen metal poles, tangled vines and brambles that had taken root and broken the asphalt to pieces. Even though the buildings had fallen and none of the artificial structures reached up more than twenty feet or so, she had the feeling of being in a forest or a maze. The old shape of the street offered space; she could look up to a gap showing sky.

She wanted to see how far the people lived. How wide the camp spread out, and if you could even call it all one camp. When she asked Star what the name of the place was, she answered, "The Winter Camp." After the rains, they would travel back north to the Summer Camp. Still, Enid kept wanting to call this a town. She kept wanting to see the people here as unified in some way. Her own experience told her this must be a community like hers, but different. A town, maybe not one like Haven, but still a town. Somehow, someway.

Voices echoed. Made it hard to guess how many people really lived among the ruins. Glancing behind, she saw that a couple of the older kids had followed them, ducking onto side streets, behind trees, giggling when Enid and Dak pretended not to see them.

She ended up being glad for their presence when once, up ahead, a shadowy figure holding a bow — arrow notched

—stepped back into the shadows of undergrowth. Enid didn't get a good look at the hunter, and when she reached the place where she had seen him, he was gone. She had the impression he was a guard of some kind. Someone suspicious of strangers. The presence of the children must have made the newcomers seem safe. That was what she hoped.

Then they found the fire. A small, lone camp, an hour or so walk away from the rest of the settlement. Or the not-settlement, rather. Enid found herself constantly bumping up against expectations. She looked around but didn't see anyone. Someone had to be nearby. The fire was small but still had some fresh flames—it had been fed within the last half-hour. A tripod was set up over it.

"Hello?" Enid called.

Dak held her arm. "I'm not sure that's a good idea."

"What? I don't know if anyone's even—"

A woman came out from around the corner of the next street. Her thick hair was pulled back from her nut-colored face; she wore leather and a felted cloak pulled tightly over her shoulders. A great bundle of branches and twigs—fuel for the fire—was slung on her back. The bundle was almost as big and thick as she was. She'd lashed it together with rough braided cord, and she seemed to just barely be managing, hefting it on her shoulder while precariously looking ahead. Two young children followed her, and they had their own, less bulky, bundles of fuel.

Enid noticed then that all the trees and shrubs in the immediate area had been cut and harvested. They must have had to walk quite a ways to find more to feed the fire.

"Mama, look!" the older child said, stopping to stare at Enid and Dak. The kids were both in tunics and leather slippers, their hair pulled back like the woman's.

The woman's eyes went round. She dropped the bundle and came forward. "What do you want? What do you want?" The demand was harsh, fearful.

"Nothing," Enid said, wondering if they should back out of here the way they'd come. "We're just passing through."

When the woman put down the branches, she revealed the baby, maybe six months old, pressed close to her body in a leather sling. Arms around the baby now, she rushed forward.

"This is mine," she said, standing between them and the fire.

Enid didn't come any closer. "That's fine."

"Why're you here?" She gestured; the kids dumped their bundles of wood with hers and came close. They'd taken on wary, suspicious looks to match hers.

Enid spoke calmly. "I saw the fire burning and wondered if anyone was around. We're just passing through."

The woman seemed to turn that over for a moment. They were tucked behind another fallen pile of concrete, and she glanced around—looking up the street, around the corner, as if searching for someone. So there were others who were part of this group, probably gone off looking for food.

She and the children all had hollow cheeks and sunken eyes. They looked tired, even the kids.

"I don't have any to share. Sorry but I don't," she said finally, with marginally less suspicion. That was probably as close to an invitation as they were likely to get.

"That's all right. Really. You mind if we rest here a moment?"

"Sure, go ahead. Daisy, get the kettle, yeah?" The older of the two children ran off. The other followed her a moment later, while the woman dragged bundles of sticks over and began feeding them into the fire. One arm always cradled the baby in the sling. The girl came back a moment later, hauling a beat-up pot that already had water in it.

The woman had a bag slung over her shoulder in addition to the baby; Enid couldn't tell where her clothing ended and various bags and pouches began, like she was used to carrying the world with her wherever she went. She pulled ingredients out of this bag, wild onions, some small knobby potatoes, and sliced them up with a small knife.

Enid wanted to help. There had to be something constructive she could do. "Can I help?" she finally asked, a little desperately.

"No. I'm fine, I'm fine."

Dak found a perch on a fallen slab overgrown with vines. She thought of asking him to play some music—everyone liked music. But he sat clenched and anxious, hands sitting on his knees in fists. Enid went to sit next to him, to watch the scene play out. The woman—was she the mother of all three of them?—told the kids to go off and leave her alone for now. The elder, Daisy, took the younger one's hand and they ran, giving Enid and Dak shy glances over their shoulders. They disappeared around a corner; shouting and laughter could be heard a moment later. The noise sounded blissfully normal, and Enid sighed to hear it.

She whispered at Dak, "There's got to be some way we can help. Yeah?"

"Help how? You want to rebuild Haven for them right here?"

Maybe that was what she wanted, to re-create Haven so these people would be safe—she assumed they weren't safe, living like this. But they must have been—there must have been people living here, like this, since the Fall. Somehow, no matter how precarious it looked. Dak was right: she couldn't exactly rebuild Haven wherever she went. Didn't have the resources for it.

He said, "I don't want to be here when whoever she's looking around for gets back."

Enid made sure to keep her staff close and wondered if she'd actually be able to use it if she needed to. Tomas could —investigators and enforcers were trained for it.

She was feeling small right now, in a world she didn't understand.

The baby started crying in a thin, choked way that made it sound ill. Enid watched the ragged mother try to balance the baby in one arm while stirring the soup in the kettle. She kept leaning in, going off balance, and having to rearrange the baby again. The two children were running in and out from the ruins, screaming at each other—playing. The woman shouted at them to come help her. The older one, the girl, paused and looked out for a moment, caught sight of Enid and Dak again, and fled.

Three children for one mother. It seemed luxurious. And also awful.

"Quiet, you! Just for a second, please stop!" she hissed at the baby, jostling it in her arm.

"Here," Enid said, because she couldn't stand it anymore. "Let me hold him while you finish the soup."

The woman glared, suspicious, but didn't argue when Enid shifted the baby out of her arms and into her own. She laid the child against her shoulder and whispered soothingly, humming a tuneless song into its ear. The baby quieted. Enid studied it; even it had sunken cheeks and seemed small. Not that she had much experience with babies.

They were all starving, or close to it. The sky was overcast, the clouds turning darker. Storm season had arrived, and what would happen when the first typhoon came in? Would they find a cave of old metal and concrete to hide in?

They must have had a way to survive. They must have had a system, however strange and poor it looked to Enid. But she couldn't imagine it, not when she knew they could all be safe, not even a couple weeks' walk away.

The woman did what she needed with the stew and took the baby back from Enid.

Enid said in a rush, "You should come with us. You should all come to the Coast Road, 'bout a week or so of foot time northeast. There's plenty of food; they'll take you in—"

"No. No." The woman shook her head. "I'd never go there. They'll take my kids away if I go there. That's what they do: they take your kids away," she said, and spat. Held her baby close, cooing over its soft, bare head.

If Enid mentioned the Coast Road to Star and Rook and their people, would they say the same thing? They take children. It's horrible. These people would never ask for help, even if help meant that crying baby would live. She stared at the woman, her endlessly mended scraps of clothing, her spitting fire and awful dinner, her children running around with limbs like rails. They were all starving, not enough to die of it, but enough that their every waking thought turned to food.

Enid pulled packages from her satchel. All she had— bread, cheese, sausage, apples—and dumped it on the ground in front of the woman.

"It's food," she said. "Have it. Have it all."

The two older children had come out of hiding and crept toward the fire, as if they could smell what she'd offered. For a moment, she wasn't sure the woman would take the gift. She stared at the paper-wrapped packages and loose apples like they might attack her. Like there might be some trick. But then she reached out. She would take it all.

Enid didn't wait to see. She turned and marched away, tears stinging her eyes, frustrated and enraged and helpless.

Dak scampered after her. "Enid. You gave her all our food."

"We can get more."

"You said it yourself: Coast Road's a week away."

"We won't starve," she said, and choked back a laugh. They might get hungry, but they wouldn't starve, not like that woman and her children.

In fact, it might be good for them to go a little bit hungry. Like it was some kind of penance. Like she had to pay a price for simply existing. Make some kind of trade. She never had before—she'd taken it all for granted.

She wanted to get out of here, get back to the Coast Road, back to the familiar. It might be a rough trip—but she was glad for it. *That* would earn her next meal.

"Enid!"

She didn't slow down, even as she knew her anger was irrational. She did glance over her shoulder to check that Dak was following, and he was, scrambling over vines and branches and debris that had settled on the ghost road. He kept a hand on his guitar, steadying it.

Eventually, she had to stop for a drink of water from her canteen. Dak caught up, and they rested. He stared at her, studying her. Probably wondering if she'd gone crazy, and that annoyed her.

"I told you coming out this way was a bad idea."

"No, you said it was dangerous. It wasn't—no one even threatened us." She didn't think coming to the ruins was a bad idea. She wanted to see what the place was like, and now she knew. And the people there weren't dangerous. They were wary, and they had every right to be.

"That's not the point. If something had happened to us, no one would ever have known."

They could have tripped and broken their necks anyplace on the road. They studied each other, now. She was sad, driven. He was scared, exhausted. Sweat dripped from his hair, dirt smudged his face, his shoulders slumped. And he was looking at her like it was her fault.

Dak wanted to be where he was safe. Where he was loved. He needed that. She wondered then if he really needed her, or just someone standing in the place she was, following him. He'd probably never followed anyone in his life, the way he'd followed her into the ruins. He didn't seem to like it much.

She suddenly wondered why she had blithely scampered off with him to the ends of the world in the first place. It must have seemed like a good idea at the time. Weirdly, she couldn't remember what that felt like.

She was such an idiot.

"Well," she said. "We're going home now. It'll be okay."

They went back to the main camp to collect their things, thank Star for the hospitality, and then they walked east, away from the ruins.

Waste and Excess

Philos was the angriest. He was the one making bribes and threats. The issue of exceeding quotas might have nothing to do with Sero's death, but once they discovered the truth of the one, Enid wondered if the other truth might also unfold. Did Sero learn something? Had he threatened to report it? Did someone—maybe Philos—have a talk with him that ended violently?

Enid asked Tomas, "Would someone like Sero contact investigators?"

"I'd have thought he wouldn't want to be the snitch," Tomas said. "Wouldn't want to draw attention to himself."

They'd never met Sero—she wanted to interview him anyway. Sit him down and ask questions, get to the heart of why he was the way he was and what he wanted. She thought she knew the answer: he wanted to be left alone. So he wouldn't have asked for an investigation. Wouldn't have even sent an anonymous message if he'd discovered the hidden crops.

"But," Enid said, thinking, "Philos might not have thought that. So, what happens if we don't find anything at Bounty?"

"There's a half-dozen cellars in this town. More barns. Did the fields look mature? Had they been growing for more than one season?"

"Yeah. They should be getting ready to start this season's harvest."

"Then someplace around here will have a hoard of surplus grain. We'll check to see if any looms are weaving burlap for bags. Don't worry, we'll find it."

He drank from his mug of tea. Shadows marked his eyes, and he still looked as tired and drained as he had last night after the altercation with Kirk.

Enid asked, "Are you coming down with something? Do you need to rest?"

"Stop babying me. You're the one needs looking after, remember?"

"I will always need looking after. Just when I think I've figured the world out . . ." Shaking her head, she let the thought go. "I will never have the world figured out."

Tomas chuckled. "Let's go knock down some walls, should we?"

They straightened their uniforms, and Tomas gathered his staff and pouch of tranquilizers. The day was looking to be hot and muggy, a late last gasp of summer. It would either make everyone lethargic or make them edgy and prone to fighting. Better they get this over with early, then.

Not two strides out the door, Dak came up to the committee house, blocking their way. His expression was set, tight lines of tension around his mouth. At some point in the last decade, he must have decided he didn't mind getting involved.

"Hola," she said lightly.

"So what happened with Kirk last night?" he said, his casual tone at odds with his stance. He glanced at Tomas but saved the bulk of his attention for Enid. Like he thought he had a better chance of intimidating her. Tomas obligingly stepped back, crossing his arms, and looked on, interested. Waiting.

"What happened *how?*"

"Everyone says you attacked Kirk—"

"Kirk attacked *us*. We settled him."

"But you must have done something to set him off."

She furrowed her brow. "Does he get set off often? Does he have a temper, then?"

"He's a kid. You know how they get. I'm just trying to clear up all the rumors flying around."

"Ah," she said. "Here for the gossip."

"Do you think he had something to do with it?"

"Not sure yet," she said, studying him. Why was he here? Like, not just here talking to her now, but in the town at all? Why had he settled down, and why here? She glanced at Tomas, and yes, he had a hand by his pouch, ready to reach for a patch if Dak decided to get squirrelly. She didn't expect him to—he would try to charm them. "Actually, I wanted to ask you . . . Ariana said you could confirm that she was at her household the morning Sero died."

His expression froze. "Did she."

"But you said you were . . . where was it, Porto? So where were you?"

"Maybe I got back from Porto the day before. It was right around then. I don't remember exactly."

"Don't remember if you were at home when news came in that a man had died?" When he didn't say anything, she moved on. "Tell me again—you ever talk to Sero? Ever have a reason to go down to his house?"

"No, none. I never went there." His hard gaze never left hers.

She didn't believe him. He should have been laughing at her, at what she was suggesting. How hard could she push him, before he just ran? Not that hard, she decided. "Ah. All right, then. Thanks. If you want to catch up on more town gossip, why don't you come with us? We're about to go to Bounty to have a word with Philos."

She walked past him, Tomas following, and Dak scurried after a moment later.

"What about?" he demanded. "What's Philos done? You think he had something to do with what happened to Sero? Is there anyone in town you're not harassing?"

"Do you know Philos bribed me with a banner?"

Tomas murmured, "Enid, calm."

But Dak's open-mouthed shock told her—he didn't know. "A banner. Really," he said flatly, rubbing a hand across his hair. He had a few silver threads among the brown. Her dashing bard was going gray. "I thought—I thought he was angry because he resented the intrusion. That he wanted the committee to resolve the problem on their own. A town ought to be able to fix its own problems." He sighed. "Does Ariana know about the bribe?"

"I'm sure she will as soon as you tell her."

"Enid . . ." He didn't like investigators on principle, she knew that. If two strangers had come here on this investigation, would he have fled like he had back at Fintown? Would he have been trying to wheedle information like this?

"Yes, Dak, a town ought to take care of its own problems.

But when someone on the committee *is* the problem, towns need us."

"Ariana will want to know what's going on," he said, and left them, trotting back to Newhome.

"I imagine she will," Enid murmured.

Tomas asked, "You okay?"

"You know the worst part? I can't remember what I ever saw in him. Why I ever wanted to follow him to the end of the world."

"It's because he hasn't sung at you this time around," Tomas said.

Yeah, there was that, she supposed.

///

TOMAS SET THE pace, which seemed slower than his usual. A calm trek rather than an authoritative march, then. Enid hadn't thought him so worn out, and she wondered if she should say something. After—when this was over, she'd talk to him. By the time they reached Bounty, word had spread and an audience gathered. A few folk came from other households when they saw two investigators walking past with a sense of purpose. Dak arrived shortly after them, with Ariana alongside. Miran was there, shawl wrapped around her shoulders even in the heat, as if it shielded her. The gathering didn't want to come close enough to get involved, but they wanted—needed —to see what was happening. Enid wasn't sure what gossip they had heard. Dak should have been as clued in to rumors as anyone, and he hadn't known about the potential quota violations.

She wished they didn't have a crowd, but she couldn't do

much about getting rid of it. Only thing for it was to behave well. And to be right.

First thing they had to brace for: Philos, storming out of the Bounty common room as soon as Enid and Tomas entered the yard. Since they expected it, they were ready for him.

"Morning, Philos," Enid said, which did as she hoped and diverted him from whatever he'd been about to shout.

He looked old. He'd aged just over the course of the last couple of days, anxiety curling his hands tighter, lost sleep hollowing his face. Enid might have felt sorry for him, if not for the malice glaring in his eyes.

"What is this? What are you doing here?"

"You offered a bribe to an investigator," Enid said. The murmurs started among those gathered. "That's only one problem. There wouldn't have been a bribe if you weren't hiding something."

"You can't do this," he said in a low voice, sounding uncertain. "This is our place. This is a violation. I'm on the committee—if anyone should be making accusations it should be me, and you have overstepped yourself!"

"You're not the only one on Pasadan's committee," Enid said. "We can get the rest of them here. Would that help? Having witnesses? Ariana's already here; it'll just take a moment to fetch Lee."

"I . . . I . . ."

In fact, someone must have already gone to get Lee, because he trailed into Bounty's courtyard along with a few more observers. "What is it? What's wrong?" Lee muttered to those in the back, as if he'd stumbled on the scene of an accident.

Philos gaped at them all. The old man stood like he could block them, even though they could just go around. Last thing they wanted was a confrontation that would end with Philos tranquilized on the ground. The old man might not survive it. Let him get frustrated; she and Tomas had all the time in the world.

"In addition to offering a bribe," Enid said, for the benefit of the observers, "we believe Philos has violated quotas for the Bounty household and has been hoarding grain for trade. We're here to find the evidence."

"No," Philos said, weakly. "It's not like that. We weren't violating anything—it's just . . . we *needed* it. To get our surpluses up. Yes, we had to go into some land outside our quota, but not much. But we needed it, if we were going to get a new banner."

"You just got a banner a couple years ago!" Lee protested.

Enid suspected that Bounty had petitioned for a raise in quotas, and the rest of the committee, including Lee, had refused. They had enough. They didn't *need* more, despite Philos's arguments.

Ariana spoke to Enid but glared at Philos. "I suspected. No, I *knew*. I just didn't have evidence."

Lee turned on her. "Why didn't you say something?"

"I did! I tried to tell you, but you didn't listen, didn't want to hear that anyone was doing anything bad; you wanted to pretend everything was perfect—"

Enid put a hand on her arm to calm her. Nothing more she could say, because yes, ideally, Ariana or Lee should have said something. Asked questions. Managed it themselves. But Philos was a bully.

All that was left was the search. Tomas leaned in and pointed. "Those two outbuildings look like they have cellars. That one's hid pretty well with those honeysuckles—I'd start there."

She turned to Philos. "I have to ask—did Sero know? Did he threaten to report you? Did you confront him about it, maybe in his shed?"

Desperately, he shook his head. His hands fluttered nervously. "No, no. I had nothing to do with that accident. This has nothing to do with that, nothing."

Oddly, she believed him. But if he had nothing to do with it, then she was no closer to discovering whose footprints those were running away from Sero's body.

One problem at a time.

"Well," she said, turning to Tomas. "Shall we?"

"Sooner the better," he said.

They hunted around the outbuilding with all the honeysuckle brambled around it; it didn't take long. The vines hid where the foundation was raised and a cellar had been dug underneath. Part of the vines grew up a trellis that could be shifted to reveal the doorway. This was no accidental surplus, no chance mismanagement of resources. This was willfully taking more than they needed and hiding it from the whole town.

Enid and Tomas were no longer the villains here.

A couple of other folk of Bounty stood with Philos. He leaned on them, rubbing his forehead. His hands trembled. His whole world was coming down, and she and Tomas would have to sort out who in the household, and in the town, knew and who didn't. How to mete out the punishments when all was done.

They pried open the cellar door and went down a rickety staircase to a dirt floor. They had to duck under a low ceiling. This was halfway between a cellar and crawlspace. Enid had her flashlight, fully charged, and scanned it around the room.

Bags. Bags and bags of grain, leaning against the walls and

stacked against one another. Dozens. The household could use them to bribe, get deals from other towns and households, make trades. Make themselves more prosperous and secure. Wealth. This was wealth. Oilcloth on the floor protected the bags from moisture. Wire mousetraps in the corners. Likely a whole mess of cats patrolling the household, too. All of it carefully maintained.

Enid tore open the sewn top of one of the bags to confirm the barley inside. Counted and recorded the number in her notes.

Philos and his household had been working hard. But they didn't *need* this. Well, Philos must have thought they did, quotas or no.

She and Tomas took hold of one of the bags—twenty pounds, she guessed—and hauled it up the steps to display it to the community. To show what Philos had been doing with the town's resources.

They dropped it at the man's feet and stepped back. Gave everyone plenty of time to look it over. To make those connections, to see what the bag meant. The whole place went silent, except for chickens clucking around them in the yard.

"It . . . it's not that much," Philos said. "We needed it."

Enid jabbed a finger at him. "If everyone here needed this much, the land around Pasadan would be tapped out in a decade. You know that, right? You understand—"

"We weren't hurting anything—"

"Gah!" She turned away, unable to look at him anymore. "Stop talking, would you? Just stop! This is why you didn't want us here from the first! It wasn't about Sero at all. This is what you've been so worried about! Does the rest of the town know? Were you doing this for everyone or just for yourself?

And what did you think was going to happen when you were found out? Did you think you'd never be found out?"

"Enid! Enid, stop!" Ariana shouted, the desperate edge so cutting that Enid actually spun to look.

Tomas had doubled over and fallen to kneeling. Face flushed red, he clutched his left arm and seemed to be trying to speak, trying to spit out words while gasping for a breath that wouldn't come. Bystanders had already backed away from her outburst; now, they watched her partner as if he were the center of some performance.

In a moment she was at his side, holding him up. He grabbed her; his whole body was shaking. His eyes were wide, like he was drowning on dry land. Blue, his skin was turning blue, and his left side clenched up in pain. He kept trying to speak. He angled himself at her ear; his lips worked, but nothing emerged from them. His fingers gripped vise-like on her arm. He was so heavy.

Enid looked up. "Tull. Someone get Tull—bring him now!" Tull, the medic. He had to be around here somewhere. Miran ran off, shawl half flying behind her.

Enid laid him flat, lifted his legs, cushioned his head under a blanket that had suddenly appeared, that someone had given her. She didn't know who. Tomas's eyes were glassy; he wasn't breathing. So she breathed for him, her mouth over his, blowing a deep breath into his lungs. Pumping his heart for him. Another long breath. Tull arrived and took over the CPR for her. Tomas's body lay clenched in pain, but there was no movement.

She knew before Tull sat back and shook his head that Tomas was gone. Enid held Tomas's hand and wept.

NO ONE BOTHERED her for a long time. They left her there, slumped in the grass, holding his hand in both of hers as it lost warmth. She knew she would have to do something soon. Sitting there, she turned that thought back and forth in her mind. Yes, she would have to do something. Make a decision, then another. Move forward. But considering that thought seemed like a great deal of effort all by itself, so she didn't do anything else.

A hand touched her shoulder. She sensed Dak. Didn't even have to turn around, and she recognized the shape and presence of him out of the corner of her eye. The weight of his hand anchored her as he knelt.

"Enid, love. We should move him. Get him out of the sun. Can we do that? Is that all right?" He spoke low. The words seemed distant, but his voice was a comfort. She used to love his voice.

She nodded and finally looked up. Two men were there with a stretcher—the same one from Ariana's cellar, the one that had carried Sero. This horrified Enid. She wanted to scream. But yes, Dak was right. They should move him.

Most everyone else had gone. Ariana stood by. So did Miran—she'd been crying, her hands clasped together. She didn't even know him, Enid thought. Why should she cry? Her own eyes felt like wrung-out rags.

The men laid the stretcher down; she helped them lift Tomas to it, and he seemed even heavier. The weight of him settling. They walked away with him. She watched them go and couldn't follow. Dak stood on one side of her; Ariana came to the other and put her arm around her shoulders, and Enid hardly felt it.

She must have spoken at some point. Given some kind of instruction. She couldn't remember, and she kept thinking she should be better than this. If it had been anyone but Tomas who had died in front of her, she'd be better than this.

Yes, she did remember what she'd said, because they ended up at Tull's small clinic, not at the cellar at Newhome. The others had wanted to take him there, store him in the chill until Enid decided what to do. But no, they weren't finished here. She had questions.

The clinic was clean, neat. A single room, diffuse light came in through a wide window. Cabinets lined one wall, a couple of chairs stood against another, and a table occupied the middle of the floor. Like any clinic in any town. When they had Tomas's body resting on the exam table, she sent them all away. All except Tull. He remained near the door, his arms crossed, his frown deep. The room was quiet, the heat of summer pressing down, humidity making breathing difficult. They should open it, let some air in. But no, not until they were done here.

The thought had occurred to her: this might have been murder.

Poison, she thought. Something that would kill his heart dead. A dart, a patch, a liquid slipped into his tea. At Haven, the medics might be able to tell what exactly had killed him. They had blood tests for poisons, infections. It had come so quickly and he didn't have a mark on him, so it must be poison. It seemed such a reasonable possibility.

But no. Why poison him but not her? They'd eaten the same food since arriving in Pasadan, drunk out of all the same pitchers. She wasn't anything like ill, except for the hole in the middle of her heart, a black space that turned into a knife when she looked at him. His dead body. His terrible still form.

"Can you examine him?" Enid asked evenly. "Look and maybe see what killed him?"

Tull answered, "I told you: if I had to guess—this has all the signs of a heart attack. I'm sorry."

"I don't want you to guess; I want you to look. Could it have been anything else?"

The man sighed, then peeled back Tomas's brown tunic, moved aside a pendant he'd worn on a thin cord. Enid looked over the medic's shoulder. Were there any patches on Tomas's skin, like the tranquilizers? Any needle marks? Any odd infected cuts? She watched Tull, making sure he was really looking, not brushing off the job because he thought she was crazy.

"What about that flushing, there?" Tomas's skin across his neck, part of his chest was red. It didn't look normal.

"It's pretty common to see that with heart attacks," Tull said tiredly.

"There isn't a poison or something could have caused a symptom like that?"

"I don't know. I don't really have experience with poisons—"

Impatiently, she said, "Then are there any other signs? Just to confirm it wasn't something else?"

"Well, yes. But based on how you said he was acting—it was a heart attack. Maybe a stroke or some kind of brain injury. These things happen. If you took him back to Haven, the clinic there is much better equipped—"

She shook her head. They didn't have time. And if Tomas had been murdered, she wanted to be here to find who had done it. "Heart attack's caused by a blockage, right? Can you do an autopsy?"

His face, already pale, blanched further. "I—I've never done one—"

"But you're qualified to perform surgery, yes? You've been

trained. You'd recognize healthy organs compared to unhealthy ones. You could tell."

"Investigator Enid, I'm not sure it . . . it will help."

He'd been about to say another word. Something like "worthwhile," or "useless." But she needed to *know*. Relenting, Tull searched through the cabinet for tools. Scalpels, forceps, a bone saw, a pile of rags. She helped him entirely pull off Tomas's brown tunic, which she clutched folded in her arms. His chest still looked like it was burned. Across the skin, a scattering of curling hair was turning gray. His sternum, the curve of his rib cage, were visible. She remembered that time when she was twelve, that storm, the body caught up in the smashed building. It hadn't looked real, either, and Tomas was looking less real by the moment. What were they even doing here?

Enid had to close her eyes a moment. This body lying here wasn't Tomas anymore. This was a puzzle to be solved. Another investigation. This was necessary.

Tull studied every inch of him, touching joints, pressing his throat, his abdomen, any place that might show symptoms. The places where diseases might reveal themselves. Enid thought when he cut, he would start with the stomach, but he didn't. He went to the chest, the heart. His first suspicion. Enid held her breath at the incision. Looked away when blood welled up. It didn't flow quickly, like it should have.

The medic was careful. Probably wasn't easy, having Enid watching him while he cut. His actions were precise, methodical. The actions of someone who wasn't used to doing this. Wasn't habit for him, cutting into people.

The cracking of ribs made Enid wince. Maybe this was a mistake . . .

Tull straightened, wiping his bloody hands on a rag, which

quickly turned crimson. His gaze met hers. "Would you like to see?"

"What? You found something? What is it?"

Tull prodded with the end of the forceps above the meaty fist of the heart. No longer Tomas's, she reminded herself. A series of small rubbery tubes branched out, veins and arteries, a visceral red, even now. He'd only been gone an hour . . .

"It's blocked," Tull said, pressing against one of the thick lengths of what must have been an artery reaching up from the muscle. The tissue didn't give, when it seemed like it should have. Gently, he sliced into it, just a little, to show a tiny pearl of a yellowish deposit. She wasn't a medic but that definitely didn't look right. Her own heart seemed to clench in sympathy.

He said, "A blockage like this is what causes heart attacks."

She sounded resigned when she said, "But he was young!" Younger, at least. Early forties was still young, even after the Fall.

"Some people are prone to it," he said. "We used to be better about fixing things like this. I'm really sorry."

The muscle seemed washed out, a grayish pink instead of vibrant. But she had no way to judge; this was the first time she'd seen under a person's skin. But she couldn't argue with what Tull had shown her.

Even if they'd been home at Haven, the medics couldn't have saved him. The heart was a physical thing, a machine, and they didn't have the spare parts anymore to fix a thing like that. She knew enough to guess what was wrong with him; but no one knew enough anymore to cure a heart gone bad. And so the loss felt compounded. A hundred years ago, she could have saved him.

The medic folded back bone and skin. Now, Tomas looked like he'd been torn into with a knife, like he'd been given a deadly wound. And would that have made her feel better, if he really had been murdered and she had someone to blame? She hated this town so much, she wanted Tomas's death to be murder so she would have someone to blame. How wrong was that?

"Thank you, Tull. Just . . . thank you."

"You want me to stitch this?"

The gesture seemed futile. What was the point of putting Tomas back together? He'd still be dead. But then, if she had to carry him back to Haven and his house there, maybe a closed wound would be cleaner. Neater.

"If it's not too much trouble."

"No trouble at all."

"Thank you."

After he finished, they dressed the body again, and his assistants came back to help move Tomas to the Newhome cellar. Once again, Enid sat with a body in semi-darkness, a lamp for company. Tomas looked shrunken. Older than he ever had. The illness had been short, but it sucked everything out of him. Everything. What would she tell the folk at Plenty? What could she possibly say to them?

He had not been alone. That must be some small piece of comfort.

"What do I do now?" she asked him. Just in case he might answer. Studied his slack face for signs.

How was she ever to bring this news back to Plenty?

"What do I do now?" she murmured again.

The job. They'd uncovered a case of quota violation that had to be dealt with. She still hadn't learned the circumstances of Sero's death. She was close—if the two incidents were connected, she might be closer than she knew. She was too close not to finish, then.

She had to do the job.

That was what Tomas would say. But she was fairly sure she couldn't do it alone.

She took a deep breath, steeled herself, and searched his body. Took his pouch with the tranquilizer patches and other odds and ends—a compass, a pocket knife. The clam shell pendant around his neck came with her. An old bronze ring on one finger. She had to work it off —his hand had swollen. But she managed it. He'd want it taken home. Searched the rest of his clothes and pockets, found no other items or artifacts that should be saved. She left his uniform with him—he'd earned it. It was a worthy shroud.

She smoothed his hair back from his head and said goodbye. Goodbye, and thank you.

//

WHEN SHE EMERGED from the cellar, Dak was waiting for her. Of all people, Dak. Who was lying when he said he hadn't been near Sero's shed that morning.

"Enid, are you all right?"

It was none of his business, she thought testily. What did he care? "Not really," she said softly. "But there's nothing to be done for it, is there?"

"I'm very sorry. I don't know if anyone's said that to you yet, but I'm sorry for your loss."

She managed a smile. "Thank you."

"Can we talk?"

This sounded like a prelude to a confession. She walked with him away from the buildings, away from anyone who might be listening. The town around her looked much the same. Nothing had changed, which seemed a travesty.

Dak said softly, "I'll go with you back to Haven. Whenever you're ready, say the word. You don't have to go back alone."

As if she needed to be looked after. As if she were fragile. He made it sound like he was doing her a favor.

But, yes, something would have to be done. Carry Tomas back to his household so they could take care of him, say their goodbyes. With the solar car she could make it back in a long day's travel, assuming the sun held out. Clouds were gathering, so it might not. But what a terrible image, her rolling into Haven with a shrouded body stashed in the back of the car. It was kind of Dak, to offer to sit with her through that. Tomas couldn't lie in the cellar forever. She couldn't sit in Pasadan forever, wondering what to do next. Dak was only offering the logical next step.

She must have looked so lost.

"Enid?" he prompted. She'd been silent for a long time.

"Yeah. I suppose that'll have to be done."

"I just want to help. We can leave as soon as you say the word."

Her grin felt crooked, painful. "You trying to get rid of me, then? Convenient, sending me off in the middle of an investigation."

He wasn't smiling. "Well, you can't continue with just one of you."

Investigators always worked in pairs. They could help each other. Keep an eye on each other. Easier to face down a whole town with two of you. Dak was right, she couldn't continue alone. Not that she even wanted to. She looked down at her hands, the brown fabric on her sleeves, the uniform that terrified folk wherever she went. Hard not to draw a line: the job had killed Tomas. The uniform. She suddenly wanted to rip hers off and bury it in a hole.

"It's not your fault, Enid."

No, she supposed it wasn't. But it felt like it.

"Can I ask," Dak said, "did Philos really try to bribe you with a banner?"

"He did."

"There's folk that'd just about kill to get a banner handed to them."

"Folk like Ariana?" she said, not really meaning to. Now wasn't the time to make digs.

He didn't laugh; Enid expected him to, but he didn't. Frowning, he looked away, and she realized she had touched something tender. She was afraid to breathe, to jostle it. He said, "Pasadan seemed like a good place for children. Part of why I wanted to settle here. I'm lucky Ariana agreed to put up with me."

Enid stared. Dak wanted a banner? She never would have expected it. But she studied the gray strands in his hair and wondered if he had started thinking of mortality. He might leave songs behind but not his voice. Surely in all his travels, he'd wooed women from households that might earn a banner and ask him to be the father? Ah, but fathering children was different than being a father, wasn't it? Did he really want to be a father? She remembered the story he'd told, how his childhood household had been dissolved because of his father's abuse.

Was that what he'd been looking for on his travels? A household of his own to replace the one he'd lost?

"She seems like she'd be a good mother."

Now, he smiled. "Well, so would you. But I missed that chance, didn't I?"

There was an invitation in that statement, if she wanted it. If she wanted to be very cynical indeed, she could go further:

with this investigation, maybe Pasadan didn't look like such a nice place for children after all. His offer to go back with her to Haven might have been more than a favor.

Enid didn't want to think that badly of him. Did he really think she could turn her back on so much of her life, and for him? Well, maybe he did, after all. She'd done it once before. She looked at Dak now and felt sadness for her younger self, who'd known so little. She ought to forgive her younger self for that.

"You did," she murmured. She didn't even regret it. "I don't think I told you—my household is called Serenity. The man I love is named Sam. We live with Olive and Berol, and the four of us have been friends for . . . for years now. And we have a banner." Just not a baby. Not yet. They only needed patience, and patience could be learned. She said, "I already have what I need."

He hadn't known any of this and seemed stricken, as if she had slapped him. "You don't need me, then."

"No, Dak. I don't."

He chuckled, and the flippant, familiar Dak returned. "Well. I am very sorry for that."

"No, you're not. Sing a few songs, you'll find a woman more than willing to sidle up to you. Most of 'em will even earn a banner in a few years, if that's really what you want." But he might have to leave Pasadan to do it.

"Sure, but none of them'll be you."

He only wanted her because in the end, she walked away from him instead of the other way around. Maybe the only one who ever had.

"Dak, can I take a look at your feet?"

"What?"

She had already knelt at his feet to study the laced leather, the rubber of the soles. This put her in quite a vulnerable position, she realized. He could so easily kick her in the face and run, and she didn't have an enforcer watching her back anymore. But she didn't think Dak would go that far, and she was right.

After she had measured the length and width of his feet against her hands, she returned to standing. She'd have to check against her notes. Later. She'd do it later. The day had already exhausted her.

"I didn't do it, Enid."

"I never said you did. I think I'd like to be alone for a little while. Thanks for the offer of going back to Haven with me. I'll let you know when I decide."

He went away without argument, for which she was grateful.

When he was gone, back in the direction of Newhome, she took a walk to Sero's house. She needed to look at that shed one more time.

///

THE ROUGH, SCUFFED prints outside the shed, near where someone had put a bloody hand on the wall while fleeing, matched Dak's footprints. It wasn't definitive proof—plenty of men in town had his height and build, and probably even wore similar sturdy boots. But it gave her some leverage.

She still didn't know why. She didn't have the story of it clear, yet. Why Dak would even confront Sero, much less harm him? She couldn't imagine him harming anyone—but that was her own bias, wasn't it?

And she still hadn't decided if she wanted to go through this alone, without a second investigator to help. Maybe she ought to send for help. Maybe she ought to leave it to someone else. The heat, the crying, had given her a headache. Her mind didn't seem to be working right, so she went back to the committee room, curled up in a chair, and tried to think of what to do next.

///

THE SUN HAD started to set when a knock came at the door, and Enid stretched, realizing she needed to go to the bathroom and she could do with a shower; her whole body felt knotted.

"Come in," she said.

It was Miran, who crept in cautiously, holding a basket that smelled of roasted something or other.

"I brought you some dinner. Fern said you should eat something."

Enid didn't want to eat, but she had to acknowledge the hollowness in her belly. She hadn't had anything since breakfast. Breakfast with Tomas. She should eat something, he would have told her. Enid invited her in, and she set the basket on the table and started putting out a dinner of mutton stew.

"Does Fern ever deliver her own messages?"

Miran smiled thinly at the basket. There were also rolls and salted green beans. "She doesn't like leaving the household much. Makes her nervous."

"Well. It's good she has you, then."

"I suppose." She finished laying out the meal, including a mug of lemonade, and Enid felt tears starting again, which she wiped away. "You need anything else?"

"Maybe company? You mind staying?" It was a lot to ask, but Miran didn't hesitate to pull out another chair and settle in.

"I'm really sorry," she said. "We're all really sorry. I know he was an investigator and all. But he seemed nice."

"He was. We grew up in the same household. Knew him my whole life." He'd always been there to pick her up when she fell. Now here she was ruining an investigation, and what was she going to do?

"Is it hard what you do? Being an investigator. Going into places where you're a stranger and no one likes you. I don't think I could do it."

"Yeah. It's very hard sometimes. But it's important work. Like digging latrines or butchering chickens. Someone's got to do it, yeah?"

"I suppose." Her hands were clenched in her lap, her brow furrowed with anxiety. She was worried about *something*. Enid set down her fork.

"Miran. Did anyone know what Philos and Bounty were doing? Did Kirk know?" He had to have his household's help. They were implicated.

She shrugged, which could have meant anything. "Folk don't much like arguing with Philos. He'd say to leave a thing alone . . . and most of us would, since he always seems like he knows what he's doing. We mostly didn't ask." Tears sprang in her eyes; she was so sensitive. "I should have known what was happening. That something was wrong."

"You couldn't have known," Enid reassured her. "Not unless you saw something specific."

Shaking her head, she said, "It wasn't anything I saw. It was . . . it was Kirk. He was so sure that Bounty would get a banner soon. Positive. Talked like it had already happened. He was so proud, and he said . . . he said he wanted me to have it, that he wanted it to be ours, mine and his, that we should have a baby together as soon as they got that banner. And I, and I

—I wasn't sure. He wanted me to come live at Bounty, but Fern needs me so much, I couldn't leave her. So I told him I wasn't sure. I'm only eighteen; I don't know that I want a banner right now. I—I don't think I've earned it, right? I'm not ready to be a mother, not yet. I know everyone's supposed to want a banner and a baby, and I'm sure I will someday. But I've got to earn it, and he kept on, and on—"

"And you told him no," Enid said.

She hugged herself, one hand rubbing the back of the other arm. An unconscious gesture, touching the anomaly of the implant under the skin. Get a banner, have the implant removed. That thing you never thought about until you had to.

"I tried to, but he wouldn't listen, he wouldn't accept. Like he couldn't believe I'd say no. I think . . . maybe he thought I was hiding something. That . . . that . . ."

And there it was, laid out like a newly made road.

"That you wanted to share a banner with someone else."

She nodded.

"Thanks for talking to me about this, Miran."

Sniffing, she scrubbed at her eyes and pulled her shawl more tightly around her. The shawl had a loose lacework pattern in a rust red yarn, pulled and worn. Enid wondered who had knitted it for her—it looked too old to be something Miran had knitted herself. There was history in that shawl.

She said, her voice cracking, "Hard not to feel like it's all my fault somehow."

Enid knew exactly what she was talking about. "Miran, one more thing. Can you find Dak and send him here?"

The Next Worst Storm

Routine carried Dak and Enid as they trekked from the ru-ins. They found water, hunted for late-season fruit and edibles. Wasn't much, but as Enid had said, they weren't going to starve, not as long as they kept heading toward the Coast Road. Once they found the road, they'd get to a settlement in less than a day's walk in either direction, or they'd meet other travelers who had food to spare. Imagine, always having food to spare. But the road was still days away.

They made camp, had sex, but it was by rote. Perfunctory, frustrated, and the physical release was palpable but fleeting. She dug fingers into his hips, kneading his skin, trying to hold on to an ephemeral emotion. Was this what it had been like right after the Fall, when Auntie Kath said they'd come up with the implants? Hungry, tired, but they still had sex because it was what they had. Because it meant not thinking so much.

After, they lay next to each other, and she was afraid to touch him. Afraid that he wouldn't like her, that he would push her away, and she didn't want to know how she'd respond to that.

Things weren't going to go on as they were, and that was a hard thing to know because she couldn't see what would happen next. At least she wouldn't have to think about it until they got back to Haven. Or until *she* got back to Haven.

Finally, they left the hills and forests leading out of the ruins, and the world opened up to the plains that they knew. Far ahead, another few days' travel, was the wide, packed dirt of the Coast Road—a *real* road, not the shadowed gaps of the ghost road they'd followed in and out of the ruins. Enid spread her arms wide, smiling, taking in a huge breath of clean, familiar air. She'd had an adventure, and she'd appreciated it, but she was glad to be back among the familiar.

"Enid, look." Dak was studying the sky behind them.

Black clouds gathered. Roiling, angry things, filling the horizon from one end to another. The kind of storm front that you knew had another storm waiting right behind it, and fierce winds pushed them all straight toward you, spawning tornadoes, prompting whole towns to flee into their cellars.

"That thing's going to pound us when it gets here," she said. "We need shelter."

"Yeah."

But they'd left whatever shelter the ruins offered a couple of days ago. They picked up their pace, driving ahead. Maybe they could beat the storm. But not an hour later, the wind started gusting. She could smell the rain on the wind. The size of those clouds meant it would come in fast and last a long time. Lengths of gray connected the clouds to the ground, rain already pouring. The ruins must have been getting soaked. She hoped the families were tucked away safe.

This all felt familiar—the brimstone scent touching the air, the tension causing her hair to stand up. This was going to be a bad one.

They were still in the wild, not near any settlements she could remember. There might be a way station nearby, if they reached the road at just the right spot. But even that much would take another day of fast walking.

They were out of time.

Best thing would be a sturdy building or cave, even over-hanging rocks. Trees would be okay—but all the trees were on low ground, along creek beds, and if the storm was bad enough, the creeks would flood and those gulches would turn deadly. They needed high ground.

"Over here," she said, grabbing his sleeve and trotting over the next rise.

The wind blew from the west, beating against her, whipping her hair. Dak held up an arm to protect his face and hugged his guitar in a way that reminded her of that woman with the baby. They needed to get to the eastern sheltered side of a rock outcrop or ravine. Ahead, Enid spotted a smudge of rocks with a bramble of scrub oak growing around it. Pathetic as a shelter, but in the wide open, it was better than nothing.

As the rain started falling, they crawled into the scrub oak, up to the outcrop, a section of bedrock that had eroded away. That gave them a wall to brace against at least, and the shrubs kept some of the wind off them. The branches and leaves scratched at them, caught at their clothing, but they picked through it until they found a cave-like space and settled in. Lodging one of their blankets in the branches above them and bracing it with her makeshift staff gave them something of a roof and allowed their little cocoon to hold in some heat. They snuggled together and waited.

The rain pattered softly at first, but quickly turned to sheets of water, solid and endless. The shelter of shrubs and blanket meant the water came to them in drips and trickles rather than buckets. They got soaked slowly instead of all at once.

It went on for hours. Wind pounded, threatening to tear away the blanket that whipped and rippled like the sail on Xander's ship. Enid held on to the edges until her hands cramped, until she was sure the wind would tear it from her anyway, it was so impossibly strong. For a while, the sound of the rain —a constant background hissing, punctuated by the odd patter and pop of drops striking their shelter or nearby leaves —was worse than the wet. The noise got louder, then started a throbbing in the back of her head. She pressed her hands over her ears, as much to soothe the headache as to stop the sound. The pounding became ubiquitous; the world would never be quiet again.

This, she decided—this was now the worst storm she'd ever lived through. And maybe the worst storms were just the ones where you had a lot to lose.

They huddled together, trying to keep warm. Enid dozed off, then Dak did, and they clapped hands and rubbed each other's arms for warmth; the movement helped as much as the friction did. But they were only going to get colder as this went on. They didn't really have space to light a fire without burning themselves up, but she was about ready to try. Clear a little space, light just a little bit of vegetation. As if they could find anything dry enough.

If they had known how close the storm was—how bad it would be—they might have tried to stay in the ruins. The shelter back there wouldn't have been much, but it would have been better than this. Still, Enid wasn't sorry they'd left. She thought of those kids, the mother with the baby, and then just couldn't think of them anymore.

Then, the storm got worse. After calming for an hour or so, the wind picked up again, and the rain turned to hail. Not just water falling on them, but punches, a million little nails trying to drive straight through the earth, the branches, the blanket, and into them. It felt like it would go on forever. She'd read about storms in decades past, the mega-typhoons that would stall out and rotate on and on, continually drawing heat and water from the ocean to dump it out as rain that lasted for days and washed away whole towns.

The sky turned dark. She thought for a moment the storm was growing worse—the clouds blacker, angrier. But no— night had fallen. And still the rain fell. It couldn't last forever; no storm lasted forever. But what if . . .

The night passed badly. Enid's legs had cramped from huddling under their soaked blanket, and she was shivering.

"I've never seen anything like this," she said, having to shout over the noise of the storm. The branches of the scrub oak lashed them; the vibrations rattled the twisting trunks down to the roots. The ground under them trembled as if the whole hillside might be swept away at any moment. But if they tried to run, where would they go?

"Me, neither." Dak's voice was taut, his jaw clamped against chattering teeth, just like hers.

"How long can we hold out like this?"

Any other time he might have had a quip, a smile. A word of encouragement. Now, he just shook his head. She was already soaked through, but a new wash of stabbing cold passed under her. Dak felt it too; his hands clenched on her.

The ground under them was turning into a river. Trickles of water the width of her hand poured down the hillside under them, carrying mud, and those trickles widened to sheets, joining together to become a solid, growing river, racing down the hill. The rock outcropping that she thought would shelter them made it worse, diverting more flowing water to the flood, driving it harder down the slope. The wider and more powerful the rivulets became, the more dirt they carried, the more slippery their footing. The ground was no longer stable, and then the scrub oak they were clinging to tilted. The mud washed away, exposing roots, which then came loose. The whole stand of scrub started sliding down the hill.

They didn't even have to discuss it. They scrambled to their feet, grabbed their packs and blankets and each other's hands, and braced against the deluge.

She squinted; everything seemed bright to her. It wasn't sun—she'd just been huddled under that makeshift shelter for so long. Daytime again, the sky was a uniform gray, mist shrouding details. As her vision adjusted to the light, she tried to make out the landscape, figure out what was happening.

The grassy hillside had turned to a slope of brown shifting mud. All of it moving downward. Their feet were sliding as the water tried to pull them down, too. They clung to each other.

"Up or down?" Dak gasped.

She thought a minute, despairing. She didn't know. The storm was everywhere; they had no place to go. The flood was traveling downhill. Torrential rivers lay downhill.

"Up," she shouted into his ear.

They slogged with no promise of anything but more rain at the top. For every step they took, the mud pulled them half the distance back again. The wind was a wall, and they bent their heads into it and pushed on. But however cold and wet they got struggling through the storm in the open, they would not drown. In a way, the desperate, panicked movement up the hill got them warm again. Nice to have something to focus on.

Dak slipped. Enid cried out, grabbing for him as he went down in the mud and half the hillside seemed to fall with him. He rolled, and there was an ominous crunching sound. Something breaking, and she thought at first it was bone. Her worst nightmare come to life, one of them breaking a bone in the middle of nowhere, and they'd have to hobble onward, or one of them would have to go for help—

But it wasn't bone; it was wood. Even as he plunged down a slick track of grass and mud, unable to find his footing, Dak scrambled after his guitar, trying to keep it off the ground, to keep from crushing it any more than he'd already done. Enid went after him, grabbing his arm, clutching the fabric of his tunic, and bracing to get some purchase. Finally, they slid to a stop, rain and mud pouring around them. Dak hugged the guitar case; Enid couldn't see well enough to tell what had happened to it. Just that something had broken. She didn't have time to think of that now, not when it felt like they were drowning without actually being underwater.

Hands digging into each other's arms hard enough to bruise and unwilling to let go, they stumbled back up the hill, hunched against the rain and making progress by inches. Enid wanted to brace with her staff, use it to help haul them up, but she'd lost it somewhere. Back in the scrub, maybe.

They fell again, got bruised. For her part she was exhausted, but if she stopped, what would happen? That didn't bear thinking on, so she hauled up Dak and herself, and Dak hauled the guitar, and somehow they made it to the top of the hill, until finally the mud wasn't trying to suck them down anymore.

Getting to the top of the hill didn't clarify anything. The rain still fell hard—at least it wasn't hail anymore—and the sky was still solid gray, rain obscuring everything but their little patch of hilltop. Enid couldn't see a break in the storm and couldn't tell how much damage the rest of the plain leading back to the Coast Road had taken. The road itself seemed an impossible goal at the moment. But it was better than no goal at all.

Continuing hand in hand—she didn't dare let go of Dak, and his grip on her was just as fierce—they sloshed and slipped along the top of the hill until they stumbled into a sheltered depression near another cleft of rocks. This gave them a moment to catch their breath out of the wind. The rush of water wasn't so bad here—instead of being caught in a river, they just had to deal with soaked ground. Surely, the world would never dry out after this.

Dak's leather guitar case was soaked through. She couldn't guess what the instrument inside looked like, how damaged it must be. He still cradled the thing close. It made moving awkward, but she didn't argue. She wasn't going to tell him to leave it behind.

They huddled there for what seemed like a long time. But every moment of the storm had seemed like a long time.

"Is it breaking off?" Dak sounded more hopeful than sure.

The rain seemed to be coming down just as hard as ever. The wind still chilled her, and her clothes felt frozen to her skin. But it might have been a little less than it had been an hour ago. The clouds were no longer that terrible, ominous black they had been, and unless she'd gotten turned around, she still knew where west was, and west didn't look any worse than anyplace else.

They should move. If they moved, they wouldn't freeze.

"Come on," she said, and noticed that she didn't need to shout over the storm anymore. That was something. Maybe it was breaking off.

"Enid. Wait. I just need to rest."

They'd been sitting for hours. But as he tried to stand, he stumbled, his legs unwilling to straighten.

"You're cramping up," she said. "You're freezing—we have to get moving, keep warm!" She was in a panic now. It would be easy to sit back down with him. But if they did, they might not get up again. They were right at the edge of failing.

She chafed his legs, trying to rub some life back into them. He cried out, tried to push her away. "That hurts!"

"I know," she said, bringing her face close to his. His hair was plastered to his head, and his face was ashen, blood-less. She couldn't feel her own face anymore. Her hands were ghostly. "But we've got to move." She kissed his chilled lips.

She wrapped her hand in the front of his tunic and pulled. He didn't have the energy to resist and stumbled after her.

Slinging arms around each other's waists, they slogged through the mud and didn't stop. If they stopped, they'd be done. They just had to find a roof and a fire. That was it. Not so hard.

The whole world was drowning. Inches and inches of rain-fall in a matter of hours. Their every step splashed on grasses mashed under a layer of water. Propping each other up, they slipped but didn't fall. Once they started moving, she didn't feel as stiff. She hoped Dak was moving easier, but didn't have the spare attention to ask. Her focus had to stay forward, always forward.

A cut appeared in the land ahead. A shadow. She thought it might be a low cloud or fog, or another flooded section where a creek had overspilled its banks. They kept toward it because that was the direction they were already heading.

And then, the grass stopped. The cut, the gap—a road cut through the plain. Wide, flat, dirt-packed. Only now more like a boggy stretch of mud. But it was the Coast Road.

"Dak, look," she said, thumping his chest. He sighed.

They didn't walk on the road but kept to the grass alongside. The grass was wet, but solid, while the road had turned to soup. Still, they had direction now. They had a long way to go. North. The shape of the sun was now visible through the clouds, and it was sinking west.

Not a quarter of a mile up the road: a way station. Just a house, garage, garden plot, and windmill—not enough to be a whole household, just a place on the road between towns for people to rest, borrow a car or a bike, water their horses, have a roof for a bit.

Perfect. The most perfect thing she had ever seen.

Visibility had improved—she could actually see ahead to where she pointed.

Dak nodded tiredly and resumed the slog. That last little bit might have been the hardest part of the whole journey since the storm began. She wondered—if they just sat in the grass, wouldn't someone eventually find them? They could wait for someone to find them.

But no, a hundred more steps would bring them to a roof, a fire, dryness, stillness. They'd come this far; they could do that much more.

"Almost there, Dak. Come on."

He chuckled. The sound was a little mad. Then he turned and kissed her on the cheek. A little rough, a little sloppy, and his lips were cold, but she laughed and appreciated the gesture.

Then, they arrived. A winding path lined with rough stones led from the road to the front door of the house. But Enid cut straight across from where they were to their goal, the straightest line she could make so she didn't have to waste a step. A sign hung on the door reading WELCOME in straight, practical letters. The windows had friendly looking curtains of yellow linen inside.

At the door, they straightened, took deep breaths. Enid knocked, wondering how pathetic the two of them really looked. A man in his thirties answered. He had neat clothes, brown skin, a rather shaggy beard. They all blinked at one another for a moment.

The way station's proprietor finally said, plainly horrified, "Oh no, were you caught out in that?"

They didn't even have to answer. The man, who was named Abe, shuffled them inside and sat them by a warm, blazing, blissful charcoal fire burning in a wide hearth. They didn't bother with chairs, but sank to the flagstones and started pulling off their sodden packs, blankets, coats. Abe pulled these out of the way and traded them for dry towels. The touch of dry fabric was blissful, clouds of pure warmth. The heat radiating from the fire was almost painful. Her muscles cramped; she might never be able to move again, but right now she didn't want to.

Rain wasn't falling. That was enough.

A half-dozen other travelers had gotten caught in the storm and had spent the last couple of days at the way station, waiting. They'd all had the good sense to stick to the Coast Road so they'd spent no more than an hour or so in rain. They'd gotten wet, but not driven themselves to hypothermia like Enid and Dak had. Everyone helped—someone brought hot tea with ginger and honey, someone else brought blankets, and everyone gathered around to hear the story, waiting while the pair of them thawed enough to be able to talk.

"There's not much to tell, really," Enid said, trying even to remember what had happened before and during the storm. The ruins seemed dream-like now. The journey back had been surreal.

Leave the performance to Dak. His cheeks had spots of red, his hair was a tangle, but he was finally smiling again. "A tale of high adventure," he said. "We went *exploring*. Great idea until that storm came up. But you could guess that, looking at how it turned out, yeah?" Folk murmured with amazement.

"You must have hunkered down somewhere," a woman asked.

"Naw, we were caught in the open," and on he went, turning their last two days into some kind of noble undertaking. If Enid had been left telling the story, she would have said that it really had been a good idea, but they'd made some mistakes and learned a lot. Next time, she'd keep better watch on the skies.

Abe poured more tea for them. "Not the worst storm I've ever seen, but it's up there. One of the worst, for sure. I didn't lose any buildings, at least."

"It's the worst I've seen, I think. Any word from other places?" Enid asked. "How bad is it?"

"Haven't gotten any messages. Everyone here was already on the road. The rain's barely stopped, so it may be a while."

"So nothing from Haven?"

"Is that where you're from?" Abe asked.

"Well, I am." She glanced at Dak, who'd gone back to staring blankly at the fire, exhaustion flattening his features.

"I'll let you know if anyone comes by from there. But you kids should get some sleep. Here, stay by the fire. We'll keep an eye on you so you don't burn up."

Dak reached for her, and they wrapped their blankets up together. She was still cold, the chill inside battling with the roasting on her skin. But she was getting better. Being dry helped, and nested against Dak she finally felt safe, and slept.

///

ONLY AFTER A couple of hours of sleep was Dak ready to open the guitar case. He'd set the instrument in the corner with the rest of their gear, but now he brought it to the kitchen table and carefully unfastened the ties. The stitching in the leather was coming apart. Even in the room's heat, it had only just started to dry out and still dripped when he held it up. It was meant to protect the instrument from a light rain. From wind and the dings and scratches from travel. It wasn't meant to protect from a typhoon.

The case opened, and he slipped the guitar out. The arm had splintered, snapped almost in half from the body, which was crushed in on one side. Loose strings twanged, bumping against each other. Dak turned it upside down and poured water out of what was left of the body.

Enid burst into tears. Sloppy, stressed, grief-stricken tears. She'd never cried like this in her life, and she couldn't seem to stop. She covered her face.

"Oh, shh." Dak put his arms around her and she clung to him.

"I'm so sorry," she managed to blubber out. "It's my fault we got caught out, it's my fault any of this happened, I'm so sorry—"

"Enid. It'll be fine. It's okay. I'll see if I can get it fixed. Or maybe find a new one. It'll be fine."

He was just saying that to make her feel better. Where could he possibly find a new guitar? He must have gotten this one from somewhere, sure . . . but you couldn't just walk into a market and find a guitar. What a terrible thing to happen to a precious object.

She kept apologizing, and he kept comforting her . . . and it was all a little ridiculous. Abe sat them down by the fire for more rest. First, Dak carefully arranged the pieces of the guitar so it could dry. Maybe he really could save it and get it repaired.

Abe made a pot of stew, and the whole group of them sat by the fire in the front room to eat. They clung to the companionship after the storm, craving safety in numbers.

Dak picked at his food. Enid ate slowly, not feeling hungry but knowing she needed food. They hadn't eaten more than a few bites of soggy fish jerky during the storm.

"Hey," he said. "It really was an adventure."

"We're lucky we didn't die."

"That's what makes it an adventure." He grinned at her and winked.

She wondered if he was capable of taking anything seriously ever.

The sun came out the next day, and the bright blue sky that shone through broken clouds made the previous week seem all the more surreal and distant. Weather was fickle and horrific. When Enid went outside, she still heard dripping everywhere. Water dripping off the roof into an overflowing cistern, trickling down the road in temporary streams, every tree and blade of grass soaked to the core. The air still felt wet, and she imagined she could see evaporation, moisture rising shimmering from the ground.

She was ready to go. She itched to get home. Her clothes were mostly dry, her stomach was full, and she was still bone tired—but she was *ready*.

Abe came out with her to look up the road. She'd been staring that way for five minutes, as if doing so would bring home closer.

"How far are we from Haven?"

"Four days on foot. There's another way station two days on," he said.

Closer than she thought. They'd made more northward progress before the storm than she realized.

"You think the road's clear all the way?"

He smiled. "If I say no, will that stop you?"

Her blanket hadn't dried yet—the thick wool would take days to dry completely and probably ought to spend some time outside in the fresh air. She tried to roll it up anyway, until Abe insisted on trading her out for a fresh one.

Dak watched her from his chair in the front room. He didn't pack, and she found she didn't much care.

When she was ready to go, she said goodbye to everyone, invited them to stay at her household in Haven, and promised Abe she'd send supplies to replace what she and Dak had used. She'd get herself assigned as messenger and bring them herself, and he gave her a hug and said that'd be fine.

Dak had disappeared through all this. She found him outside, after she slung her pack and rolled blanket on her shoulder and was ready to set out. She figured he was hiding so he wouldn't have to say goodbye.

"Hola," she said. He stood a few paces out on the footpath, arms crossed, looking off at the horizon like some hero in a story.

"Are you sure you shouldn't rest a few more days? You still look off."

Off? And what did that mean?

"I really have to get back. They'll need help," she said, thinking of Peri and Tomas and everyone at Plenty. If the rains had been as bad there as they'd been here, roads could have washed out, trees fallen, who knew what else.

"They'll be fine, Enid. There's plenty of people there who can take care of it. They don't need you."

That punched her in the gut. By that definition—could they survive without her?—then no one needed her. No one needed anybody, not really. But that wasn't the point.

"You saying you *do* need me, is that it?" she asked wryly. Because it sounded like he was asking her to stay. But she didn't believe him. Wouldn't, unless he asked outright, and he'd never do that.

"Dak, I want to go home." Then, more calmly. "Do you want to come?"

"No, Enid. I can't. I can't go any farther, not right now."

He seemed to be pleading with her. Like she was supposed to tell him she would stay, just because. And if she wanted him to come with her? What about that?

"Well. Good luck, then," she said. "Maybe we'll run into each other."

"Yeah."

They should kiss or something. Or hug? There wasn't a guarantee they'd ever see each other again. Well, he would always know where to find her—just go to Haven and ask. But by the same token, he would always know how to avoid her, and that would say something, too, wouldn't it? This ought to be a sad moment.

She reached out her hand because that seemed like a good compromise. He clasped it, then leaned in for a kiss, warm lips pressing against her cheek. He lingered, waiting for her response. For her to tilt her head toward him, invite another kiss.

All she did was give him a thin smile. She walked away and didn't look back.

///

BY NOW, ENID had spent a lot of time walking. She might have been so tired her muscles felt like wood, but she kept going, because the movements were so familiar. Easy, really. Sometimes easier than stopping. And the sun felt marvelous. She turned her face to it, letting it paint her skin with heat and turn her closed eyelids red and glowing. Part of her had worried that she would never feel it again.

A few days to get to Haven. If she walked faster, might she make it quicker? If she kept walking through the night? That probably wasn't the best idea. Or maybe it was—she'd never find a dry spot after that storm. Gullies that had been nearly dry a few months ago were roaring. Mudslides had taken out some hills. The slash of a fresh temporary creek bed cut a swath through one ten-foot stretch of road. Enid noted the location as best she could, so she could get word to a crew to come out to shore it up. And see what she had to do about helping restock the way station. They'd be out of supplies, after helping so many people. She was sure Plenty had some surplus stores they could send. Assuming Plenty was all right and hadn't washed away in the storm.

She walked faster.

Other travelers were on the road, too, more as she approached Haven. A woman about her age cantered up on a sturdy gray horse, sloshing through mud, and pulled to a stop to greet her.

"What're things like farther on?" She was dressed for weather, a hat hanging on her back, with a heavy cloak and saddlebags stuffed with supplies.

"Wet," Enid answered. "Road's washed out in a few places. The way station half a day's walk is in good shape and taking care of folk. They haven't gotten word from farther out yet. You been through Haven?"

"No, I'm from out east. We're okay, looks like the hills got the worst of it, but I thought I'd get out and ride my usual rounds, see if anything needs doing." She was a messenger and knew the roads around here well. But Enid wished she had word from Haven.

"I'm headed for Haven if you have anything for there," Enid said. She did, a couple of messages, folded squares of paper marked for Haven's committee. She'd planned on dropping them at the way station for the next messenger going north, but Enid would do just as well.

"What about you?" the rider asked. "You have everything? Food and water?"

"I'm good, thanks."

"Bien. Travel safe, then."

"You too."

And she was off, her horse splashing in puddles as she urged it forward.

No solar cars were out—the roads were likely too treacherous for them, and the sun was still spotty and unreliable. Every time she passed others on foot, similar conversations happened: what's it like, how are the roads, are you all right, and do you need anything? She gave her packets of raisin bread to a couple of men who were hoping to reach the next way station—they had a sheepherding station that had washed out and needed help. At least she was able to tell them that they were close.

No one from Haven came along. Not until the next day.

She ended up stopping for a few hours under a stand of cottonwoods that somehow hadn't blown over in the storm. It was the driest patch of ground she could find, and she needed the sleep. But the night turned cold, and she didn't think trying to start a fire was worth the effort. Despite it all, she managed to let go of enough tension to sleep for a little while, but as soon as she started awake, she figured she might as well keep moving. She'd stay warm if she walked.

She wondered how Dak was doing, and where he'd decide to go when he left the way station. Maybe he'd come to Haven. She wasn't sure how she felt about that. It might be easier if he stayed away forever. Then she wouldn't have to think about him anymore.

When a lone figure came down the road toward her, she took notice. She was on a rise and saw him first. Whoever he was had a brown uniform—an investigator, out on some official business. Likely storm-related, and she wondered what. Was he coming from Haven? What was the news? She picked up her pace and got a better look at the shape of him, hair in a tail and a lanky stride. Then, she recognized him: of course, it was Tomas.

Shouting his name, she ran. Somehow, after all this, her muscles were able to run. Time enough to rest when she got home. The man looked out at her. Laughing, he opened his arms, and she collapsed into a powerful hug. She had never clung to anyone so tightly.

Finally, she let him go and he held her at arm's length. She was almost as tall as he was; she'd forgotten, in the few months since being gone. Had too many memories of being a child around him. But now, it was almost like she was a real adult or something, no matter that she didn't feel like it.

"Enid! Are you okay? Please tell me you had shelter during that mess." He glanced over her shoulder, surreptitiously looking around, but no, this stretch of road was open and no one could hide. Obviously he was curious, but he didn't come out and ask where Dak was. She supposed she ought to explain that.

"Um. We kind of got caught out in it. But I'm fine. Really, I'm fine. I just want to get home because no one's had word about Haven and I got worried." It came out in a rush, and she had so much more she wanted to tell besides—too many stories to tell. In the end she just said, "I'm fine. I'm fine."

He pressed his lips in a thin smile and nodded, maybe not satisfied with the answer but willing to accept it.

"Haven's a mess right now," he said. "Some buildings down, roads washed out. Couple of injuries. It'll be okay; folk are already cleaning up. I'm taking messages south to see if there's anyone worse off needing help. Any news?"

"Way station a couple days south has a lot of folk sheltering. They'll have news if anyone does." She held on to his arms. "What can I do? I want to help—what should I do?"

"Get to Haven and start working. That's it for now. You sure you're okay?"

She grinned wide. "Am now. It's so good to see you, Tomas."

"And you! When I get back in a week or so, I want to hear all about your adventures."

She almost asked if she could go with him. She was so happy to see him, to see anyone that she knew, she didn't want the reunion to end.

But Haven needed help, and that was something she could accomplish right now.

"All right," she said, still beaming. "Be careful, yeah?"

"You too."

They waved each other off and continued their journeys. For Enid, though, the world had righted itself. Everything was going to be fine.

///

FOR THOSE OF Enid's generation, it was the worst storm any of them had seen. A full typhoon, it had lasted some three days and generated winds that blew down entire stands of trees, stripped fields of grain and orchards, knocked off roofs, and collapsed buildings. Older folk spoke of the last worst storm, and the one before that, trying to decide if any of them had been worse than this one. Enid didn't understand how they could be.

But no, previous storms had washed entire cities away. Haven still stood. They all still had a place, and if the harvest fell short this year, they'd make do with stores, get help from other towns, and they'd be all right. This had been a bad storm, but not the worst.

It was Tomas who first suggested she think of becoming an investigator, a couple years after the storm. She'd become a messenger to the northern households and way stations, and did that for a year or so. Never ran into Dak again, and had stopped worrying that she might. She'd met Sam by then but hadn't slept with him or fallen in love with him yet. Meeting Olive and Berol was still a little ways off, and building Serenity another little ways after that.

"I think you'd be good at it," Tomas said. And also, she

thought, the uniform didn't scare her. Maybe that was all it took. So she started the process, which wasn't as hard as it might have been since folk already knew her from her messenger rounds. She got the recommendations. Met Nan and started as her assistant. Kept on with it. Started wearing the uniform and mostly worried that she might disappoint Tomas. She spoke to him often about the job, about the effect the uniform had on people, about what she should look out for and how she should respond. She picked his brain and was grateful for his patience.

"What's the most important thing about being an investigator?" she asked. She was about to go off on a case as Nan's enforcer for the first time. She was starting to build her own household. The world had gotten bigger than ever, and she sometimes felt very small indeed.

Tomas hadn't had to think about the answer.

"Kindness, Enid," he said. "We have to be kind."

The World Might Not Remember

In Auntie Kath's journals, the transition from the old world to the new one had been gradual. No declarative note announced, "And now it has happened, this is the Fall." She'd write of empathy for folk living in places half a world away destroyed by storms, Pacific islands vanishing under rising sea waters. Then the disasters moved closer. A pair of cousins displaced when tornados raged through their town. Family friends losing jobs in an economic recession that looked like the previous one, but this one became a depression and kept going on and on until it was normal. It was all so awful, but then it had all been so awful for such a long time, they hardly noticed a change in degree. Like a frog sitting in water slowly turned up to boiling. There wasn't an anniversary of the day when the Fall happened. The process lasted years.

When Kath's parents died—that might have been the end of Kath's old world, Enid decided. Not when the power grid failed, not when airplanes stopped flying. Their death marked a definitive date for the Fall, at least for Kath. Enid had this idea after Kath had died and so couldn't ask her about it. But it was such a personal moment of destruction. The end of Kath's old world, certainly, but for everyone else the tragedy would have been more distant, like Pacific islands drowning.

Kath herself marked the end of the old world when she came to live at the clinic. For her, that was definitive proof that things would never be the same again, that the old world was truly gone, that the Fall had already happened and no one had noticed. Kath and other diarists of the time didn't talk about the new world yet, the culture that grew up on the Coast Road. They hadn't been convinced they would survive that long. They went from one day to the next, grateful to have made it so far.

They began marking time according to seasons and harvests as had been done centuries past, because it was easier. None of the first survivors could remember exactly when they'd built the barricade to protect the clinic from marauders, or when they'd torn it down because the marauders were gone. They could remember the last Super Bowl and World Series and Olympics and the last movie they'd seen or concert they went to, but not when it was decided that there wouldn't be another. The Fall didn't leave a definitive mark on the memory of society, not like such a disaster should have.

But personal memory remained. Kath always remembered exactly when her parents died, exactly the last time she spoke with her brother, and exactly when she herself left the old world behind. Right to the end, she'd been able to tell stories about her friends, the people who'd helped her and taken care of her, and spoken of where and how they died, from accident, disease, or simple old age. The world might not remember, but she would.

The worst storms were the ones that changed you. The

ones you remembered not for how bad they objectively were, but for how much damage they did to your own world. Banners, planted in memory.

///

ENID WAS SURPRISED when Dak actually showed up at the committee room, after their last talk and all she'd implied. He knocked on the door, and she called him in. It was late; he carried a lantern. She had another pair of lanterns resting on the table. The light spread to the edges of the room, but it was muted, casting both their faces in shadow. Reminded her of those old days around campfires. In dim light, they probably both looked younger.

He stayed by the door. "Miran said you wanted to see me? You ready to take Tomas back to Haven, then?"

Ah, that was why he'd come so easily. His offer was still on the table, and he expected her to give up the investigation. Just like that. "Have a seat, Dak. Please."

She had a chair pulled out and waiting. His look darkening, he set down the lantern and sank into the seat. Clasped his hands together and watched her closely. She didn't think she'd ever seen him so nervous.

What did he know? And how much would he tell her? Or would he storm out of the room if she pressed too hard? He'd always avoided her hard questions. He'd always fled rather than face difficulty. Then why was he here? Why had he stayed?

"What is it?" he prompted, after she'd spent too long considering. "What's this about?"

"I can't figure it out," she said. "Why did you decide to settle down? You used to hate complications. Couldn't sit still for them. Yet here you are."

"People change." A pat phrase, easy to say. He watched her steadily.

"I suppose," she said. "Was it love? You fall in love with someone and couldn't bear to be parted?" That would have been romantic, to think that he had fallen in love—really and truly this time—and changed because of that.

He chuckled. "Love means lots of different things, Enid."

Another easy answer. She wondered if he'd ever loved her. She couldn't remember him ever saying the words to her. Not that it mattered. And what would he say if she asked him that now? Another easy, poetic answer, no doubt.

"Then why?"

"Another interrogation."

She shrugged. "If you like."

"Maybe I just got tired."

Dak likely didn't know himself. Maybe he was trying to re-create that thing he'd lost as a child, without even realizing it. Maybe he wanted something he couldn't get from wandering, and maybe Pasadan was just the place he happened to be when he decided to stop.

Sometimes, you could interrogate someone for hours and never get the answer you wanted to hear. Sometimes, people just went silent.

"Never mind. It's none of my business. Not what I wanted to talk to you about."

"Then what did you want to talk to me about?"

She inhaled, considered the words she wanted to say yet again—she'd come up with several different versions of this speech—and finally said, "How long has Ariana been thinking about how to summon investigators to go after Philos?"

His whole body was so rigid he barely flinched. He schooled himself to calmness. "Well, you've been busy."

"And to think, everyone thought I was just going to go away."

"What do you think happened here, Enid? What sort of scenario have you come up with?" He'd recovered quickly; his voice was light again, like he was telling one of his stories. An entertainment, light and frivolous. As if none of this mattered.

"Ariana didn't feel she could confront Philos directly. So when an opportunity to call for an investigation presented itself—she took it. I want to know if she saw an opportunity, or if she'd been planning this. If she'd *created* an opportunity."

"And why do you think I know the answer to that? You know I'm almost a stranger here myself." He spread his hands, a gesture of innocence. A simple man, a humble musician, entirely blameless. If he could keep asking questions, he would never have to answer one himself, and he'd be so friendly about it, you might not ever notice.

"You're right, Dak. People change. And I no longer have the patience for your charm."

His smile froze. She let the pause drag, and drag, until he finally chuckled. "At least you think I'm charming."

She almost—almost—chuckled with him. "I need an answer, Dak. Forget I'm an investigator. I'm just a person trying to figure out what really happened, so I can do what's best for the whole town. Help me."

"You never could let go of a mystery," he said.

"Ah. You do know me."

He looked away, maybe even blushed. "Yeah. A little."

"How long was Ariana planning to lure investigators to Pasadan?"

He bowed his head. "As long as I've known her. We . . . we talked about it. She confided in me, I suppose."

"And you agreed to help her?"

His smile twisted. "The price for joining her household. She didn't want to be the one to confront Philos, to submit a complaint against him. She worried about it affecting her own standing in town. Worried Philos might take some kind of revenge. But if she could get someone else to do it . . ."

"Someone who was already on the outs with everyone. Sero."

"And she couldn't be seen talking with him, so I did it. If you could call it talking. Man barely said a word, seemed to resent every moment I spent with him. Never met anyone like him. I think he only tolerated Miran because he didn't want to scare her. Sweetest person any of us know. He refused to help Ariana, of course. She even offered him a place at Newhome. We could have all been one . . . big . . . happy . . . household." He sounded bitter. Like the gray in his hair, the tone didn't suit him.

He might have thought it was good fun, conspiring to manipulate investigators, to point them like a weapon. And then it had all gone so terribly wrong.

She said, "That was you, who'd run from the shed. Who got the blood on the wall."

"I didn't kill him, Enid. He was like that when I found him . . . you have to believe me." He leaned forward, balanced on the edge of his chair, nearly falling out of it.

"I know, Dak," she said softly. He slumped, back curling over his lap. The breath went out of him.

"I—I went to talk to him one more time. Ariana thought if we just pushed him enough . . . but no, she never talked to him, she didn't know how he was. How . . . willful. But I went, to make her happy. He wasn't in the house, which meant he was working in the shed. The doors were closed. Weird, because he never closed the doors when he was working. Left them wide open, for air. I knocked. No answer. So I looked in . . . and there he was." He gave a weak, sad laugh. Wiped his eyes, which were shining. "I went in to check, to see. Touched the pulse at his neck, but he was already cold, you know? Must have got blood on me then. Didn't even notice. I closed the door behind me, and . . . I ran. Just ran. Wanted to get away from there, didn't want to be anywhere near there in case someone thought it was me. I didn't want to have to answer any questions."

"Why didn't you just tell me you were the one to find Sero's body? You could have told me what you saw."

He spoke to his hands, folded in his lap. "I didn't trust you. Not in that uniform." The statement sounded like an accusation. She should have expected him to say something like that, but it still came as a blow. He'd trusted her once. He *knew* her. Didn't he? Maybe not.

"What did you do next?" she asked.

He leaned back, now slipping into his usual easy manner. The worst was over; he could relax. "I went to Ariana and asked her what to do. And she . . . she said we could use this. Said to keep quiet. I'm sorry, Enid. I should have told you everything, I'm sorry—"

She held up a hand. Spoke as gently as she knew how. "Do you have any idea who might have been inside that shed when Sero died?"

When he didn't answer immediately, she resisted leaning in. Grabbing the collar of his tunic and shaking until his brain rattled.

Then he shook his head. "Or maybe he just fell. Maybe . . . maybe he closed the door and fell, and it was an accident—"

"Did you see Miran there?" Enid asked. "She went to talk to him one last time that morning. Did you see her?"

"You can't think that poor sweet girl—"

"I don't know; that's why I'm asking."

Except Enid did know. She did.

"Enid. Just . . . stop. Just go home. Haven't you done enough to wreck this town?"

"Dak. It wasn't an accident," she said.

His mouth hung open. "You—you're sure?"

"I think . . . I think I might need your help for this next part. Sero deserves what little justice we can offer, don't you think?"

She thought he was going to focus on the uniform again. Make some jab at the brown cloth and tell her once again how much damage she'd done, how much damage those other investigators had done to his young self and family. Say that one person's death didn't matter in a world that had lost billions. If he got up to leave and never spoke to her again, she might not have been surprised.

But he finally said, "Yes. What can I do?"

///

LATE THAT NIGHT, Enid went to the household that had managed Sero's pyre and asked them if they had the resources for another. "I'm very sorry to have to ask you to prepare another one so quickly. I can make sure your fuel supplies are restocked from Haven. Will it be possible?"

The man who had tended the pyre before gaped at her for a moment, blinking in the light of her lantern, then nodded. "Yes, should be. We can have it ready in the morning, I think. I—I'm sorry about your partner."

"Thank you."

"Does the committee know? That you've asked for a pyre, I mean."

Enid's smile felt toothy, predatory. "They will."

The next morning, Ariana was the first to find out, when Enid and the pyre-tending crew arrived to collect Tomas's body. Enid hardly looked at Tomas before covering him with a shroud. She had said goodbye already and didn't want to keep saying it over and over. As they left the cellar, Ariana and half of Newhome poured out of their kitchen, confused as sheep in a storm. Dak stood off to the side, wary.

Enid got between the onlookers and the stretcher and its bearers. Shielding Tomas.

"What's this? What's going on? Investigator Enid?" Ariana asked, hands on her hips.

"We're burning the pyre for Tomas this morning," she said. A wind was starting to pick up; clouds gathered on the horizon. They needed to get this taken care of before weather moved in.

"But . . . I thought . . . We assumed you would want to take him home. That you would want to carry him back to Haven as quickly as possible—that his own household would want to see his pyre. That would be more . . . proper. Wouldn't it? We all assumed you would be leaving." She spoke like she was try-ing to convince Enid. Push her out the door, even.

That was hardly surprising. The woman had requested an investigation to get at Philos, with no real understanding of what she was bringing down on her people. She might have deserved pity, but Enid didn't feel inclined to it.

"He died during an investigation," she said. "They'll un-derstand. And I'll be finishing what he and I started."

Ariana's mouth opened at this. "But . . . but . . ." Gaped like a fish, she did.

Dak stepped in. "Let her do what she needs to, Ariana," he said calmly.

Ariana stared at him with apparent disbelief, and Enid wondered what kind of betrayal she thought was happening here. Did she wonder whom Dak was working for now? "But —" she started, and her voice broke.

Enid turned her back, discouraging argument, and escorted Tomas's stretcher to the pyre built just outside of town. The stretcher bearers carefully arranged him, and it might have been her imagination, but they still seemed to flinch from the uniform, even though the man wearing it couldn't harm them now. Symbols, it was all symbols.

The man tending the pyre offered her the torch, which she lit from a lantern, then touched it to the fuel of the pyre and stood back to watch. The flames rose, engulfing the body until it was just a shadow, and she whispered goodbye, over and over.

Ariana and Lee came to watch with her, standing a short distance away. Respectful, but out of reach. Neither wore their gray committee sashes and hadn't since her first day in town. They probably only wore their sashes for hearings and the like, and this—they didn't know what this was.

Philos did not come. Miran did, but not Kirk. A good number of folk from Pasadan watched from farther back. Not necessarily anyone who'd interacted with Tomas, and no one here really knew him. But it was likely they'd want to say they were there when the investigator died at Pasadan. That would make an excellent bit of gossip. A good story for the fireside. They were welcome to it, and Enid ignored them.

A familiar shape came to stand beside her as the flames did their work to the sound of cracking wood and the scent of ash. Dak, who didn't make a move to touch her. She'd have liked to be held by someone just then, but she was thinking of Sam.

"You all right?" he asked.

"No, not really," she said. "Eventually I will be."

"You're the strongest person I know, Enid," he said, looking away and returning to stand by Ariana, who seemed to be fine with him there.

It was time, Enid decided. She wasn't getting anything done standing here watching the fire. As soon as she finished this, she could go home, and she desperately wanted to go home. She thanked those tending the pyre one more time, then went to speak to Ariana and Lee.

Enid wished she still had Tomas looming at her shoulder. Would anyone listen to her, without him beside her?

Well, Dak had.

"I'd like to meet the committee at Sero's homestead now," she said to the pair. "Will you come with me?" Enid looked over the gathering again, just in case, but still no Philos.

Ariana stared. "You did it. You found out what happened."

"I might have. But I need confirmation. Philos needs to be there, too."

"I—I don't know if he'll come," Lee said, wringing his hands. "Right now—he's despondent. I think he's aged a year just since last night."

Enid felt no sympathy for the man. "I'll go get him myself, if you think it'll help. And where's Kirk?"

"Haven't seen him," Ariana said.

Enid hadn't seen him since the day before yesterday. He wasn't there when she and Tomas had uncovered the hoard at Bounty. Had the boy actually fled? And what did that say?

"Miran." Enid turned to find her right there. Not eager. Her shawl was stretched tight across her shoulders, from hugging herself. Whatever happened, she would see it through.

Braver than her beloved, she was. "You know where Kirk might go if he wanted to hide?"

She hesitated. "No. No, I don't."

Lying, Enid was sure. That was fine. "Right, then."

//

ENID FELT LIKE a magician, revealing wonders.

First, she went to Bounty to find out the state of things. She wouldn't have been surprised to see that the entire place had burned to the ground. That Philos would turn out to be one of those types who would destroy what he'd built rather than see someone else knock it down. But the place was just as it had been yesterday, the pretty sign still standing, the buildings and gardens just as they should be. The door to the secret cellar and the honeysuckle vines had been put back to the way they were, all neat and innocuous.

The usual bustle of a busy household was absent — everything quiet. No one seemed to be working; the loom was still. The only sounds were the murmuring chickens.

"Where is everyone?" she asked Ariana.

"Common room, I think," she said. "Are you sure this is necessary? I was hoping we could just leave Philos be."

Enid turned on her, glaring. After all Philos had done, after he'd potentially undermined the entire community, she could still say that? Would she argue that Philos and his household should avoid punishment, too?

"Not angry at him anymore? I thought you wanted this."

Anguish pulled at her face. "I didn't think . . . I didn't expect . . ." She gave a frustrated sigh. "It's the whole town. I thought it would just be him and Bounty. But it's spread out to the whole town."

Enid stared. "It always does. That's how it's supposed to work." She marched on. "Philos needs to see this."

He was there in the common room, sitting at the kitchen table, bent over his own hands. One of the household's women —middle-aged, her frizzy gray hair cut short—was with him, hand on his shoulder, trying to impart some comfort. Lee had been right—Philos had aged. Whatever force of will had been holding him straight was gone now, and his hands were so bent, the fingers so twisted, they didn't look like they could hold a cup of water. He still wore his gray sash, though.

Enid wasn't about to let his appearance influence her.

When she entered, the woman flinched, and that made Philos look up. He seemed to need a moment to focus on her, and his frown deepened.

"I thought you were leaving."

"Philos, I need you to come with me to Sero's shed."

He hunched back over his hands, his gaze turning inward. "I want nothing to do with you."

"Can't you leave him alone? Haven't you done enough?" the woman hissed at Enid.

Enid's anger became such a useful tool, times like this. She tempered it and honed it into a weapon.

"Hasn't *Philos* done enough is the better question. Philos, you will come with me, or I will dissolve your household and scatter you all up and down the Coast Road. *Don't tempt me.*"

Philos alone might have tried his luck. Might have pushed her to see how far she'd really go, and part of her desperately wanted him to try. But his companion spoke to him in a low voice.

"Maybe you'd better go. Just to get it over with." Protecting the household rather than the man, which gave Enid some heart. Helped her make some decisions about what would happen next. She gave the woman a thin smile of thanks.

Ponderously, Philos rose from the chair, leaning on the table, and made his way to the door. Bent over, unwilling to look Enid in the eyes.

Back in the courtyard, she'd picked up observers: the committee, the rest of the household, a few other folk of the town, including Miran. Dak stood by, hands folded before him. Much like the usual stance of an enforcer—he knew how to play a part if he needed to.

Still no Kirk. Enid turned to his father. "Where's Kirk?"

"I don't know. If he's gone, then good. You can't touch him." He glared defiantly.

She took a breath, managed her temper. Imagined Tomas standing nearby, whispering, *calm*. "Oh, I think I can. You think he needs to be present to be shunned? You'll see he doesn't."

"I don't know where he is." He pressed his lips together, sealing his mouth. She'd get nothing more from him.

Enid could solve this. She looked around a moment, giving herself time to think. She needed a solution and needed to maintain her authority. She needed to appear omnipotent. Now, how to do that?

She didn't believe Kirk would flee the town. He was close to his father, attached to his household, if he'd thought he was going to earn a banner there. More than either of those things, though, he wouldn't leave Miran. He cared far more about Miran. So, that meant he was hiding.

Scanning the courtyard again, the gathered faces, she came to the building with the cellar, the carefully placed trellis, the perfectly hidden door. And why not?

"The cellar," Enid said. "We'll check there."

It was a sickening moment of repetition, finding herself on the precise ground where Tomas had died, going through the same motions. She set the feelings aside for now, because she didn't want to cry during this. Time for that later. Working by herself this time, she pulled back vines and uncovered the door. No one stepped forward to help her, and she didn't ask. This was the job of the investigator, to be the outsider exposing what no one wanted to see.

Finally, she swung open the door. Didn't go down the stairs, just in case. She hadn't brought Tomas's staff with her and began to wish she had. Never mind. She'd figure it out.

"Kirk?" she called into the dark space. Her voice echoed. "You mind coming out now?"

No one answered, but she listened and heard an intake of breath in the close space—sound carried there. She could wait for him all day if she had to. But he could wait all day as well.

So, they waited. A minute, another minute. The tension in the group behind her rose, people growing restless. Something would have to give, and she didn't quite know what would do it. She'd go down there and drag him out, if she needed to.

But she had a secret weapon. "Dak?" she asked him.

The man came forward, standing at the edge of the doorway beside her, and called into in the cellar. "Kirk. Why don't you come out?"

It took another minute of them standing there, but Kirk finally came to the stairs, looking even more slumped and despondent than his father. He'd been crying—his eyes were red, the skin around them puffy.

The sooner this was all done, the happier Enid would be. This wasn't going to be easy.

"Come, Kirk," Enid said. "I need you to see something. I need everyone to see something."

Miran rushed forward, taking hold of Kirk's arm as he emerged, whispering comforts to him. He didn't seem to hear her. At least she'd get him to their destination—he couldn't run away now.

"Right," Enid announced. "If you'll all come with me?" She had a real procession now, following her to Sero's shed. She arranged it so she walked next to Dak. "Thanks."

His look was wry, like he wasn't sure helping her had been a good idea. "Aren't you going to say something about what a good investigator I'd make?"

"I wouldn't insult you like that."

He opened his mouth, closed it, and she marveled at leaving him speechless.

//

THEY COULDN'T ALL fit in the shed, so Enid chose her witnesses to stand at the wide-open doors and look in: the three committee members, Kirk, Miran. Dak, because he'd hear about it one way or another. And if she could convince him, she'd be able to convince everyone.

She could still be wrong about this. Picked up the wrong clue, imagined the wrong thing. It could all be wrong. No—it was already wrong. She was just trying to explain the wrongness. Understand it. However this fell out, she would understand what had happened a little better and give the memory of Sero some little peace.

The open doors let afternoon sunlight pour into the place. An apt metaphor. She would have liked to point that out to someone. Tomas, ideally. She swallowed back the tightness in her throat. Grieve later. Plenty of time for it back in Haven, with the people who knew him. How terrible it was to mourn alone.

Her witnesses studied the interior of the place. As if she might have written the solution out in secret ink, if they only knew how to read it. And maybe it was a little like that.

No one had touched the scene, not in the handful of days she'd been here picking over the town. She'd told them exactly what her evidence was, the blood on the wall, and no one had interfered with it, for which she was grateful. She realized now Philos and the others were worried about her discovering so many other infractions in the town, they had been thinking little of Sero's death in the end. That made her all the more angry.

"Someone was here when Sero died," she said. "More than that, that person knows exactly what happened."

She felt like she was putting on a play. Dak ought to appreciate that. Ariana clutched the musician's arm. Her expression had gone taut and fearful. She was afraid of what Enid was going to say, whom Enid was going to accuse. She couldn't trust Dak's calm. All she knew was that Dak had found the body. And maybe she didn't believe him when he said he hadn't killed the man.

Enid walked through the scuffed dirt to stand at the table. She put her hand on the pieces of broken hinges he'd been working on. "Sero was here, working like usual. Many of you had probably seen him working just like this, when you came to ask for his help on a job? Miran?"

The young woman's eyes were round, but she nodded quickly. Yes. He stood just like this. So Enid did, in front of the table, hands clenched as if she held a tool.

"Someone came here and confronted him," she said. "Someone who was angry at him."

Ariana said, "What could he have possibly been doing to make anyone that angry?"

"Oh, refuse a request?" Enid said pointedly. "Refuse a job? Not do what someone else thought he ought to?"

The committeewoman ducked her gaze and pressed closer to Dak, who merely glanced at her, scowling.

"But no. He talked to Miran," Enid said, matter-of-fact. "Miran was kind to him. He might have looked forward to her visits. Even if they were awkward. Even if she didn't like coming here. Maybe she resented it. But she couldn't say no to Fern. She couldn't stop delivering meals, talking to the man. Unless Sero died?"

"No!" Kirk cried. "That isn't what happened!"

"Be quiet," Miran hissed at him, even as tears fell, streaking her cheeks. They stood shoulder to shoulder. Kirk had folded in on himself, arms crossed.

These two were protecting each other.

"Miran?" Enid prompted.

Her voice choked. "I didn't mind bringing him food when we had extra. I really didn't." Her head shook slowly. "No one should have minded it."

"Someone did, though."

"But what harm—" Ariana started. Her voice fell, and she looked across at Kirk.

"So Sero was here, and someone came to confront him for spending too much time talking to Miran when he didn't have a right to. At least that's what he thought. He was determined to tell Sero to keep away from her. He looked at the shed and saw the doors wide open. Marched over to confront him. Do you remember, Kirk? Were the doors open when you got here?"

"I don't know," he said, sullen. He glared at her as if he could wish her away with the power of his will.

"Why don't you show me where that person must have been standing? I think he was just where you are now. He would have come straight in, right for Sero, here. Come on."

She coaxed him like he was a stray dog, step by step. Just a little farther.

"Sero would have been surprised. He liked to be alone, didn't much like people coming at him, right? So he would have stepped back." She did so, toward the spot on the two-by-four that still showed a stain of blood. "Maybe it happened even more quickly. Why would anyone be angry at him? He might have put up his hands. We all know Kirk has a bit of a temper. He might have taken advantage, maybe pushed—"

"No, it wasn't like that, it wasn't—"

He rounded on her, and right at the last, he saw it. They all saw it. He stepped in; she stepped back. He didn't raise a fist, not this time. He stopped himself. And she was expecting it so was able to keep her balance, her awareness. Was ready to block him if he followed through. Sero wouldn't have been ready. He wouldn't have expected it, not from the son of a committee member, from a place like Bounty. Sero might even have been confused as to why Kirk came here to yell at him in the first place, and when Kirk lunged, he would have dropped whatever he held, thrown up his arms, stumbled back in confusion—

"A bad step. That was all. One chance in a hundred, that step threw him back against the one spot on the wall that would kill him." Enid took that step back, but carefully. Still, everyone could see the trajectory she was on. If she had tripped, if her whole body had swung as if on a fulcrum, it would slam her skull against that piece of wood and crush it.

"Sero wouldn't have taken that step if Kirk hadn't pushed

him," Enid said. "And then Kirk carefully closed the doors, so no one would see. If it had truly been an accident, the doors would have stayed open."

Kirk wore a look of despair. He knew and was sorry. His father — Philos showed no surprise at the image she presented. He'd known all along. Kirk had told him. The two of them together had hoped it would all just . . . go away.

Enid nodded at him. "Is that what happened, Kirk?" She didn't mean to sound gentle. She meant to be furious at him. He'd been angry, but had this really been worth any anger at all? The boy was clearly broken.

Miran — she was crying, but she wasn't looking at the tableau Enid had presented. She hadn't been surprised, either. She'd known, and she hadn't been able to protect him.

Kirk put his hands over his face, which muffled his words. "I just wanted to scare him a little so he wouldn't get any ideas. It was an accident. How could I have meant for that to happen? I didn't mean it! I didn't!"

Enid believed him. Still, she couldn't absolve him, assure him that of course they all understood, that it was all right, that there'd be no consequences —

"It was an accident that never should have happened," she said. "That was only the first infraction committed here. The second was not telling what happened straight off. If only you had done that —"

Philos was furious. "How could you expect us to, knowing how he'd be treated by you —"

"You don't know how he'd have been treated if he'd just told us straight off, do you? But you'll know how you'll all be treated now, hindering my investigation for three days. All of you." She pointed this last at Miran, who Enid really thought would have known better.

Kirk still tried to argue. "But Sero—"

"Sero was yours. He was part of Pasadan; he helped build this place, no matter what anyone thought of him. You should have cared for him. Accidents happen, yes. But you should have *cared*. All of you!"

At least no one was arguing with her assessment of the events. At least no one tried to tell her this wasn't what had happened. She was at least satisfied with that part of it: she'd learned what had really happened. *I solved it, Tomas.* She thought she might have heard a response, an echo in the back of her mind: *Never doubted you would.*

She moved to the door, pushing past the gathered witnesses to get out of the shed. "I'll have my judgment for you in an hour."

Marching up the hill, she waited until she was out of sight before brushing away her tears. All that, for a bit of jealousy and misguided anger. Jealousy was a nebulous thing until you were the one feeling it, she knew that well enough. But they were supposed to be *better* than that. Better than the old world.

Leave it to Dak to follow her. He caught up with her when she reached the committee house. She only wanted to go inside and pack, to get out of here as soon as she could. But she waited for him to say what he wanted to say. She planned to just let it wash over her, because she was tired of being the voice of authority.

They stared at each other for what seemed a long time.

"Well?" she asked finally.

"You proved it," Dak said. "The rest of us might have suspected, but you proved it."

Was he praising her? Accusing her? She couldn't tell. She wasn't sure she'd ever been able to read him. "What do you want, Dak?"

"Would it have hurt anything to just let it go?"

"It would have hurt everything," she said. "You really think Sero wasn't worth defending? You think Philos gets to flout quotas just because he thinks he deserves it? Maybe it won't hurt anything now, but what about five years from now? What about when the next big storm comes? Or when the next person who dies because of an accident that isn't an accident is someone you love? And the whole town tries to cover it up? The plan has to be for everyone or it fails; we all fail."

She waited for the argument, for his insistence that investigators did more damage than good. But it didn't come. His smile seemed amused, and she wanted to slap him.

"I've missed you, Enid," he said finally. "I've been lonely these years."

"No. You have folk in every town happy to see you. You're never lonely."

"You're the only one who was ever willing to travel with me."

He still had the charm. The gentle, wheedling, bardic charm. He simply showed up, and people fed him and cheered for him. And all she could think was how much she didn't miss him. It seemed cruel to say it out loud, however much he likely deserved to hear it. But the silence stretched, and that was answer enough. He heard the words she didn't say, and ducking his head, he chuckled.

He hadn't changed, and she didn't care.

"I've got to get home. If you'll excuse me." She went inside to pack. Soon now, she would tell all this to Sam.

He wouldn't laugh.

///

THE HOARD OF grain wouldn't be wasted. It would be passed along to the regional committee, and from there it would go to households that needed it, places with blight or a bad harvest that had put them behind quota.

As Pasadan had shown it could not care for its people, there'd be no banners. Not for some years at least. Kirk and his household would never get one, not as long as Philos and Kirk were there. And Miran . . . that was a harder question. She had known; she had lied. Did Enid punish her whole household, then? Was the punishment for the rest of the town enough? Maybe it would have to be.

But whatever Kirk had wanted, he'd lost. That seemed a more apt punishment than locking him away in some dark room, like in the prisons the world had built before the Fall.

Kirk could run, but she'd send messages and inside a month there'd be nowhere he could go on the Coast Road where folk wouldn't hear of who he was and what he'd done. What they'd all done. All the investigators and all the folk of the surrounding towns, households, and markets would know if Pasadan tried to duck out of their shame. They wouldn't need an enforcer standing over them to keep watch. The wider community would do that themselves. That was the real punishment, the real consequence.

Enid was still angry as she passed judgment. But she was satisfied.

///

A STORM WAS coming up. The clouds on the horizon were slate gray, tinged with green. They gave Enid a sick feeling in her stomach because they reminded her of the ones from a decade ago, of the storm that she and Dak had been caught in, and the one that had destroyed Potter before that. She had to stave off the sense of panic, that she needed to get to shelter *right now.*

She had time. A day at least. She would get back to Serenity before the storm hit, and all would be well.

At the way station at Tigerlily, she stopped to trade news and to deliver the first of many copies of her report on Pasadan. The place was bustling; they'd also seen the clouds building and thought the storm looked like a big one, so they were preparing. Shoring up structures, covering windows, gathering supplies, taking care of folk caught traveling who needed a place to shelter.

Enid wanted to take the solar car all the way to Haven to speed up her trip. She made sure no one else needed it more, and no one did. Besides, once the clouds moved in and the vehicle's battery ran low, the thing wouldn't be much good anyway. It would stay safe, parked in Haven.

She talked about the case to a couple of messengers and the head of the way station. She wasn't really in the mood for it, but she needed to do it, to start word moving. The responses were either aghast or enthralled. Maybe a little of both.

"So it really was a murder?" the head of the way station asked, more than once.

"I think in the old days, they would have called it manslaughter. Maybe wrongful death," she said.

"Dead's still dead, and what a wretched situation," a messenger from the south muttered, and Enid agreed. Before the Fall, they had the time and energy for semantics and fine gradations of meaning. She passed along a couple of copies of her initial report, which would be copied and passed along in turn, until all the regional committees knew what had happened.

"I'm very sorry about Tomas," the head of the way station said. "I liked him."

Enid smiled a thanks and gritted her teeth. She was going to be facing those condolences, and offering them, a lot over the next couple of days. Made the wound hurt more, not less. She wanted to be home.

The drive back to Haven gave her plenty of time to mull over questions. Decide if she'd learned anything, or if the town had learned anything. If *anyone* had learned anything about what had gone wrong and what they could do better.

Banners were a scarce resource. People fought over scarce resources. But they'd already known that, hadn't they? Would anything have kept Kirk from thinking Sero was about to steal something from him? Or would he have thought that in any case? If Kirk hadn't been so possessive of Miran, would he have staked a claim on something else? Sero's auger, maybe? It was all just . . . exhausting.

Part of her never wanted to arrive back at Haven at all, because then she'd have to tell everyone about Tomas. She didn't have a satisfying reason or explanation for his death. He just died, as people do. Too soon, too young.

And there, she started crying again.

She had it all planned out. She was going to drive the car straight to Plenty, call as many people as she could get into the common room there, hand over Tomas's staff and belongings, and lay it all out as quickly and straight as she could. Offer what small comfort she could, then bow herself out and flee to Serenity. Hope Sam was there. If he wasn't, she would make a cup of strong tea and wait for him.

It was a good plan, a solid plan for which she could brace and shore up her emotional reserves. Be the dispassionate investigator for just a little longer. But before she could get to Plenty, she met Olive, coming up the road with her basket on her arm. Probably back from trading bread for eggs at one of the other houses. She was looking good, color back in her cheeks, energy in her stride. She felt good enough to go out, which she hadn't a week ago. Already, the world looked better.

"Olive!" Enid called, and parked and spilled out to greet her friend. Olive laughed and gave her a one-armed hug, taking care of the basket.

"You're back; it's so good to see you!" she gushed. Then she glanced over at the car and asked with total innocence, "Where's Tomas?"

Well, that finished her off, didn't it? Enid folded, right there in the middle of the road.

Olive sat with her for what seemed a long time while Enid just sobbed, and Enid worried about the image—investigators weren't supposed to lose it like this; she had fully intended on taking off the uniform first, or at least getting out of public. But Olive kept saying things would be all right until Enid could at least pretend to believe her.

"Want me to go to Plenty with you?" Olive asked gently.

"No, I can do it. I have to do it, tell them what happened . . ."

Olive frowned. "Maybe you could come home first and get cleaned up. It can wait another hour, yeah?"

Enid thought a moment, then nodded. Some of the pain fell out of her, just having someone she trusted to lean on. She let Olive help her up, and they took the car to Serenity.

And Sam was there, right at the front of the cottage. He saw her and smiled. She stopped the car, nearly falling out of it to get to him faster. If he was surprised at the fervor with which she threw herself at him, well, he didn't seem to mind.

"I missed you," he murmured in her hair, holding her close, then squeezing even tighter when she leaned into him. She needed him, needed this.

"You have no idea how much I missed you," she murmured back. Straightened, took his face in her hands. "I love you so much."

He kissed her, then said, "That bad, huh?" He looked over her shoulder to see Olive coming up, arms close in, her expression drawn.

"It was bad." She had to tell him about Tomas. But maybe not right this minute.

"You all right?"

She had to think a minute. "I will be."

"I love you too, Enid."

"How're things here? With the storm?"

"Orchard's called for help harvesting apples before the wind knocks 'em all down. You up for it?"

The task sounded clear, simple, and productive. It was perfect. "A job. Oh, yes, I'd love to. But let me change clothes first."

"Come on, then," he said, grabbing her hand, and they jogged inside as the wind picked up.

Acknowledgments

AS ALWAYS, no book is an island, and I had help. My thanks to Seth Fishman and John Joseph Adams for taking a chance on me. To Daniel Abraham for reading the first rough—very rough—draft. To my Monday-night dinner crew—Wendy, Anne, Max, and Yaz—for getting me through some rough patches. And to my longtime readers for sticking with me. Thank you all.